The Lichfield Incident

By

August Quinns

To Audrey
with best wishes

August Quinns

Also by August Quinns

The World's Most Exclusive Club
Caroline

August Quinns

The Lichfield Incident

Lichfield Citizen.

31ˢᵗ August 2001

Circulation 10,090

Issue 1125.

Free.

Explosion damages Cathedral.

At 6 am yesterday an explosion severely damaged the 'Ladies of the Vale' the spires of the cathedral and there is grave concern for the future of the beautiful, ancient structure. The Dean said he had no idea what caused the explosion, but felt it had something to do with the site of alterations to the hotel and conference centre opposite. The police have issued a bulletin saying that access to the Close is restricted on the grounds of safety, while an investigation is conducted. Amazingly there is only one injury reported, a passer-by was blown over by the blast and is in hospital with minor injuries. He is not available for comment; a report given to the media stated that he is Mr Albert Fradley, the MD of Arraye Electronics, a specialised small firm in the old town. His associate, Mr Huddleston refused to say anything until he had spoken to Mr Fradley.

Our reporter has been unable to obtain any further information, but was told by a workman from the building site that there was nothing stored which could have caused such devastation. He also pointed out that the swathe of damage is very odd. It is almost as if there was a giant breath, blowing everything in its path to bits. The damage to the priceless ancient Herckenrode glass is impossible to assess, but appearances are that it is totally destroyed. The bishop is said to be in shock, too stunned to make a statement   .

TIC faces cuts.

The Tourist Information Centre is under threat due to council overspend, according to the Finance office. They are (cont'd p 3)

ARRAYE

ELECTRONICS
SECURITY CATEGORY 1AA.

AUTHOR A FRADLEY
DOCUMENT – PERSONAL LOG
9/9/01

SCHEDULED FOR DESTRUCTION 9/9/02
RESCHEDULED FOR DESTRUCTION 9/9/03
RESCHEDULED FOR DESTRUCTION 9/9/04
RESCHEDULED FOR DESTRUCTION 9/9/05
RESCHEDULED FOR DESTRUCTION 9/9/06
RESCHEDULED FOR DESTRUCTION 9/9/07
RESCHEDULED FOR DESTRUCTION 9/9/08
RESCHEDULED FOR DESTRUCTION 9/9/09
RESCHEDULED FOR DESTRUCTION 9/9/10

OK

CANCEL

I gazed at the stark choice. I knew that try as I might, I could not click 'OK' and erase that episode ... no, not an episode. Rather the beginning of my life. I had dithered and re-read the transcript until I could see it anytime I closed my eyes. For an instant the cursor hovered over the way out. But I knew, as I'd known in '02 and every yearly review since, I never would. I was avoiding the issue as usual, desperately trying to convince myself that it was for my son, Albert Fradley to do that after he had read and understood. Albert, the fifth Albert Fradley, was sleeping as any four year old did at four a.m. Liza was God knows where, away on one of her 'business trips,' the absences that twisted my guts in knots the whole time. Albert, 'V' as he had been nicknamed, should know the truth. Or so I convinced myself for the sixth time.

I clicked 'CANCEL' and re-opened the document, re-living that day the earth tilted.

Chapter 1 The Awakening

In the early hours of that unforgettable morning, the explosion rocked Lichfield Cathedral to its medieval foundations and sent shards of the ancient glass from the Great West Window scything down the aisle in a lethal storm. At the east end the 16th century Herckenrode glass in the Lady Chapel was restrained by the security mesh, but mostly collapsed like discarded confetti. The whole ancient fabric of the building shook and cracks appeared in the main tower. The Dean at his prayers in St Chad's Head Chapel thought the end of the world had come.

But it was the controversial, nearly completed, and fortunately closed, Conference and Leisure extension to the nearby hotel that took the main force. If it had not been there it is likely that at least one of the three steeples, the 'Ladies of the Vale', would have fallen. The Dean shuddered at the chilling prospect that had been narrowly averted. The stark, twisted girders, tumbled brickwork and roofing sheets tossed aside as so many used sweet papers told their own story. He had been one of the leading lights in opposing the development. But if it had not been there. He shivered again. Of the temporary, portable building that had been the site of the blast, there remained so little that there was nothing for the forensic team to focus on. There had been no gas cylinders, no fuel stored, no incendiary devices: they were baffled.

There were those who looked beyond the obvious, those who wondered at the odd linear form of the swathe of destruction: the Darwin Centre had lost most of its roof, but most of the surrounding buildings were untouched.

Some said the explosion was Divine Retribution for British Telecom's desecration of the Cathedral. There were those with their own ideas that nobody listened to: there were those who knew, or thought they knew.

Despite my injuries, the explosion came to me as more of an emotional shock than a physical one. It also turned round my whole life.

It made me into a wanderer, seeking with little hope of finding what I sought and not knowing if I would still want it when I found it. I am recording this for the future if I have one.

My past has died, just as I thought Dad had succumbed to cancer two years ago; we don't realise the effect childhood experiences have on us. My mother's ill temper left me with a reluctance bordering on fear to become emotionally involved with a woman. When she finally stormed out Dad turned his frustrated feelings into a love affair with the cause of her temper, his Jaguar XK 120. I thought that was my lot too.

Until I met Liza.

Dad turned his life into a monk-like existence and developed a tiny, specialist niche in electronics, making sub-miniature surveillance devices and detectors. It wasn't easy; the market is small and highly competitive. He concentrated on tailor-made gizmos, innovation being the main selling point.

He died of cancer two years ago, leaving me the business and the still immaculate Jaguar. I have built up an impressive reputation in the bizarre, shadowy world of Intelligence. The professionals find it hard to realise that the stocky, fresh-faced character with unruly red hair can give them the goods. Speak to the field operatives, the real spies, and they know better. But then that requires an odd sort of person anyway. I know because I fell in love with one.

I can still vividly remember the time when it happened. I'd always scoffed at love at first sight, but that heart stopping moment will burn within me as long as I live.

Fighting the early evening crush in the Bearpit, "The Duke of Antrim" as it is listed in the tourist guide; I was heading for my usual corner, as far away from the bar as possible, when I was jolted violently in the back by a tourist, an enormous Texan.

He apologised so loudly and profusely that all eyes were on me.

Waving aside his apologies I muttered that it was all right and turned back to my corner and stopped as I was pierced - that is the only word I can use - pierced by a woman's eyes, so dark as to be hypnotic.

The face round them was not beautiful, but it was ... the usual words, 'striking' or 'memorable' were totally inadequate. It was amazing, addictive! I could drown in those eyes.

Her cheekbones were angular in the Slav look now so popular on the fashion catwalks; smooth cheeks as creamy as Irish Coffee were framed by black hair shot with a blueness that shimmered. It was unfashionably long, but formed the perfect setting for that wonderful, totally unique face. It did not strike me at the time, but she was unusual in not wearing ear rings.

Neither of us spoke, time and place ceased to exist for me. Conscious of nothing but the total and instant recognition of a force stronger than reason, lust or longing, I could have stayed there for ever.

I was rudely jolted into the present as Suzie's voice boomed in my ear; I turned as in a dream. "Come on Dozy, 'ere's yer pie!" Now I love teasing that voluptuous waitress, but at that moment she was wished in hell as the contact was broken. As I turned back to my corner, the face was gone. She had disappeared as if she had never been. I vainly scoured the press of diners and drinkers, but there was no black hair, no creamy oval face, no deeply disturbing eyes. She had just gone.

The pie might have been sawdust as I ate mechanically. The taste in my mouth was bitter; I had tasted love at first sight, I was hooked, and I wanted, no I needed more.

Chapter 2 The Colonel

"Bert! Snap out of it." Bill Huddleston looked down at me from his six feet three height, "The buyer's due any minute and you're mooning about like Goofy."

My passion up to then had been the Jaguar. It had been bought second-hand by Dad in 1975 when he discovered that a Le Mans driver had been Bert Hadley. He did this instead of taking my mother to Florida; it was ostensibly this that caused the irretrievable fracture that led to her abrupt departure a year later. Bill's love was Disney - the real Disney of the early years, the flickering images, not the smooth, computerised present day fluidity. He looked at me worriedly, "You're not doing a Donald are you?"

I snapped back, "No! I'm not ducking out." The truth was that I wanted to throw up everything and look for that face. But then, being the Managing Director, I could not do just that. I had responsibilities, a life to live. One of the chores was the monthly 'Buyer's Visit' from SIS, or MI6 as most people know it, to see our latest toy or adaptation. In truth I hated this part. It was like a form of prostitution or selling a child into slavery; not that I was ever likely to know what that was like.

Pulling myself together, I growled, "OK, get the Earl Grey out again. I suppose we must make a living."

Bill looked at me quizzically, but said nothing. I detested the clipped tones of Colonel Heward, his military style of suiting, tightly-rolled umbrella and pigskin brief-case, in fact almost everything about him; and it showed. But he did know his business and knew his exact requirements. That way we both tolerated each other and wasted no time on meaningless niceties.

We heard the chime of the clock tolling two as our door bell rang with the double ring pause double ring that he always gave. Bill glanced at the monitor, "Here he is, regular as Olive Oyle." There was a pause, "Oh! He has company this time." He operated the remote locks to admit the Colonel.

We heard his footsteps mounting the stairs, the outer door open and shut. As the door to my office opened, I rose to greet him but froze and stopped dead. I don't think my mouth dropped open, but don't remember it. Conscious of only one thing I held my breath.

Instead of the Colonel's lean features and bowler hat I saw that face.

For the second time in that day I stood transfixed, unable to move. Our eyes were only aware of the other's shock. I was paralyzed by the indescribable sensations from wonder and stripping away of all, but the awesome, mysterious chemistry of real love.

How long we stood I have no idea, but gradually I was aware of Bill's quiet voice, "Are you all right?"

I was not all right; in deepest shock, I forced myself to listen as the Colonel introduced Bill and me to Liza Vancyk. He pronounced it *Leezza* in the east European way. That name rang as sweet as any bell.

Gradually I became aware that Bill was speaking, "... sorry to hear that, Colonel, we've grown to know each other over the years; I hope that the next tests are better news."

While Bill was talking I saw Liza's hand outstretched. In a dream I took it, it was cool. It was as smooth and cool as a chilled Cinzano and as intoxicating. I reluctantly let it fall as my eyes said things that could not be put into words. She smiled as if slightly amused, but there was something else in her eyes. I knew that my world had suffered a massive shift and would never be the same.

With a slow recovery of senses I took in the rest of her appearance. A lightweight, charcoal grey business suit in understated simplicity spoke of excellent taste, the skirt ending just above her fine boned, dimpled knees. Her small feet were fitted with deep blue, low-heeled shoes that were unmistakably Gucci; she had no handbag, just a slim, leather document case. I drank my fill of this as I once again looked at that face. Her slender neck rose from a touch of white lace in the V of the elegant jacket moulding her upper body so beautifully. She was poetry in shape and motion.

I was never so aware of my battered, tweed, sports jacket and rumpled, twill slacks. As I felt a faint redness creep up my neck, I subconsciously straightened the collar and momentarily went cold; all thoughts of Liza instantly vanished. There was a minute lump that should not have been there. I said nothing then, but gave Bill our secret sign that signified 'bug'. He blinked an eye in recognition and pressed a discreet button on the desk. Colonel Heward gave no sign that he noticed, but his words became even more clipped than usual: Liza gave no sign that there was anything amiss, but continued to look deep into my soul.

Dear old reliable Bill, said, "I think this calls for a drink, what about it, Bert?"

Numbed in double shock, I must have nodded, because in no time at all we were in the hushed atmosphere of the Central Hotel sipping a passable champagne.

I made a mental note to put it on Bill's account, not mine, but then changed my mind as Liza removed her jacket to face me in her white, lacy blouse that had me feeling utterly scruffy and uncomfortably warm. What with the champagne, the warmth of the day, the heady company of Liza and the shock of the discovery of the device on my jacket, I was in a daze, a dream world where nothing was what it seemed.

It was a good job that Bill was on form or poor Heward would have thought I was drugged. I was, drugged by the intoxication of Liza, and it showed.

I can't remember what we discussed, it was all perfunctory and superficial, but, as we parted, it was left for Liza to call the following day to, as Heward put it, "find her way around." So we parted; the Colonel to his train, Liza to her hotel and Bill to lead me back to the business. Automatically from habit, I checked the integrity of the premises, but Bill went in first to set the Radiation Seal and only then spoke, "What the...?"

Holding up a hand before removing my tweed to hang it on my swivel chair, I slowly turned back the collar to be rewarded with widened eyes as he saw the tiny grey blob.

He reached out to remove it, but I seized his hand, "Don't touch it! Let's see what we have first."

We both looked at the device and each other, before looking again at the Radiation Seal glowing SAFE. Bill spoke first, "Well! Let's not take all night about it. What d'you think?"

Thoughtfully, I mused, "It's the first one I've seen and I'm taking no chances. If I pull it off, it could self destruct, or at least warn the sender." So I spent the next three hours carefully dismantling the bug. First, I cut out a piece of the collar, which meant that I needed a new jacket. I put it under the microscope and slowly peeled back the covering plastic.

At the end of those three exhausting hours, I was satisfied that I had sorted it out, and I was impressed! It was good; it was almost as good as mine. Almost. But there were some deficiencies. For one they relied on an internal power source, mine has (well that's a trade secret) and as far as I could see there was no memory to cover those times like now, when transmission is blocked. But it was good.

Bill and I looked at each other; I spoke thoughtfully, "This has all the signs of the CIA!" Bill nodded, "Who do you...?"

I jumped up, "The Texan."

Bill's eyes widened, clearly alarmed, "Who?" He listened as I related the events in the The Duke of Antrim, the 'Bearpit'; he whistled as I finished. He also spoke quietly under his breath, but loud enough for me to hear, "And you had to fall for her."

Open mouthed I stared, started to speak and stopped. It suddenly burst on my brain that something was going on that I did not like.

As quickly as events had lifted me to the heights, my emotions collapsed, my world started to fall apart.

Not only had I been struck by Cupid, but I was being sucked into the world of intrigue and deceit where treachery was a way of life; a world that I had kept out of as a participant as long as I could. I was only a technician. Or so I thought then. My mind was in a whirl, thoughts flew as flakes of snow in a blizzard.

Was Liza in with the CIA? Was the Texan for that matter? Did she see me as a bumbling fool, all too easily beguiled? Who was watching who? And who managed to put that damned bug on my tweed? It was with a cold fury and blackness in my heart that I started to reassemble the device and to stick back the piece of tweed into the collar.

Chapter 3 The New Man.

The following morning I took the tweed to the Oxfam shop, speaking firmly in case anyone was listening in, "I wondered if you could make use of this, it isn't very smart, but it is a good jacket." I dropped my voice and gave a nervous laugh, "I've met a girl and I need a new one, so it's good-bye to my old friend."

She took the jacket with a brittle smile that spoke volumes; she said "Thank you, I am sure someone can use it." She might as well have said as she thought, *if they are desperate enough.* I smiled as I thought of some remote eavesdropper groaning. "Serve them right," I gritted; I was fond of that jacket.

The next call was at Burton's. Not their usual type of customer I was, however, in a hurry and wanted something better than old Harry, my tailor's idea of fashion. I ended up with a bottle green, fuzzy kind of velvet jacket and shapeless slacks that they assured me were meant to look that way. I was also assured that I needed a fancy shirt and some sort of snakeskin shoes. I felt that I looked like a poor version of Elton John or that Welshman on TV. It certainly had an effect on Bill.

He whistled. "Cinderella *is* going to the ball then?" I turned to him with a cold stare as if he suffered from foot rot, "Are you addressing me my good man?" We both burst out laughing. Then I looked serious, "It was one way of throwing them off the scent, whoever they are."

Bill looked equally serious, "I was worried you'd lost your marbles for a moment there. I mean. She is a cracker."

I said nothing, gave nothing away in my face, but my mind was racing, full of conflicting thoughts. The very thought of Liza's wonderful face was still enough to quicken my heart rate. Was I being paranoid about security? Was it likely that a buyer was double dealing? Was I losing my marbles as he said?

And over it all was the reawakened memory of those eyes meeting mine. I shoved the whole lot in the mental 'pending tray'; sure only of very few facts at present, time would tell the truth of at least some of the others.

We got down to preparing for the return visit of the new buyer, Ms Vancyk. It suddenly struck me that I did not even know if there was a Mr Vancyk, I only knew that I had been sure in that brief and searing contact that there were no ties, that she was her own boss, that she would not cheat on anything she had put her hand to. It became clear that as time was to prove, although I was basically right, I was too simple minded: she was much more complex than that.

The following day I rose to the too jolly voices of Radio Two; not for the first time wondering how anyone could be so cheerful at six in the morning.

I opened the heavy curtains to be met by a belligerent sun, bright enough to make me wince although it was just rising over the tall elm at the bottom of my garden. The term 'garden' can only be loosely applied to my modest, tree-fringed estate. The wielding of hoe or rake, much less a spade, was not my idea of an absorbing pastime. The state of the gently overgrown ground was more of the damage limitation sort than gardening. On the other hand, the blinding sheen on the Old Ivory White of the Jaguar was a banner declaring to the world where my devotion lay; at least, it had up to then.

I reached for my dressing gown to cover my usual feeling of vulnerability after my cosy bed and saw the green, velvet jacket thrown over the bedroom chair. It suddenly hit me like a brick; all the events of yesterday came flooding back. Still feeling the impact of those eyes, dark as mountain lakes in winter, I went hot and cold at the same time.

And that forceful face still raised my heart beat. I remembered the Texan and the feeling turned to a hateful unease at the unknown factors suddenly thrust into my life. I swore to myself. I was a fool! There was no reason why I should let anyone get under my skin, least of all a woman or an agent or whatever he was.

Suddenly stripping off the silk dressing gown, I stood naked, no longer vulnerable, but resolute and firm in mind. I was my own master, nobody's lackey! I would make of the day what I wanted! A cold, stinging shower proved my point. As the needles of cold water pummelled my skin I felt ready to take on the world. Dry, I reached for my trusty tweed and then cursed again as I recalled where it was. My face reddened and I damned the cause. That jacket had been a part of me for years! The day was going to go my way. I was determined it would.

It started well enough. The sun shone brightly on the colourful shops of the busy, old lane as I strode confidently to the anonymous door of my domain. The security was undisturbed. I entered my kingdom and settled down for another routine day. Then I recalled Liza's coming visit.

I straightened my IN tray, paused and stopped. It was not going to be like that today. Determined to relax I made a cup of coffee and waited nonchalantly - or tried to. Bill arrived. He waved at the monitor, before ascending the stairs behind the book shop. Leaning back and I sipped the coffee and began to feel better. He seemed to have lost yesterday's tenseness and set about his drug dose.

The coffee he makes is so strong that I can't call it anything else, but it seems to have done him no harm; as long as he doesn't try to foist it on to me, it doesn't worry me.

He stretched as he sat at his console, "It's a Mickey, today all right! (Mickey as in Mouse - bright and cheerful). This had frustrated me at first, but now it was just part of the furniture, normal and friendly, like my now dead tweed used to be.

The green velvet just did not have the same feel at all. I would just have to try old Harry again later today.

Bill set my calm aside with one sentence, "I want to clear up the AD/C 45 before our buyer arrives. Could you deal with the post?" He looked hopeful, a boy wanting to play truant or scrump apples. I nodded, but I was suddenly no longer relaxed. My heart had started to beat faster, my palms went moist, the fancy collar was tight.

No matter what I told myself, even the thought of her was enough to start it all off again. I scolded myself, "Grow up you idiot, you're thirty, not some spotty teenager, drooling over Scary Spice, Get a hold of yourself and get down to work." It did no good. Dad always said I was inattentive.

Anyway I settled down to open the secure e-mail, which was surprisingly light. The two memos from suppliers only needed the acknowledge code, Bill need not have worried. The paper junk was a different matter. As usual, three-quarters went in the bin, I did not want a free On-line CD (I suppose that some people are still using them), nor was I about to support the Salvation Army, nor the Save a Tree Campaign. I sighed. Maybe I should have been in advertising. The gas statement went into the spreadsheet, the Accountant statement into the safe and that was that. All nice, steady routine. I sipped my cooling coffee and sat back to the accompaniment of the comforting creak of my well-used, snug, leather chair.

A glance at the monitor made me freeze. Someone with black hair in a pony tail was approaching the door. I stared. Was this teenager, Liza? She reached up to the bell push and gave the ring, now no longer needed by the Colonel. I glared at the clock. She was a minute early! I did not realise that it had taken so much of my time. In a daze I operated the remote locks.

As she entered, I mentally kicked myself into life, '*You were going to be decisive today. Well ruddy well do it!*' By the time Liza pushed open the door facing me I was cool again.

It all totally evaporated as she breezed in with a face that glowed from the morning sun, life and a tinge of excitement.

She wore no jewellery, seemed to have no make-up; if she did it was very skilfully done, her Irish Coffee cheeks had the merest touch of blush, her red lips had the subtle shading that no lipstick can simulate. Casually dressed in a muted green, angora sweater and pale stone slacks she positively oozed elegance.

She made me feel like one of those Victorians in a smoking jacket and funny round hat. Once again I flushed embarrassingly. I waved her to the seat, not trusting myself to say much.

She looked at me with those deep eyes. They did not waver from mine, but I swear there was a smile lurking at the corners of that delicious mouth.

She opened the document case and spoke in her slightly throaty way, "I'm not too early, am I? But I wanted to complete this new contract, (I mentally started at the sinister overtones) so that I can have the afternoon free while it's so nice."

"Not at . . ." I swallowed and tried again as my throat dried. "Not at all, it's certainly a day for being out and enjoying it." She smiled, her cheeks dimpled and the last dregs of my resolve ran unheeded into the metaphorical gutter. With difficulty I dragged my mind back to the conversation, "What is this 'new contract' you just mentioned?"

She placed several sheets of the usual specification papers on the desk. The heading hit me straight away -

DEMOLISH. The acronym was Distant Electro Magnetic Orientation Line In Safe Houses. Pondering the exact meaning, I began to experience a chill crawling up my spine. Unable to put a finger on it then, I wish now that I had torn up the papers there and then as I was tempted to do. Vague rumours had reached me through the 'trade' about this crazy idea and the loss of two good men in the field in, even for the Intelligence world, very blurred and hushed phrases.

Not for the first time I wondered who thought up these crazy Star Wars schemes.

My thoughts were ended as Liza turned the documents round, "I'm not asking for an immediate response, I'll just go over the main points, the requirements and delivery times." She paused, "It's a big one. This comes from Downing Street, not Horseguards." She used the old name for HQ. It didn't matter that it had moved many times, was now in the monstrosity of Vauxhall Cross. To us it was still HG.

She sat back; her mouth had lost its softness to become firm. "I've used your work many times and I've wanted to meet you, well now I have."

I wanted to say '*Well what do you think?*', but I was dumb. So I just nodded and mumbled, "It's always nice to meet the users, I hope you were satisfied"

This time there definitely was a smile, "Oh yes. I'm satisfied."

Once more I went red in adolescent embarrassment and silently vowed to go to Oxfam to buy back my tweed. We spent the next two hours going over the specifications and delivery dates. My misgivings slowly left me, as did my feelings of distraction.

I began to see a woman of clear mind and purpose in that young-looking body.

The flush of first love began to mellow into the warmth and assurance of the coming together of intellect and spirit that is the foundation of true love. In her presence I started to relax, to feel she might want to know me better.

I hadn't realised how long we had been until Bill entered with the modified AD/C 45. He looked at my cold coffee cup and turned an accusing eye on me, "You haven't forgotten to give the lady even a coffee?" I blushed at my lack of thought. Bill turned up his eyes in mock despair.

He turned to Liza, "You just can't get the staff these days!" We all laughed, but I felt a twinge of jealousy at his ease with Liza.

I jumped up, "I am really sorry, Miss Vancyk, please allow me to treat you to lunch as recompense." Dimly it registered that she didn't challenge the 'Miss'.

She stood up, laughed, stretched. I felt myself flush again. She spoke lightly, "I really didn't notice the time myself. Lunch seems a good idea."

Bill looked glum, "Sorry, but I've to meet Sheila at one. It will have to be another time, sorry. But don't let me stop you."

I blessed Bill! Sheila never met him for lunch, she was always asleep. She was a Night Sister at the Staffs Hospital. I thought, '*I owe you one Bill.*' Instead I said, "Oh, well, another time then." So Liza and I had our first date. The occasion warranted it, so I shunned the Bearpit and took her to the hushed luxury of the Central.

As we went together I was in paradise dismissing the feelings of mine earlier that morning. Was it only this morning that I had thought I was my own master? I felt that Liza was incapable of any duplicity.

I was wrong on both counts.

Chapter 4 First Encounters.

The lunch was a huge success, the food was, as always, beautifully prepared and well served. The only flaw was that green velvet jacket! I had to remove it to my mental discomfort to ease my physical discomfort. My rising temperature had a little to do with Liza's presence and a lot to do with the warmth of the day and an inappropriate garment. Liza's angora sweater was clearly covering the bare essentials and was also light enough to be comfortable. She was at ease and enjoying herself. I was enjoying the experience, but that jacket had to go.

Removing it I hung it on the back of my chair. Liza even suppressed a smile as she saw the fancy shirt, which made me even more overheated. I was glad when the time came to settle the account and to emerge into the pedestrianised quiet of Dam Street. As I was about to make my farewells the Texan appeared, head and shoulders over those in the thinly crowded street. He saw me and waved. My heart sank like a stone.

His voice boomed in a deep, gravelly bass, "I never got a chance to properly apologise the other day. Guess I'm like a steer in a pottery, as you say." I saw Liza smile; dimples in her cheeks making my heart skip a beat. He went on, "I should at least buy you a beer or something." He paused, "Are you coming in?" He waved a ham of a hand at the door to the Central, "I'm staying here, so you're welcome."

I looked at Liza then him, "We've just had lunch, thanks. But think nothing of it. No trouble I assure you."

He looked pained, "What about dinner tonight, then; say eight?"

It was more an order than a request, but for some instinctive reason, I did not hesitate. Liza looked surprised as I replied with a laugh, "Why not? Drinks on me."

He hesitated fractionally before shaking my hand vigorously and laughing. "Great! That's swell. I'll look forward to that." He started to go then turned suddenly. "I never asked your name. Mine's Clinton, Aloysius Clinton the Third." He stuck out his big hand again.

Wincing at the pressure as I took it, but managing to keep a straight face I said, "Albert Fradley," I paused, I could not resist saying, "the Fourth. And this is Liza Vancyk."

I know I detected an instant of stillness, but it was gone in a twinkling and he boomed out, "Gee that's wonderful; see you at eight." With a wave of that huge hand he strode into the hotel.

Liza looked blankly at me.

I spoke briefly, "We literally bumped into one another in the Bearp... the Duke of Antrim yesterday." I finished lamely, "You know what these Americans are like, impetuous and generous to a fault. But I thought I would bring a decent bottle of Moët with me, I was not impressed with theirs."

Liza's smile emerged to warm her face again, "Well! I was about to issue my own invitation, but it can wait." We parted, each with our own thoughts. I was wondering exactly why I had accepted the invitation so easily. Still musing about CIA, Liza and unknown links I turned into the lane leading to my workplace.

I was brought to an abrupt halt in both stride and thought, by the sight of a fat, jolly looking man in a pink shirt, waving around a calculator and looking closely at it. The sight itself was unremarkable; it was just that he was pointing it at my office. As I stood unheeding of the people round me, he put it into a pocket, took out a pad and made a note, before walking away down the lane.

It was with sweaty palms that I opened the door and climbed the narrow stairs, to be met with Bill's grave face. He growled, "You saw him too!" I nodded distractedly.

We both looked at the Radiation light, still glowing "Safe" and the Integrity light which was steady. "He doesn't seem to have been active, but I'm worried," I said to Bill. We double checked the monitors and detectors. Nothing had been registered.

I relaxed slightly after this, but it was Bill who spoke first, "Perhaps he's just a nut case."

It seemed unlikely as I mulled it over, "Perhaps." But neither of us believed it.

Chapter 5 Social Engagements.

I bought my Moët and Chardon before going home to change. I had no compunction at all in taking my own drink. They knew me well enough at the Central to get away with it, and I knew that we would order something else as well, so they would just shrug it off. The choice of clothes was not so easy. My final choice was a silk, polo necked white sweater and navy blazer. If it was too hot, as expected, I would at least look formal, not a film set escapee.

Parking the Jaguar in my reserved spot off Frog Lane I walked through the shopping precinct. It was quiet at that time, too late for shoppers, too soon for the evening strollers. My follower was heard, but not seen. I promised myself to wear my 'hearing aid' tomorrow; it is very useful to know how far back your 'tail' is! He was not intent on mischief, yet.

I arrived safely and unfazed at the Central. Antonio greeted me in the Green Room; he took my Moët carefully as befits the vintage. It would re-appear at the right temperature and time - perfectly. There was no sign of Clinton, nor of Liza, so I sat in the foyer placed to observe the traffic of Reception. There was not long to wait and I was lost in admiration as Liza arrived in a royal blue dress, with a narrow skirt, accentuated by the bow at the rear. The neckline was hidden by a light evening jacket of pale gold lamé which shimmered as she moved. Her movements were sheer wonder to watch; I felt a catch in my throat as she saw me and approached with a dimpled smile that would have melted stone - it did much more for me.

"Not kept you waiting, have I?" Her voice was gentle and soothing, not a seductive purr as one of my ex girl-friend's had been, but enough to warm my crusty old heart. Before I had time to reply, the lift doors opened and Aloysius emerged.

He was a big man, and he dominated everything in sight by his sheer presence.

In all honesty I could not see him being CIA. There was no way he could ever merge into the background; he would have dwarfed the Statue of Liberty.

The foyer became suddenly overcrowded as he came to us, holding out a hand. I took it to be pulled close and hugged by his free arm. I will never take to this American habit. It is both too intimate and insincere at the same time to my way of thinking.

Disentangling myself I watched as he gently raised Liza's hand to his lips. I did not like the look in his eye. Was I jealous? It was stupid, but I was, and that after only hours of her acquaintance. She's always had that effect on me. As we were escorted straight away into the Green Room, I wondered.

This man knew how to command attention. He also had the best table by the tall Georgian windows, overlooking the Minster Pool. I don't know about Liza, but I was impressed.

The meal was one of the best in my memory, the Beef Wellington was true ambrosia and the delicate offering for dessert was a froth of meringue, whipped cream, angelica, cherries and sugared swirls. I've forgotten the name, but the sight is etched indelibly in my memory bank.

It is still all so clear, but it was completely overshadowed at the start as Antonio accepted Liza's gold evening jacket to reveal a strapless neckline to the royal blue dress. That sight has been with me ever since, I doubt if it will ever leave me. There was nothing provocative. It was decorous and beautifully revealing at the same time. It did a lot for Aloysius, whose eyes revealed his feelings. The sight of the blue against that creamy, lightly tanned skin made the meal pale into mediocrity, which only goes to show the state I was in. The meal was memorable in other ways.

Aloysius told us he was researching his family tree.

He was convinced that he was descended from the Bishop Roger de Clinton and that the family had connections with the Irish clan Clinton. I made the assessment that he was travelling in hope more than in certainty but he was prepared to spend lavishly in the quest. He was 'in chemicals', was suitably vague as to what. He laughed it off, said he left that all to those who knew what they were doing.

He had inherited the money, not the ability, from Aloysius the Second. Generous and charming he was suitably discerning of the Moët, so he was not the usual brash, newly-rich Texan. For my part I told him in equally fuzzy terms that I was the fourth of my family named Albert and I was in a small way in microwave radiation detectors; he accepted this without attempting to pry. He also accepted Liza as a 'buyer', though what he thought of the relationship he kept firmly out of sight under his breezy banter.

Although it was bliss to gaze at the dream of Liza opposite, I was not sorry when the time came to depart. I'm not up to all this business of half-truths. The devious way of telling someone what you wanted them to know, while trying to find the truth is alien to me.

There was nothing definite, but I felt that Clinton was a phoney. However, he was telling the truth when he referred to his business as dealing in 'rodent bait'. I should have realised that there is more than one description of a rat.

Chapter 6 Down to work.

For the next two days I was hard at the specifications as defined by the remit from, or rather through Liza. It was clear to me that she knew what she wanted from the device, but she had no real knowledge of the technicalities of production. Parts of the basic theory behind were very odd. For one thing we were working in extremely long waves, something I had left in the Ark. But, not it would seem, the brain that designed DEMOLISH.

As I worked on the hardware problems of fitting the seven stages of exciter/amp/reactance/modulator/f.multiplier-/-inter-amp/power/harmonics into the tube of 100 mm by 15mm I became more than a little uneasy. Something just did not seem right! The potential for interference from solar wind for one thing was too high, apart from the security aspect. I supposed that they were counting on the opposition being unaware of there being anything in that range. But what was the reason for 2,875 m as the chosen carrier medium. Still that was not my problem; you know what they say, 'Ours not to reason why ...' Except I had no intention of doing any dying.

I was forced to fall back on AM because of the Kilocycle range, but it was all good for the grey matter. It was certainly a challenge!

In those two days we saw our jolly fat man wandering round and making more notes, but never a squeak on the detectors. That is, until I recalibrated an old AM meter in preparation for the testing of components prior to construction. Bill had just said, "Here he comes again." when the meter needle went off the scale. I stared mesmerised for a split second before I switched it off. Bill sensed my startled movement. He hurried over, "What's the matter? You're as white as a sheet."

For reply, I switched the meter on again. There was nothing!

Wiggling the connections still produced nothing.

Rushing to the window I was just in time to see him disappear down the lane. I turned to Bill. "What was he doing when you saw him?"

He looked blankly back, "Looking at that calculator thing of his as far as I could see. He wasn't looking this way, if that's what you mean."

Switching off the meter I sat down, "Come here a mo', Bill, I want to talk."

He listened as I described the sudden life of the meter that coincided with the presence of the fat man. His concerned expression was answer enough. For once Disney was forgotten as he said, "I don't like this, Bert, not one little bit." That, I thought, was the understatement of the year.

Liza came to check on progress soon after that unsettling event. She wore light slacks with a pale blue blouse, hair in the girlish pony tail, lacy sandals. I reported everything, including the fat man. She did not seem to be worried. It was only as I knew her later that I came to detect the signs of stress. She would have made a fortune at poker. She said that it might have been a fluke, but was genuinely pleased that the first drawings were rapidly coming together.

I must have shown more stress than I thought, because she surprised me by saying, "You need a break. It's a wonderful day. What about a run in that old jalopy of yours? My eyes widened as she went on breezily, "Blow out some of the cobwebs. I'll bring the goodies at one, so be ready." Before I could object she had swung out of the door and was gone.

Bill grinned, "Lucky for some." I sounded more irritable than I felt, "Oh go and ... and do a Ham Gravy!"

The startled stare he gave me, at my reference to Olive Oyle's first boyfriend, made me burst out laughing until my eyes watered. I spluttered, "Go home and wake up that sleeping beauty of yours and give her a cuddle or something."

He drew himself up to his full height, "You randy devil!" As he spoke, I felt that there was a break in our closeness.

There was nothing I could pin-point, just an unaccustomed coolness. It was as if a cloud had passed over me. He seemed about to say something, to argue. Instead he shrugged and looked slightly hurt.

But he still went.

As I prepared to leave, I stopped. Who said anything to Liza about my car being old?

Chapter 7 Time Off.

Liza arrived at one as promised. I noted she was not surprised as we loaded the Jaguar, lowered the soft top and drove into that glorious sunshine. I wondered what else she knew about me.

We motored gently down sleepy lanes to Ashby de la Zouch, where I parked the Jaguar in the Castle car park. As I switched off the engine, I savoured the sunshine and the sight of the busy street, lined with buildings that seemed to have stood still for centuries. My usual dining place was the Queen's Head, where I enjoy the half-timbered structure's feeling of solidity and strength. But today I was going to shun the cosy interior for the outdoor pleasures of Liza's picnic basket. She looked with interest at me and undid her head scarf to shake her black hair. She looked lovely.

"Come on," I said lightly, "let's look at the shops for a moment." She simply smiled in reply, before swinging her elegant legs gracefully out of the small door. We dodged the heaving main street and the non-stop traffic; I headed for one of the passageways. As we walked slowly along the alley, admiring and gazing we came to one of the 'antique' shops. In it I saw a crystal XK 120 on a black stand. I pointed it out to her and went in. I browsed for a time, before asking the price of some terrible glassware, then I priced and bought a little posy basket. Then I pretended to notice the Jaguar in passing and haggled a little over the price before I bought that too. It didn't fool the proprietor for a minute, but it was fun. Liza accepted the posy basket, which she admired, but she was genuinely pleased that I had bought the car. It felt good and I had no qualms about playing truant. We strolled back to the car, chatting of inconsequentials when I stopped dead. Liza took my arm, but said nothing. The fat man was wandering along with his eyes on his calculator.

Quickly turning my back I looked blindly in a shop window. He was reflected in the glass. He did nothing but walk along, stop, make a note and continue along the street.

I was trembling slightly as we turned to hurry to the car.

Liza said nothing until we were out of the town. "What was all that about?"

"Tell you in a minute," I said as I shook my head,

I drove into the car park at a nearby reservoir and stopped the engine, "Let's picnic over there." I pointed to the bank well away from the snack bar and boat club. We took the rug and basket to sit sprawled in the sun. I looked her in the eye and said, "What's going on? Tell me now before I get in any deeper."

She looked into my eyes, "Please explain what you're worried about."

She did not speak again as I told of the meter, the man and his odd behaviour. Finally, reluctantly she muttered, "Would you believe me if I said I can't say?"

I nearly said I'd believe anything she told me, but simply agreed, "Yes, I would."

She leaned back on her elbows, hair thrown back, face up to the sun, "There's really no need to worry. There's no danger to you, I assure you."

I sat up straight, "What about you? Are you in danger?"

She sat up, put her hands round her knees and gazed over the water, "I don't think so. Up to now I was sure that I was not. Now I'll have to do some fact-finding, before I can say yes or no." She turned to face me, smiling as she opened the basket, "Today the only danger is from starvation. Let's eat."

She was right on one point. Fears vanished; I was ravenous.

For the rest of that blissful two hours we ate, talked and walked in the warm sunshine, at peace with each other and the world. We knew it couldn't last; we shut our minds to the future and lived for the present. I can't remember how it happened, but we walked back to the car hand in hand as naturally as a married couple and as unashamedly.

Chapter 8 Annie.

Liza had to go back to London the next day, to report on progress. Bill and I worked flat out on the project now called DEMO 1. Although we still worked as a team, there was something between us that had not been there before Liza arrived. It was worrying me, but there was no time to ponder too deeply.

It was demanding to be under the pressure of a strict deadline. I'd just been peering into the microscope for an hour when I stopped for a coffee. I called to Bill, "Could I have a coffee, please Bill - and not one of your semi solid ones."

He stuck his head round the door, with an unaccustomed scowl on his face. I was taken aback by the look and the grunted remark, "If you feel that way, perhaps you'd best do your own. " His voice became almost a snarl, "I'm not the wicked queen you know and you're not Snow White. Others are working as well!" This startled me, but I was also very stiff and stressed.

I snapped back, "Oh all right! Cut it out, Bill. Not asking too much am I?" I took one look at his face and spoke wearily, "Never mind, I'll do it myself."

He spoke one word, "Good!" and slammed his workshop door.

I managed to pour hot water on my hand and roundly cursed Bill, the intelligence service, Liza and the world in general. Hearing the row, Bill rushed in all concern. He stuck my hand under the cold tap, dried it and inspected it with a worried look. We swapped apologetic glances; Bill spoke first, "It's time for us both to take a break. Why don't you go over to the Duke and relax before something worse happens."

We didn't know it, but the worst was just about to happen.

Cursing myself for my clumsiness I stood nursing my smarting hand. He was right. The pressure was getting to us both. But other pressures were building up too.

"OK. But it's for both or none. Pack up and go home early to Sheila. You need some time off more than me. At least Sheila's at home." He went without any further prompting.

I went to the Bearpit out of habit, not because I particularly wanted to. It was snug and warm without the claustrophobic atmosphere of some of the more 'Olde Englishe' pubs. I could never stand the sham and overcrowded clutter of the ones that catered for the undiscerning. There are those that specialise in brassware, those that are a danger to unsuspecting craniums (or should it be crania?) with their heavy oak beams and some that are all plastic and chrome. To me the Duke has just the right balance of old and modern.

After all, who wants ale in a leather and tar tankard anymore? I certainly would not like to return to the days of no refrigeration and no disinfectant. Anyway I trudged in feeling sorry for myself and a fool to boot. I looked forward to tweaking Suzie's cheek and a bit of banter. I missed Liza, but I had to keep living.

It was a disappointment to find a new girl, Annie, an American, behind the bar. In so many ways she was an improvement. As I allowed my attention to focus on her, I realised that she was attractive. The truth was that she was very attractive in an immature way, especially for an American; she almost seemed too young to serve in the bar, but I supposed that the landlord valued his licence too much to take risks. She was eager to impress and she did. As I talked to her, letting her faint American accent lull me, strangely I found myself thinking less of Liza and beguiled by Annie's youthful exuberance. My visit was longer than I had meant it to be, but I began to enjoy my chat. I could see why the landlord had taken her on - the prospects for the future looked good as long as Suzie wasn't put out. Annie had that fresh-faced glow that seemed to have vanished from Hollywood. Not only was she was good to look at, but did not seem to either notice or resent the attention I was giving her.

I compared her pale-blue, wide eyes with the bottomless dark pools of Liza's and began to wonder which I preferred. I kicked myself and it hurt. She was at least ten years my junior. Still, with her pert figure, frank, blue eyes, short, brown hair and bubbly personality she was going to make someone happy. As I thought on these lines, it suddenly struck me; she was cute and sweet, but there was no pain of Cupid's arrow, no heart-warming chemistry. I thought of Liza and ached for her magic.

Annie was still on duty late that night as I returned and started to eat my steak and ale pie. I wandered over for some sweet to follow it. "Don't they ever let you off duty?" I asked, hoping it sounded guileless.

Her eyes crinkled into the smile that was never far away, "Well, the truth is I need the money for college back home." She laughed lightly, "Anyway I've nowhere to go and no-one to go with. At least here I meet people and time passes so quickly." Her face fell just a little, before she brightened again. "It's not for ever anyway, only for this summer."

I thought of the trouble she could get into with some of the lads who came at weekends and before I could stop myself, I said, "Could I show you the city some time when you're off?"

Her eyes widened as if I had offered her stardom in films, "Would you do that, just for me?"

Feeling like a silent film villain I said, "Sure. Just say the word and I'll see if I can be there."

She gave me a dazzling smile, but was cut short by the presence of a gang of four lads, who swept up to the bar as a pirate ship pounces on to a prize galleon.

Watching from a distance I saw the way she deftly averted their comments with telling, but light hearted ripostes. I thoughtfully ate my meringue and cream; she was not as naive as she projected or seemed.

I was surprised to see Antonio stride into the bar; order a beer and turn to lean his back on the rail. He saw me and weaved across to join me. "All on your own tonight? No lady friend?"

I ignored the jibe. Shaking his outstretched hand I asked, "What are you doing supporting the opposition? I thought business was good."

It was his turn to grimace, "Too good in the short term, I've become a training manager to try to turn the Green and Rough they've hired, to cope with the extra load for the summer." He sipped thoughtfully, "Most of them seem keen, but there's one guy I just can't get through to. He's the oldest, but there's something deep I can't feel comfortable with."

An unexpected shiver slithered down my spine. I shook myself and the feeling passed. Antonio felt my chill; the moment wriggled away. We commiserated and spent the next hour decrying modern youth. As we looked at the new barmaid, he said ruefully, "Now I could just do something with her."

I stared at him in mock horror, "You don't mean?"

He flushed, "Of course not! But I reckon the Duke will benefit nicely." Smiling I knew exactly what he meant.

Chapter 9 Progress

Bill and I got on better the following day. The new components from the suppliers fitted like a glove. It began to look as if we might finish on time and with a little to spare. Liza called just after ten as I was running a test on the oscillator; the extra long wave length really was a pain. Despite the tension of the work I was still susceptible to that smile of hers; my heart did not quite somersault, but I was still very pleased to see her creamy complexion crinkle into the welcome I was beginning to recognise as special to me. I began to dare hope Liza felt as I did. She must have seen the tiredness in my own eyes, because she put down the usual buff envelope without a word. She put her hand on mine and spoke softly, "Let's take a break; in the Jag if you like. What about Chasewater?"

I grimaced, "Too busy and noisy. No. Let's go somewhere more peaceful." She was clearly pleased, so we decided to drive out into the country where some churches were putting on a flower festival about then. It was a sight to see in a slow and unhurried way. It was just the thing for my jaded nerves. We had a quick bite at the Cathedral Coffee shop before strolling to the car hand in hand.

We left in the crush of traffic and thankfully headed for the relative peace of the east beyond the ring road. I drove steadily, the open top letting the breeze ruffle our hair in the sunshine. It was wonderful and a life saver. I really enjoyed the calm of Clifton Campville church. We had a light tea in a little café and I began to feel human once more. Liza seemed to be less than her usual lively self, rather preoccupied.

I did not push it, but let it flow in the hope that she would open up.

She did not do so, but she did recover some interest in the different approaches to flower arrangements in the other churches we visited. By the time we saw the last one we were sated with the sight of colour and form.

Partly to lift the silence between us I played a piece from Bartok's Concerto for Orchestra on the CD deck I had surreptitiously added to the Jaguar's comforts. As the dancing notes flew out into the wind of our passage, I felt at peace and glanced at Liza. I was shocked to see a tear run down her cheek. Pulling into a layby at the first opportunity I turned off the music. She blinked and looked at me with brimming eyes, "Why did you do that?" As the notes drifted off in the breeze, a bee buzzed his annoyance. I was at a loss, I stammered, "Well, I thought ... well, you seemed to be upset. "

She smiled a genuine smile, "It was lovely; it was so moving I couldn't keep it in." She brushed her cheek. "Would you mind playing it again, louder?" For answer I complied and drove on, the weaving notes combining with the sense of Liza's loveliness, the sweet running engine and the warm breeze. It was with regret that we neared the Birmingham road. Liza touched my arm, "Is there a country hotel we can eat at? I'm not ready for the city yet. I want some space right now."

I swung north. "I could try Rafter's, I suppose," I said hesitantly, "but I'm not dressed for company."

She shook her head, "No I don't want a big place, let's just look."

In the end, we found a little pub on the banks of the Trent and Mersey canal. We stayed there for hours, mostly just sitting and watching the narrow boats passing. Liza was amazed at the variety of designs; she was captivated by the decorative painting on the traditional styled boats. It was something I had never thought too much about; being born in Fradley they were just part of the scenery.

It was darkening slowly in that soft, intimate, June night as we reluctantly rose to leave. Liza took my hand naturally and without hesitation. It was all too good to last. On the way back to Liza's hotel I played 'The Swan' by Saint Saens. The languor of the stately melody suited my mood exactly. The tinge of sadness was part of it too. The summer air washed our minds, calming, soothing, and relaxing. Even the hands of the car clock were reluctant to move too fast. But others were seething and about to erupt.

Chapter 10 Confidences.

At her hotel, she said, "Please come in for a moment, there's something I want to show you." I wondered, but there was only one thing to do. I followed her. She had a typical hotel room, one that could be anywhere in the world. She took off her light coat and opened the window. I could see her standing, back-lit by the hotel floodlights, her hair turned to a halo by the sodium glow. Dimming the room lights, she walked over to the dressing table and lifted a portable CD player on to it. She switched it on and stood once again by the window as the sad, sweet strains of a Chopin Nocturne drifted out into the warm night air. For once the city noises were muted as if in deference to the delicacy of the emotive air. As it finished, neither of us spoke, neither moved for many minutes.

I broke the spell as I stood, "Thank you for that. It was wonderful, the perfect end to a perfect day." She remained, tantalisingly silhouetted at the window, an enigmatic goddess in a golden world.

I held my breath as she spoke softly, "Do you ever feel that something is too good to last?" Stupidly I nodded in the dark before speaking.

"I haven't felt that for some time," she murmured, "Until today." Nothing else was said, needed to be put into words, but I just knew that we had reached a crossroads in our lives. I let my love send out a tendril, it seemed to me that it met and entwined another equally fragile contact.

I don't know how long we stood. I dared not move for fear of breaking the fragility of the moment. In the end it was Liza who spoke of the music, "I am sorry it was only on my portable, but it is lovely."

"Why did the music move you so much in the car?" I whispered. She came to me in the golden dusk, an almost ethereal presence in an enchanted kingdom.

"I haven't told you, but I'm Hungarian by birth. Bartok is able to lift my soul back to Hungary. He died in America a wandering soul far from his homeland. I feel that he wrote purely for me and my longing to go home." Her voice trembled as she spoke. I wanted to take her into my arms, to embrace her to reassure her. But I did nothing. There was no part for me in that area of her life; I just had to let her be alone with her solitude and melancholy.

But I did do one thing. I spoke softly, "Would you like to hear those discs on my system some time? I've a Bose that's quite good."

The reply was equally soft, "Yes, I would like that very much!" I left then, quietly, leaving her in the darkening room, still standing at the window.

She seemed to be a world away from the Liza I had first seen. Which, I wondered, was the real Liza?

* * *

It was as I was going to work the following day that I saw the Texan leaving the Central Hotel. It was a sight to wonder at, more of a Royal tour departure with the porters rushing out with enormous cases, all under the authoritarian eye of the doorman. I wondered what his excess baggage charge would be and I was glad I wasn't responsible for it. His deep growl reached me over the chaotic bustle, "I'll be back soon as I've gotten this little old problem licked! Be back before you can brush the steps." It was clear that the search for the Roger de Clinton connection was not yet over.

As the overloaded taxi headed for the Birmingham road, I checked the office integrity and entered as usual. Bill was not due for another quarter hour so I made a cup of instant coffee and munched breakfast, a half chocolate-coated, wholemeal biscuit. There was still a fullness in my torso from the meal last night.

There was also a warm, comfortable glow from the savoured memory of Liza's nearness. Smiling to myself I remembered the sight of her silhouette in the golden glow. I felt relaxed and calmer than I had for ages. Thinking back, I suppose I hadn't been at peace since the time it was clear that Dad was going to die. It was a pleasant change.

I strolled over to the window and was amazed to see a police car arrive at the Central. Two uniformed officers went in, accompanied by Antonio. Idly I wondered if the Texan had gone off with the silver. It didn't seem a feasible premise; I dismissed it as Bill strode up to the door. As I unlocked the remote, I was dismayed to see the fat man behind him. He was walking along with his strange device again. It suddenly became imperative to find out what it was. Before I could do anything about it, he went off towards the Cathedral at a quick walk. I was still frowning when Bill came in.

"Morning Grumpy!" His obvious good spirits made me smile.

"Have a good day yesterday, Bill?" I asked. A big smile was the answer, "Great! Sheila was up and about, when I returned so we went to Chasewater. It was a bit crowded," I mentally gave thanks for my choice yesterday, "But we rowed a boat and had an ice cream. We were like kids from school. It did us a world of good." He paused, "You look as if you had a good time too."

I nodded, "Felt better than for years. Good music, good company, the hood down and too much food. Yes, I did have a good time."

I sighed with pleasure, "For once I'm ready to work. I want you to look at this carrier wave generator before you go back to that ADV. Can it wait?" Bill nodded. I went on, "I

53

can't seem to keep it steady for long, I suspect this chip might be faulty."

There was a definite cooling of Bill's good humour. At the time I put it down to the problem in hand. After about an hour, Bill sat back and stretched, "It's not the chip; I'll stake my life on that."

I was getting very frustrated by the elusiveness of the answer, so I let my frustration come out in annoyance, "So what the hell do you think it is? Gremlins are out of fashion."

There was a hardening of Bill's mouth and he let out a long slow breath and he started to drum his fingers on the workbench. This was too much. "For God's sake, Bill, cut it out, I've had enough."

He stopped drumming and stood. There was a steely glint in his eyes, "There is no need to take God's name in vain. There is a problem that you couldn't find right? I'm only the hired help trying to find it."

"Don't be so touchy," I growled back, "I thought we could still work as a team. If you can't I'll slog on alone."

"Don't think you're the only one with problems."

"I suppose you want to get back to your hidey-hole. And there's no need to come over all religious with me. If you feel like that I'll probably be better without your help."

Bill strode to his workroom, "Good!" He slammed the door. I sat wondering how we had gone so far from our normal harmony. So I turned back to the hateful project. Was that the reason? I was tempted to pitch the lot. But of course my professionalism came to the fore and I plugged in another meter. The rest of the day went in eliminating possible causes until I traced it to the simplest thing, a dry connection.

As I was straightening my stiff back, the bell rang and I saw Liza on the monitor screen. She was in wearing her business suit; hair was loose, framing her face, not in the becoming pony tail. She had been carrying the local evening paper, which she dropped on the desk. I stiffened as I saw the headlines, MAN ATTACKED IN CENTRAL.

She saw my glance and grimaced, "Someone beat up the old night porter last night." She shrugged away the unpleasantness as if it did not matter. But it was clear that she had been ruffled by something.

Her smile to me was genuine, but brief. "I have to take the transmitter to an evaluation test tomorrow, if it's ready. Can I collect it tomorrow?" My face must have registered my incredulity, for she went on, "There's been some pressure to advance the date by a week to next month." Bill came in as she dropped this bombshell.

I nearly swore, my peace of mind went out of the window, "You can't be serious. It isn't on!"

She went quiet, before speaking softly, with a steely edge, "I don't like it either, but it really is necessary."

She suddenly softened, looked appealingly at Bill and then me, "I will say no, if it really is impossible."

I massaged my brow, "OK! I'll stay here tonight and wind it all up. What time do you want it?"

"Six o clock in the morning."

My jaw dropped, "Tomorrow is Sunday, if you have not noticed. What the hell's the rush?"

She was calm as she spoke, "Yes I know it's the Sabbath, and that should tell you what the rush is like. Can you do it?"

I nodded wearily, "Yes, yes. OK! I get the message. I'll be here."

She gave me a warmer smile that put some of the warmth back in me, "Why don't you come with me, it might be fun?"

I ruminated momentarily. 'Why the hell not?' I thought, the idea of fun at six-o-clock on a Sunday morning was rather incongruous. I simply nodded and said, "OK!" At that she smiled. It was not exactly the warmest smile I have seen, in fact for a moment, it made her positively impish; the sort of imp that has a red hot, toasting fork. The look vanished in an instant.

I should have been warned.

Chapter 11 Fun and Games.

I was at the office by 5 am that quiet morning. It was almost eerily quiet in the Three Spires Centre, only the subdued cooing of the pigeons met my solitary footsteps as I yawned drowsily past the sleeping populace. The sun was lightening the sky, which promised another wonderful day. On a day like this I did not want to be anywhere but in the English countryside, preferably in my XK 120 with the hood down, burbling happily along a lane in the unspoiled area to the north. Idly I wondered what the official car would be like that Liza drove; could I persuade her to come in the Jag instead. I breakfasted on my usual coffee and biscuit after packing the prototype in a bubble wrap and then impatiently watched the door monitor.

Just before six, I saw Liza's slim figure, dressed this time in a dark blue trouser suit, step confidently along the lane. Quickly shutting the office door I met her as she reached the shop next door. I was rewarded with a dimpled smile that gave me a happy, warm feeling. Today was going to be good, I could feel it. I carried the long box easily under one arm as we walked side by side to Frog Lane car park. The sun was beginning to reach the ground between the narrow lanes. I said persuasively, "Let's not waste the day, let's go in the Jag - I can lie about your expenses if you like." There was the flicker of a mischievous smirk as she said, "I couldn't do that. You never know who might see us." I waved at the empty streets, "Like who, for instance?"

She still shook her head as we neared the deserted space, "I really want to drive myself for once." Resigned, I capitulated. '*Ah well,*' I thought, '*at least I can watch Liza.*'

There were few cars, mostly box-like Repmobiles, my Jag stood aloof as befitted her pedigree. Liza pressed her remote key fob and the hazard lights flashed on her car.

My eyes popped. What a car!

It was no boxy Repmobile. It was jet black, with a huge spoiler at the rear, tyres as fat as paint rollers and an air of menace that only the Porsche Carrera Sport can exude. The 3.5 flat six is a vicious beast, it can eat you up and spit out the bits faster than a Striking Cobra. Liza laughed gleefully at my expression, "Do you still want to go in that ancient chariot?" Dazed, I shook my head, ignoring the derogatory description of my first love.

I stowed the box in the minuscule rear seats and strapped myself in the red leather, bucket seat in the front. Liza slid in and turned the key. It was a good thing I didn't know what was to come.

There was a grinding and a bellow, which immediately slowed to an uneven rumble as the highly tuned engine slowly flexed its muscles.

My eyes scanned the instruments, all set for the driver's convenience. In addition to the usual dials there were one or two oddities; there was a key pad near the driver's left hand and two push buttons near the right. However, I did not have the time to ponder as Liza, with a squeak from those fat tyres, spurted out into the ring road. It was not now totally deserted, but there was still nothing to pose any obstacle to quick travel. Liza swirled round the roundabout at a speed that would have left my Jag spinning wildly. The narrow live axle and skinny tyres of mine need a careful touch. The Porsche seemed to be stuck to the road with superglue. The acceleration was enough to thrust my head hard against the headrest. I was grateful for the four point harness instead of a seat belt.

Liza was quick; there is no doubt of that. We did not exceed the speed limit by more than ten mph until we reached the M1, but it was twice as quick as I would have been in my Jag.

In the corner of my eye, I saw her profile and watched her more than the scenery - not that there is much scenery on the M1. There were more cars and an occasional lorry trundling along by the time we reached the boring bit.

We had not exchanged more than six words by then, I was content to sit and watch her drive. She drove as well as she walked, her action was fluid, smooth and seductive in its confidence and poise.

I felt rather than saw the surroundings passing very quickly, glanced at the speedo. My eyes opened, 140! I did a quick mental calculation. 140 kph was roughly ... say ...84 mph. I pointed to the speedo and spoke loudly over the wind noise, "140 K is over 70; it wouldn't do to be caught speeding!" The grin she turned to me definitely was impish, "That *is* miles, not kilometres!" She laughed out loud at my face as the realisation sank in.

A quick glance at the rapidly vanishing rear view penetrated my calm appreciation of her features; I squeaked in alarm, "Slow down, you'll have every policeman in the Thames Constabulary after you."

She laughed, a wild, carefree laugh, but did not slow down. Just then I realised that we had passed a Volvo Police Car, which pulled out, to chase us, blue lights flashing. Not surprisingly, I couldn't hear the siren.

I jerked thumb rearwards, her wicked smile broadened. I noticed her left hand toy with the keyboard. The next moment, her foot went down hard and I was thrown back against the bucket seat. Dimly it registered that there was a new note, a form of scream from behind us as the speed shot up to 160, 165, 170 and continued to rise - rapidly.

The few other vehicles were disappearing behind us in a blur, it felt as if we would be airborne any moment, but the speed did not slacken for several miles.

I was terrified. I don't think I shut my eyes, but I can recall little but the impression of being in free fall, with no control over anything.

It ended when she suddenly swerved to the nearside, slowed as if we had an arrester parachute behind and dived off at Junction 9, towards Redbourn.

There was a minor squeal from the rear tyres as she flashed into a service station and stopped dead round the back of the reception. She was grinning like the Cheshire Cat and more alive than I had ever seen her up to then. She reminded me of a member of a visiting team at a Christmas party. She'd been high on crack! I suppose that Liza was high on adrenalin. Whatever it was it left me a quivering heap of jangled nerves. I just sat, stunned, while Liza's face threatened to split in two from the excitement bubbling from her grin.

As I sat, slowly gathering my shattered equilibrium, the manic grin turned to concern, she seemed to collapse a little, "I'm sorry if I frightened you, but I needed that."

I slowly struggled to sit up in the close-fitting seat, my voice was a trembling quaver, "What about the police car, they must have your number at least."

She started to chuckle, it turned into a real laugh. With a delicate handkerchief she dabbed her eyes, "Fat lot of good it will do," she coughed and wiped her eyes again, "he'll recognise it ... it's his own!" She looked at my shocked face and doubled up laughing and choking. Eventually she calmed down and spoke between giggles, "The plates are LCDs I changed them to his number when I saw him." I was speechless. Of course, the Key pad.

It was then my turn to double up with laughter, the thought of a policeman calling up for the owner of his own number struck me as so ludicrous that, combined with the relief at still being alive, I went almost into hysterics. It was Liza's concerned "Bert!" that stopped my fit.

I looked at her in wonder and admiration, "I'll say one thing. By heck, you can drive!" From me that was true praise indeed. Later, of course I was to realise that this was just one aspect of her incredible control.

We sat for some more moments, listening to the clicks from the cooling engine. I suddenly sat up, "Just what have you got in the back of this thing?"

She was slightly embarrassed, as if caught out bragging, "Well, it's not too much really, it has high lift cams, hot valves and a supercharger that comes in at seven thousand." She lowered her eyes, "It's good for 195 on the flat, but I've only done it once."

She looked me straight in the eyes and I felt again that sensation of being stripped of every mental barrier, her soul met mine as no-one else has ever done. It was at that moment that I came closest to knowing the real Liza and it was when I wanted to be with her for every moment of every day. It was not sexual in the least, just a total meshing of mind and spirit.

Leaning over I pulled her to me and kissed her on the lips. I was unprepared for the slight saltiness on them. She surprised me more by the hungry way she responded and seemed to be reluctant to let go.

We did draw back; we drew back as if looking at a chasm opening before us. We saw the widening gap and had to decide which side we wanted to be on. I hesitated to return to my old life and the choice was made for me by there being no way back. What had started out as an instant infatuation had become a way of life that was permanent, which could never be changed, no matter what came to us in the future. The love I found then is eternal and indestructible; it will last to the end of time, beyond life itself.

At that moment I found something that very few are privileged to even see, even less to experience.

We had a sort of coffee break/breakfast in the plastic café at the service station. Ordinarily I would have avoided such a place like the plague. But on this momentous occasion no nectar of the gods tasted so sweet. It was all due to Liza and it was utterly incredible.

We drove relatively slowly to the testing station, an anonymous cube-like building on the small industrial estate near St Albans. DEMOLISH was given a run with a large, box-like object attached by heavy duty cables. I wondered at the need for such amperage. There was some muttering from the white-coated technician. He sent us off for some lunch while he analysed his data. For some reason that I could not precisely pinpoint, I did not take to him; he was abusing my baby and I did not like it. We went to a little tourist café that was too crowded for my state of mind. The wonderful day was fading. We ate in a quiet mood, I knew that Liza was in a sort of withdrawal state after her adrenalin-driven high of the morning, but she too seemed to be reluctant to leave the transmitter with the white-coated tester.

We went back to the square building with a sense of foreboding. It was obvious that the feeling was justified as we were met by the bald statement that it was all right as far as it went, but to be on the safe side it had to take more power.

I fussed and grumbled, I objected about the resizing that would be needed, but all to no avail. It had to be done. Despite some not very subtle probing about what was being transmitted, and why the wavelength was so long, I left the testing station annoyed and frustrated. Outside the weather was glorious, but it might as well have been midwinter for the gloom in my heart.

Liza drove back sedately, but the journey seemed endless. I hated the project and wished I had never taken it on; but then, I thought, I would not have met Liza. It was not a happy homecoming and we parted in almost silence.

Chapter 12 Breakdown.

I was no happier on the following Monday morning as Bill came in singing, "We dig, dig, dig, we dig, dig, dig, we dig the whole day through." Waspishly I commented, "We're not digging, we're rebuilding. Guess who thought they needed more power!"

His face fell, he swore, which was a very unusual event for him, "What the hell do they want to do? Blow up the Cathedral?"

At the time it seemed a totally ludicrous idea. I shrugged, "That was another thing; they don't seem to be very forthcoming about what they do want to do with it." I scowled at the desk, "I have a nasty suspicious mind on this one, Bill. It's a case of '*You don't need to know so we're not telling you.*'" Savagely I went on, "What I can't stand is that they're up to something that's risky, they're involving me and they won't even trust me enough to say what it is. All this power they want, it's more than the NEC uses. What are they up to?"

Bill was no longer in his normal easy going frame of mind, he almost snarled, "Hasn't that girl friend of yours given you what you want?"

There was a shocked silence for a full minute, Bill had the grace to look unhappy for some seconds, but then his face hardened.

I spoke softly, with menace, "Just what do you mean by that remark?"

Bill turned as if to go, but I repeated louder, "Come on, what did you mean?"

He turned a red face to me, "Nothing, nothing at all!"

It was an obvious lie, so I snapped back, "Well why say it then?"

He stiffened and turned back, "All right then, it may have sounded coarse, but I thought you and her were buddies, as close as Tweedle Dum and Tweedle Dee. Don't tell me you haven't heard something in your cosy chats."

I almost spat back, "What I do is no concern of yours, and keep Liza out of it!"

He smirked, "Oh! Liza is it, no longer the correct Ms Vancyk. Have you had her in bed yet?"

The instant he said it he knew he had gone too far. But it was too far for an apology, a retreat. He stood his ground as someone facing a firing squad. At that moment I could cheerfully have shot him where he stood.

"Bill ... Mr Huddleston. That remark is totally uncalled for. I suggest you go and think carefully what you are to do next. In all our eight years of working together there has not been an occasion like this one."

I stood up and moved to the door, "I'm going out for ten minutes to give you time to think. What happens when I return is up to you."

I left; Bill still glowering with a face of thunder.

I walked to the Cathedral coffee shop and back, I entered the nondescript door, mounted the stairs and entered the clutter of my domain. Bill did not seem to have moved. He stood irresolute, growled from his boots, "I apologise unreservedly. It was stupid and crude. I had no right and no cause to say what I did. It's just ...well, this is getting to me as no other project has and I thought, I thought I was being shut out. With you and Liza ..." He let it tail off lamely.

"If only I knew, I would tell you. But I don't." I looked him straight in the eye, "Do you believe me?"

He was not too sure of anything, that much was obvious; he heaved his great shoulders in resignation, "Look what's happening to us."

We returned to work, but it was hard and not satisfying.

I wondered where it was to end.

In Liza's absence I worked day and night at the modifications to boost the output. It was difficult, but after a week of intense effort, Bill and I managed to fit it all in the same dimension casing.

I was concerned about the possible effects of the output causing overheating. As we were still in the dark as to the usage and purpose, we could only guess at the current drain and duration.

There was something missing in the relationship between Bill and myself. We had recovered from the fireworks of the blow up of a week earlier, but there was a reticence that had not been present before Liza's appearance. I missed the easy rapport that we had, but there was no way back, even if I'd wanted there to be. The truth was that Liza had started to be part of my life in a way that I would not have believed possible. I'd not been so deeply involved with my various girl friends over the last ten years. My mind ran back to Margaret. It seemed for six months that we were settling into a steady state of togetherness that would lead to marriage or at least the modern equivalent. Although I was brought up in the Methodist tradition, it all seemed to be irrelevant to my life after my mother left. Dad never said as much, but there was a hint of censure from one of the ladies of the chapel when he started to visit a friend, a quiet widow.

He was seen by the Minister several times and told that there was no stigma attached, but it seemed to cast a shadow over services he attended.

In the end he just stayed away and the Minister's visits stopped. They ceased altogether when the Stationing Committee did its work and Ministers changed at the end of five years.

Looking back, I was sorry for Dad, he might have struck up a new friendship with that gentle lady if the disapproval had not been there. As it was, he died in his own quiet way and Jean is still gentle and alone. To tell the truth, I would have liked them to marry; she was clearly drawn to Dad as he was to her.

The feelings died under the chill of one dour person. The tragedy was that both were too gentle to fight hard for something they needed, too afraid to suffer any rebuffs. Now I learned from this. I thought I was falling for Margaret and her for me.

It was all going along steadily, days out in my Metro, just occasionally in the Jag, and nights out at the cinema or even events in the NEC. Once we went to London for The Phantom of the Opera and stayed overnight, separate rooms of course, but it introduced a thrill into the trip that put us firmly into the 'couple' bracket in the eyes of the church and Dad as well, bless him. It all went wrong when she suggested we visit a new housing development on the old Maxtock Grange estate. Without thinking too deeply we were starting to plan for the unspoken tying of the knot. It was as the cheerful salesman was talking of mortgages, earnings multiples and terms of loan that it suddenly struck me that I was getting in too deep without being certain it was what I wanted. It didn't help when Margaret described me as an electrician. I could not tell her exactly what Arraye Electronics did produce. She wasn't very inquisitive. She was beginning to show signs of restlessness. The description 'ball and chain' was beginning to sound too real for my comfort. I did not want a repeat of history, to be drawn into a situation where there was no strong reason for a life together. I wanted companionship, but merely being good friends wasn't enough. Margaret didn't actually break off the affair, but she cooled and didn't try too hard to stoke matters up again. It was as a result of that as much as Dad's unhappy divorce that made me keep a guard on my emotions. Then there was Joan of the high heels and low neckline, she did not even rate as a serious girl-friend; she thought of herself above anything else. Then there was Brenda. She was afraid of a commitment; she's still afraid, uncommitted and single.

I thought I was armour-plated as far as women went. There had been too many rejections. I was happy enough in my dedication to work, especially as Dad's early death had made me take up the reins before I wanted to. Until Liza appeared!

Now, I wanted to be with her above all else, even at this stage of not knowing all about her. As I thought about it, I knew precious little.

But I didn't care, I was as sure that I wanted to spend the rest of my life with her as I had ever been sure of anything. The past week's activity had taken my mind off her for a time, but now that the time was approaching for her to return, I was edgy and impatient.

Bill knew this and was unsure what I really was thinking, what the future held for him and for me. We still got along well, but there was no longer the feeling that Bill was my best pal.

Chapter 13 Developments.

I was still in this frame of mind when Liza came back to check on progress. The weather had gone from the regular succession of fine weather that we dream of, to the usual English mix of showers and sun that we try to ignore. It was the show season with the English optimism that persists in planning outdoor events and hoping that this year will be better than last. The car show had been dampish: the Arts Festival, being indoors, had done better. It was in the bustle of preparations for the Medieval Market that, through the hidden monitor, I next saw Liza, black hair swinging, coming to the door of our office. Waiting for her had seemed endless and now I felt a tingle of excitement as I saw her stride confidently along the lane. She was as welcome as a summer breeze; her smile had a warm and personal quality, setting my senses soaring. Our touch of hands was slightly longer than absolutely necessary. Possibly due to the slight mugginess her hand was warm, not its usual calm coolness. She was genuinely pleased at the readiness of DEMOLISH Mk. 2; to be honest I didn't think she believed we could do it. If it hadn't been for the chill between Bill and me, I don't think we would have. Ah well, every cloud has a silver lining. Liza was not so pleased to see my tiredness, she remarked, "You're not heading for some illness are you?" I reassured her, "Only short of sleep. " I nearly added, '*and a shortage of my favourite customer,*' but didn't.

She must have sensed this thought, she murmured for me only to hear, "I need to deliver the unit tomorrow, but there's no rush this time." There was a pause as she went on almost persuasively, "I never did take you up on your offer to play your Hi-Fi for me. Could I invite myself tonight to play some of my discs?" She went on in an apologetic tone, "I could bring a bottle and a pizza."

Despite my tiredness, life flowed back into my brain. There was no way that our first meal in my house was going to be a pizza!

I had become used to cooking for myself and developed quite a skill in quick, but interesting dishes.

It was with both a touch of pride and anticipation of an evening together that I replied, "Bring the bottle by all means, but you're going to sample the Haute Cuisine à la Fradley."

She did raise an eyebrow at this retort, but simply said, "What time and where do you live?" I said to be there at seven, and drew a sketch map. She took it and left leaving a trace of a perfume I couldn't place, but which was very pleasant, not heavy. I was no longer tired and Bill noticed as he came to say he was going home.

Most people are surprised at the smallness of my concern; they think that a manufacturer needs a factory, imposing premises and a huge research budget. I had followed Dad's lead in keeping a firm hold on every stage personally.

Bill and I so were tuned to each other's thoughts that we had an almost telepathic insight for the answers to the development problems. In essence listening devices are simple, all they have to do is to change sound waves into radio waves and send them somewhere. It's the need to avoid detection that poses the problems. With the growth of the 'in ear' type of hearing aid, there are any number of chips, processors and resisters that fitted the majority of our applications, it is only the very special applications that need the secret ones, they come from Silicone Valley via HMG. I do also have a contact with a research department at Newcastle University that they don't know about. That helps me to keep one step ahead of the CIA, Mossad and the rest. I want MI5 to have the best. They do as long as their employer pays me enough. I was not out to make a fortune, but I tried to safeguard my future, you never know when there might be a change of mood or a new head of department. On the personal side I ran my Jaguar and a Rover 400 that was rather faster than the usual, my small cottage was on the outskirts of Whittington, I'd moved there from the family home in Fradley when the RAF base became an industrial estate.

I bought the old orchard and some acres of rough woodland as an insurance against creeping development to keep the house secluded and hidden. My whole life was in low profile. I lived quietly and just got on with my simple life as a bachelor.

But this was about to change in the preparations for Liza's evening visit. I collected some ingredients from the supermarket and a bottle from the Dog Inn as I went home. I was still tired, but the aim to please Liza drove the fatigue to the back of my mind. Dinner was going to be my own version of Beef Wellington, it involved some shortcuts that would have had a purist horror struck, and I didn't care. For me the joy was in eating, not spending ages in the handling of pastry and sauces. I'm sure that many of the TV chefs and cooks are just show-offs. Anyway, I wanted to be ready in good time.

The smells were becoming tantalising by seven o clock, so I was pleased and more than a bit relieved as I heard a car engine burble up the bumpy lane. There was a knock on the door.

I was not prepared for the sight of Liza in a cream, silky gown at the door. It was sheath-like with the thinnest of straps, which revealed her beautifully formed shoulders. The delicate, soft material had a subtle tone that made her skin look attractively and evenly tanned.

The contrast of my open necked shirt and rumpled, fawn slacks made me warm with embarrassment.

I flushed a little more as she leaned forward to kiss me on the cheek and I caught a scent of the perfume she had left lingering in my office. Covering my discomfort I turned to allow her to enter my lounge/living room. It is not really a lounge, but it is where I spend most of my leisure time. It's, well, sort of rumpled and comfortable; a bit like me really. It's rather too cluttered to be elegant, but it's fitted with the best in audio and visual electronics so that I can watch or listen in both the lounge and bedroom equally well.

The ceiling is low-beamed and rustic. I like it and it suits me fine.

Liza gazed around. She didn't speak for some seconds. She turned to me with a soft smile, "I like it." For some unaccountable reason this pleased me as she went on, "It's absolutely wonderful. Have you lived here long?"

I blushed at the accolade, "Three years now. I couldn't stand the family home a moment longer when Dad died, this turned up and I've been making it my own ever since." I suddenly said, "I hope you had no trouble finding your way, most people don't even know I'm here."

She grinned, "Yes, it's not exactly on the M1! In fact I grounded once or twice. If you'd warned me I might have come in a Land Rover."

We both laughed at that. "That's one of the reasons I bought it, I like to be out of sight at home."

The atmosphere was becoming warm and informal, despite the effect of Liza's dress on me. The sight had unnerved me at first, but now I watched her with unalloyed pleasure. She saw my eyes and her cheeks dimpled. I wasn't sure, but thought I detected a very faint touch of pink on her cheeks. She was gorgeous and she knew it. I put on a disc of Chopin, can't remember which one, but it was clearly a good choice for her, her eyes sparkled in the low lighting. The meal was a marvellous success, I'd been nervous carving the beef, but it was every bit as good as I'd hoped; Liza enjoyed everything immensely and said so without being fulsome. I can't really remember what we talked about, but it was not about surveillance devices. The bottle she'd brought was a Hungarian red that was fruity with a touch of sharpness. She looked pleased when I complimented her on the choice, but there was a sad and faraway look in her eyes then for a moment.

The dishwasher swallowed the debris and I closed the kitchen door as we drank coffee to the final strains of the Chopin. She leaned back contentedly into the softness of my sofa. It is easy to sink into, not so easy to get out of, it's a place to relax and let the world go by. As the silence descended I struggled up to change the disc.

Liza looked round her, "Is this the Bose you mentioned?" She spoke in a slow, low voice as I nodded, "Could I hear one of my Bartoks?"

"That's the reason for your coming."

She passed me the disc from her carry case. I read the label, "Concerto for Orchestra." I looked at her lounging comfortably in the sofa, "It's a world apart from Chopin, but I like it." We sat and listened as the composition rose and fell in tone, volume and intensity. At first I'd not been at all sure - I was much more at ease with my Chopin collection - but after a time the feeling of sadness was replaced with a sense of strength and power, the power of endurance and inner strength of hope for the future. Don't ask me to explain it; it just seemed to grow in my understanding of his labour of love and his breaking away from the rigid strictures of classic composition.

As the last notes trembled away, Liza was trembling too. I turned in some concern, wondering if she was cool. The look on her face wrenched my heart. There was a deep yearning, an unsatisfied longing, a look of loss. It did not seem real that the music could affect her so much, but at the same time it made me hesitate to interrupt what was clearly a personal sensation. A tear slowly trickled from her eye and ran down that soft cheek. She suddenly brushed it away and, as if a switch had been touched, her face lit up and she smiled. It was a smile of peace, not poignancy. She murmured, "That was wonderful! That system of yours brings out the very delicate nature of the score as I've not heard it before. I loved it. Thank you."

I scrambled out of the sofa again to place one of Chopin's Polonaises in the deck and returned to flop beside her, "I was worried for a time, I thought you were unhappy. I wondered if it was a disappointment."

She seemed to be surprised at this, "Not in the least. In fact I was in the realm of the spirit of longing for his homeland." She paused, and then continued, "I'm Hungarian by birth, I suppose that is why I feel as he did. I have not been there since I was 10, but I feel as if I'm just lodging here until I can return home. Does that seem stupid to you?"

Gazing into those deep eyes, I tried to see into her soul, "I would never think you stupid. I've only known you for weeks, but I'm sure as I am sure of anything that you know exactly what you want and the way to get it." She grinned wryly at that. I reassured her, "I know how I feel about people and I'd trust you with my life."

At this her smile froze, she seemed to put a solid screen between us, "Those are strong words, strong and not too wise. I warn you not to take everything on trust, you need to be aware of the dangers and keep your wits about you."

My retort was foolishly confident, "I know all about that, I've been aware of the pitfalls there are for a long time. It's made me wary and rather lonely. Not because I can't stand company, in fact I want to be able to share my innermost feelings with someone who trusts and sees me in the same light."

Releasing her hand I wriggled out of the sofa again, "Ever since I saw my mother walk out of the door, when I was five, I've been afraid to trust anyone completely, until now." My words were inadequate to express my conviction, "Don't ask me how, but I know you can be trusted with that most vulnerable part of me that I've kept apart all these years." Looking down at her reclining in the nest-like sofa, I laid my feelings bare, "Tell me one thing. Do you trust me?" There was a mixture of emotions for the merest fraction of a second, before she held out a hand. She said nothing as I sat uncomfortably, but examined my face as if seeing it for the first time.

When she did speak it was a little uncertainly and gently, "I think you need to know me better, but ... yes, I do trust you. I've been unable to trust anybody for nearly all my life; it's been so long that I've nearly lost the ability to do so." I sensed that this was a revelation of herself that was not at all easy.

This was a critical moment in our relationship so I said nothing, but waited. She spoke lightly, breaking the spell, "Could I have another glass of wine?"

Feeling dismissed, I flushed, "Sorry! I've a fresh bottle of Asti, would you like that? It must be nicely chilled and is a good one." She simply nodded as answer.

I went to the kitchen to take the bottle from the 'fridge, but sensed her behind me before she spoke, "Could I use your bathroom for a minute?"

I apologised again for my failure, "Let me show you round. It's not a stately home, but it is interesting. This once had three bedrooms and an outside loo. I made one of the bedrooms into a decent bathroom, another into a study cum tip. Down here there is this kitchen, a laundry room, pantry and the living room." Rather aggressively I went on, "It's cluttered, but that's how I like it and how I expect it to stay."

She smiled disarming my prickliness, "I don't care about any clutter, what I do care about is the 'lived in' feel, I can't stand fussiness. But I'm not a minimalist and like somewhere to surround me with the empathy of the house. This house has had many happy times in its past and it's happy you're here now." She hesitated then went on, "Unfortunately, I haven't been able to find that aura as I'm always on the move." My heart jumped as she went on, "I could settle here given the chance." I looked, but there was no coquettishness, no hint of an undercurrent. To assert my domestic dominance I cleared my throat and led the way to the bathroom.

As I waited in the kitchen, my mind was racing, imagining and wondering. I could find no answer.

There was a swish from her dress as she descended the narrow stair with a sparkle in her eyes, a touch of peach on her cheeks. In that setting, the sense of intimacy was almost overpowering. The swirl of her dress only served to emphasise her slender figure. The urge to hold her, to embrace and to kiss her was powerful.

Resisting the impulse I still hesitated and did nothing; we sat once again in the depths of the sofa.

Chapter 14 Family History.

Liza sipped the Asti appreciatively and told me of her life.

"I was born near the city of Gyor, one of the tribe of Magyars. It's near the Duna, the Danube to you, on a plain that's well watered, crossed by canals and streams. The Magyar are wonderful horsemen, I rode as soon as I could hang on to the mane of my pony." She went on wistfully, "My parents were poor, and Papa was a pastor in the Lutheran Church, popular with the farmers. It was not popular with the government and hated by the local Communists. For one thing it had always been independent of the state; I suppose that's one reason. It's also why there was the trouble that led to us all leaving in the night one spring." She looked into her glass as if she could read the past there. There was a hiatus until she continued in a musing tone, "The troubles always seem to be in the spring, it must be the rebirth of life." I could sense the threatening forces.

"Anyway, we were told by the village policeman that it would be prudent to take an extended visit to Wien, Vienna, right away. He was a Magyar first and a policeman second." I nodded and still said nothing. Liza sighed and stretched. She went on sadly, "At first Papa refused to go. I was only ten, but can still remember the cries of my mother. In the end, it was the local Communist leader, of all people, who persuaded father to go." She smiled at the thought, "He'd been opposed to religion, but still admired father more than some of the jumped-up politicos." I thought that it wasn't only in the East of Europe that there were pretentious, self-important officials.

"We went to Austria, but there was so much pressure on the Austrians from Beograd that we slipped away again and came to England through the church contacts. Father filled the pastoral need for a congregation of exiled Hungarians at

Hednesford and would have still been there, but for his feeling of guilt at fleeing."

There was s fleeting pain on her face, but it vanished quickly, "In the local school my lack of English was soon changed. I learned quickly through being befriended by the girls of my class. It was all so new, exciting and fun going to their parties; I sang Magyar songs that they loved. I went to Staffs Poly and gained a degree in Electronics. It was a bit unusual, but I was unusual!" With that I could find no fault, but I had no idea how unusual then.

"While I was there, I met Stefan. He was a Hungarian too, but he was bitter about the regime. His family, Islic, had been aristocratic, traced their history for centuries. They had been forced to leave after the fall of the Austro- Hungarian rule of Ferdinand. There had been the usual intrigue at court and the outraged husband took the opportunity to settle the score." She gazed into the past again, before continuing in a firmer voice, "Stefan was tailor-made for the Intelligence Service and was actually recruited at the Poly."

Her eyes darkened, "He was so intense. I fell for his dark looks and dark moods. It was like playing with fire or experimenting with drugs, the sense of danger was heady stuff."

I smiled to myself at this phrase. She went on, "He was always pestering me to prove I loved him. He would sulk or glower for days each time I refused his enticements. He didn't believe I genuinely wanted to love him, but it had to be right, wonderful and true, not just a quick and passing moment. He couldn't accept that I wanted it to be within marriage with the blessing of my church, that it was very important to me."

I mentally noted this.

"He was persistent, but he finally brought matters to a head when he told me he was returning to Hungary as an agent, to locate the centre of unrest, to bring the names to

England for the setting up of a network reaching into Czechoslovakia. He stressed it was dangerous, he might not return to give me the chance again."

She paused as if to gain willpower to go on, I just sat and waited. There was no chance I was going to ruin things by speaking.

It was silent in the cottage, the disc long since finished. Outside we heard the trees gently moaning in a freshening breeze, it seemed as if the muggy weather was about to break.

She sipped again and sighed, "I was an immature twenty two. Finishing my years of slog and looking forward to a job with good pay, I was in love with a glamorous man. It was only my parents that stood in the way. I could never have told father what I wanted to do." She put down the empty glass, "And then they had the chance to return. The village church had been given the chance to re-open officially so father just packed up and went, almost overnight. It was a terrible blow to me. They said I could come as soon as the graduation was over, but they insisted that I finished the course." She folded her arms as if chilly, "I was told of the 'trial' for treason, their conviction and being shot on the very day of the ceremony for awards here."

She looked at me as if for assurance that I understood, "The next day I moved into Stefan's flat."

The words hit me hard, but she went on calmly relating history, "I was there only three days. Days that Stefan made love as if there was no tomorrow. He swore that he would let nothing stop our love."

Hatred for the ruthless, predatory, arrogant Stefan burned within me; 'love' for him meant mere selfish dominance of will. Liza was conciliatory, "I think he really thought he was invincible. But he was careless; he disappeared after a visit from the KGB. He was just never seen again."

I gently touched her hand, she seized it fiercely, "I blame myself for his death and that of my parents, I betrayed their love, they went worried and distracted by their concern for me. I was sure that Stefan was thinking of me and not himself, that if I had not moved in with him, he would still be alive."

Her face was screwed up at the inner turmoil, "I killed them by my selfishness. I can never let myself do the same thing again. If I ever let go and betray the standards of my upbringing, I know that tragedy will follow." Silent, I simply held her hand.

We both started as there was a flash of lightning, I sat up, "Did you shut the Cabriolet top?" She too struggled to rise, "No! I thought it was too hot." I ran for the door as the rumble of the thunder reached us, flinging it back I heard the patter of drops. Rushing over to the Porsche I fumbled with the open top. It was not cooperating and seemed to resent being handled by a mere male. Large drops started to splash ominously on the gravel as I wrestled. Liza appeared beside me, I yelled above the rising wind, the thrashing of the trees, "Get inside, you'll be soaked, I'll manage. There's no need for two of us to get wet."

She shook her head, "You'll never do it alone, it sticks at the windscreen end; it must have been bent at some time." She was right. It took both of us minutes to get it snugged down. By that time, my shirt was sticking to me, cold and damp.

As we dashed back into the warmth of the cottage, the heavy drops turned into a torrential downpour. We had been only just been in time. I felt cold, needing a dry shirt. Liza was trembling; her thin, cream dress was drooping at the neckline, wet as far as her waist and heavily spotted from the hips down. It looked ruined. With her hair plastered round her face, she looked pinched round the mouth. I ran up to the bathroom, seized the bath towel and dashed down to where Liza was shaking visibly, wrapped it round her shoulders and held her to me. "You're cold," I said unnecessarily.

She smiled thinly, "I didn't want the seats ruined and I know what that top's like. It's my own fault; I shouldn't have left it off." She shivered again.

I pushed her to the stairs, "Now go and get out of that wet dress. There's a thick dressing gown of mine in the bathroom, put it on while I make a coffee. You need something to warm you. Now go and do as I tell you."

She slowly went up the narrow stairs, rubbing at her wet hair as she went. I thought there was a twitch of a smile at the corners of her mouth before she turned away.

Chapter 15 Complications.

After putting the coffee on I went to my bedroom to find a dry shirt. I briefly stared at the closed bathroom door, but decided to use the kitchen towel on my own short hair. My slacks were very damp, but would have to do for now.

In three minutes we were sitting at the dining table sipping hot coffee, listening to the beating of the rain outside. It might have been the coffee, but her face was pinker than I'd seen it up to then. Against the dark blue of my smart, terry dressing gown, she was decidedly cuddly. She seemed to be no longer shivering, I noted, "Warmer now?"

My reward was a gentle, relaxed twinkling of her eyes, a crinkling of her lips. She was at ease, domesticated even, and I felt proprietorial about her as I'd never felt about Margaret, Jean or the other girls I'd known.

We sat and chatted of the way the weather had changed, the good spell we'd had, the effect on the summer activities in Lichfield, but not once did we mention the project. It was an unspoken agreement that we shut out the world, as we'd shut out the storm.

After nearly an hour, the rain eased off, but it was still heavy. I looked out of the low window, where it was obvious that the rain wasn't stopping yet. Liza yawned and tried to hide it. Contritely, I spoke, "Is that dress very wet? Can I get you something to put on instead?"

She looked back with eyes that were narrowed with a laid back quietness. "It's drying in your bathroom, if you don't object."

My eyes opened, "Oh! No." I swallowed at the thought of Liza in nothing but my dressing gown, "Can I get you something to wear? I don't have much to offer."

She laughed gently at that, "I don't suppose you do! No I will be all right for a time in this." She snuggled it round her chin, "It's lovely and warm. Thanks for the use."

I am not a lecher by any means, but I'm still human. This situation was causing all sorts of thoughts to run in my mind. Most of them were instantly dismissed.

The time on the carriage clock suddenly caught my attention. "Good grief! It's nearly two! If I get some slacks and a shirt, can you make it back to the hotel?

She looked positively sleepy, so I quickly, hopefully, yet fearing the answer, changed the question, "Unless you'd prefer to stay over?" I must have sounded hopeful, because she stood and grinned that mischievous look I had seen in the drive to St Albans.

Flustered, I began to say, "I didn't mean," I let the thought peter out.

She smirked at that, "I didn't think you did." She stood and stretched, revealing some of her neck and upper body then drew the dressing gown round her, "You've given me a lovely evening. I would like to stay if you don't mind. It would ruin it to have to drive back in this, and I'm tired."

My thoughts were not altogether coherent as I mentally rearranged my plans. It would be uncomfortable on the sofa; it was wonderful to sit on - in - but altogether the wrong shape for sleeping. Still, the delicious thought of Liza being under my roof for the night was worth it. "I'll just clear these coffee cups and I'll get some blankets. You can have the bed."

Her next remarks stopped me dead and made my palms sweat, my pulse throb, "Whatever for?"

I stared daring to hope and hoping in another way that I'd heard wrong, "Well, you know ... it's not as if ..." She smiled, "Your bed is big enough for two isn't it?" With a dry mouth, I said uncertainly, "Yes, well it is, but I thought ..."

"Don't be silly, that sofa is totally unfit to sleep on and why waste a perfectly good bed? Anyway, we can keep each other warm." She was making me uncomfortably warm right then.

"I can't offer you any pyjamas, I never wear them, myself, but I can give you a shirt."

"That's all right; I sleep in the nude too."

A turmoil of totally conflicting emotions engulfed me. Hopes and fears vied for dominance, I said with a dry throat, "Are you really sure about this?" She was getting me really hot, not sure that I wasn't dreaming. Also I was not sure I was overjoyed. The easy acceptance was a bit worrying. Liza had said earlier that she blamed someone's death on her unethical love for Stefan; I was totally mixed up. The thought of Liza's naked body was exciting beyond belief, but the lack of reticence on her part just did not fit. Not for the first or last time, I wondered what was going on in her head.

She sounded a little short as she replied, "Yes, I am sure." She stopped and her face lightened, it was untroubled as she said, "You didn't mean sex?"

I definitely went red as I lied, "Certainly not!"

"So you promise faithfully not to do something we would both regret?"

What could I say? "Of course I do."

She stood there looking down at me from the bottom stair, explaining as to a small child, "To my people, the Magyar, it was strictly forbidden before marriage. I personally believe in total integrity; to me sex is the ultimate intimacy, a union of spirit, more than merely an animal act."

"I'll go along with that," I asserted, "some folk these days ..."

Throwing back her head she laughed, "You sound like my father," she crossed herself, "rest his soul."

Somewhat put out, I wondered just what she did think of me.

Seeing my frown, Liza looked at me tantalisingly, "Of course, I loved my parents in a very different way."

My already confused state was in turmoil, "And how do you feel about me?"

The coquetry vanished instantly, "With me it's all or nothing. I am a child of my people and live by rules. The foundation of any relationship is faithfulness. To enter into a contract without integrity is a betrayal of yourself as well as the other involved."

A dark, brooding expression settled on her creamy brow, "I was betrayed once. And I can't forgive that."

The intensity made me shudder. But the mood lightened as she lifted her eyes to scrutinise me as if seeing for the first time, "The freedom fighters in Nazi controlled Warsaw were men and women who lived together for months on end in cellars, ruined houses, anywhere they could. There was no privacy, no separate space. Everything was communal. But they respected each other. The virgins were still virgins as they lived and died together." She was sombre as she spoke with finality, "There was no betrayal of trust."

But then she came back to the present time and her eyes sparkled, "But now is the time for rest, yes?"

Mutely I nodded; I was worn down by the force in her.

She smiled her dimpled smile that always turned my heart, "My whole life is spent reading people's intentions and deciding if I can trust them." She looked deep into my soul again, "If you say something you mean it. I know that you won't try anything silly, that you won't spoil it all. You said once, you wondered if I trusted you, well the answer is, yes, I do - implicitly."

With that she turned and started to climb the stairs, "You don't mind if I go first?"

Speechless, I just nodded.

Later, as I slipped into bed, she said dreamily, "Turn your back." As I hesitated, she repeated, "Turn your back to me." We lay in close contact as I obeyed, Liza wrapped around my back. She fell asleep quickly, breathing steadily and deeply. It was some time before I could still my thoughts. What sort of woman was this?

She had the most wonderful sense of right and wrong, she was a fantastic driver with incredible control, she was involved in the twilight world of Intelligence, yet she could trust me to sleep in the same bed. She was racked by an awful guilt complex, that was all wrong, but she couldn't see it. The enigma was not resolved by my muddled thoughts and my mixed emotions about that warm, soft body pressed at my back.

I slept little and dreamed wildly. I was in a nightmare world where up was down and nothing made sense; hanging over it all was the feeling of imminent tragedy that screwed my brain to pulp.

After all the chaotic events of the night and the wearing effect of the nightmares, I woke late, confused in mind and soul, muddleheaded and felt deserted. The bed was empty. She'd gone as if she had never been. All that remained was the memories and that faint scent of hers on the dressing gown.

Chapter 16 Down to Earth.

I struggled into the office, but it was not a good day. It started badly as I found the remains of some reveller's over indulgence on the doorstep. The Cleansing Dept huffily said that I was not the only one, but they would deal with it as soon as possible. I noted a police car with two plain clothes policemen follow a patrol car with uniformed men to the front of the Central Hotel. This was followed by a flurry of movement outside the grand front door until, after much shouting and noise; the aggrieved staff followed the officers into the staff entrance. I saw Antonio in the middle of the shouting factions; waving his arms in true Italian style.

Bill came in, his usual cheerful self rather blunted by the uncleared mess. It did not go at all well when he jokingly asked me what I had been up to the previous night. He realised that it was not the best thing to start with, when I replied very crossly, "You wouldn't believe me if I told you!" To tell the truth, I was wondering if the whole business was a nightmare or not. My head ached from the lack of sleep and I was thoroughly mixed up.

As the project was now on its way to another test and I'd nothing pressing, I shouted to Bill that I was going out for some air. His laconic reply of, "OK!" was clearly an exasperated comment on my ill-humour.

The Bearpit drew me, more out of an instinctive reaction than for any set purpose, but the day took a turn for the better as I entered to be met by Annie's innocent smile. She was a ray of sunshine in the darkness of my soul and I began to feel human again, "You're looking a bit gloomy this morning," she chirped.

I was not so morose that I could grunt back, so I allowed a wan, faint smile to curl my down-turned lips ever so slightly up, "I've had a trying time, I'm rather baffled and frustrated by a, er, a colleague and I didn't sleep too well last night."

She leaned closer to me, eyes round and frank, "I was frightened out of my wits with all that thunder." Her eyes turned to twinkling ovals as she giggled, "I had my head under the quilt and got hot and stuffy."

It was my turn to feel hot as she confided in a low tone, "I got so hot I had to take my nightie off, I felt really naughty."

My blushes were spared as Antonio gave me a dig in the back, "It's all right for some! I've just about had it up to here with this lot! Half of mild Annie, I'm parched."

He turned to me, serious of expression, "This is the second of these thefts in the staff lockers. They think the attack was someone caught in the act. There's been only a few pounds taken, but it's causing terrible suspicion among the staff. The parti-chef has threatened to leave if it happens again and I don't want to lose him! The trouble is that everyone's in and out of there, day and night. I'd need a security man for twenty-four hours to be any use, and I know the Manager won't wear it. It's not his fault I suppose, Head Office always carping on about the rising costs and dwindling margins. I just hope the police have frightened him off; I suppose I should be politically correct and say him or her. Ta, Annie."

He sipped, sighed and continued as a germ of an idea was growing in my mind, "The truth is, I feel it in here," he tapped his chest, "that this isn't just a sneak thief. It's not like some occasions in the past - it's almost as if someone's searching rather than stealing." He sipped again and sat facing me, "You wouldn't believe the problems with the Sex Equality and Anti Race Legislation."

I'd no wish to be regaled with more dark thoughts, so I interrupted, "I might be able to help in a small way, if you think it would help."

He put down his half empty glass, "Now that's the first bit of good news I've heard all morning."

Trying to look doubtful, I said, "Well, it's only a thought, but it might help."

"Well, go on then, don't keep me in suspense."

I leaned back, "By the way I was about to have the Steak and Ale pie, would you care to join me, or are you due back?"

"Blow that lot for an hour. Why not? OK, Annie, two of your best, we'll be in the corner." He took the remains of his beer and headed for my corner seat. "Now," he said confidentially, "what's the deal?"

I raised my eyebrows in mock horror, "No deal, just trying to help." I'd no way of telling if he was fooled or just accepted my lie at face value. The truth is, I'm not good at lying, especially to a friend. "It happens that I've come across some electronic devices that can record the happenings in a small area, they ..."

He interrupted, "Not security cameras; the union won't allow the management to put them anywhere in the staff areas."

"I was about to say that they're a sort of security device, but they are, well, should I say, very discreet." I leaned closer, but stopped as Annie came with two steaming plates. After she had smiled warmly and wished, "Have a nice meal." I continued, "They actually look like energy saving bulbs, so they can easily be accounted for. I'd put them in and only I would know how to recall the memory."

He chewed on the pie, "I wish our chef could cook like this. Is that all, no free dinners, no secret girl friends?"

I looked suitably shocked, "Good heavens no. This is just helping out in a difficult situation." I smiled blandly, "I suppose I can still bring my own Moët?"

His face was mock serious, "Oh! I don't know about that, what with the pressure from HO and all that." He laughed, "I know you, you schemer, come on what do you want?"

"Nothing, nothing at all. In fact you'll be doing me a favour. My source wants me to test them in a live environment; this could be just it."

He accepted without further ado, but I was sure he saw through my amateur attempts to lie convincingly. He simply said, "I'll let you in this afternoon, about three, it's quiet then, OK?" I nodded and said nothing.

Chapter 17 The Test.

Bill was incredulous, "The AV 4's not been screened yet, and you're going to put it where any Tom, Dick or Harry can get their paws on it. I give up! I never took you for Dopey. Grumpy and Dozey, maybe. But never Dopey!"

"OK, OK! I know what you mean, but this isn't the Kremlin, this is the Central. It's likely to be the best chance we have to put it into a true test area. I've wanted to try the retrieval system 'in-house' so to speak before the spooks get their hands on it. Have we two in stock?"

He blinked, "*Two*? Now what do you want two for?"

I was not a good liar and Bill knew me too well, but I still tried, "For two locations of course, in case one's not properly sited."

"Hummph!"

"I've to go this afternoon, so you'll have to hold the fort again for some hours."

"Hummph!" and he shut the door firmly as he went to the secure stock room.

Was I being paranoid? Could it be that the Texan wasn't CIA after all? I shook my head, this was not my field at all and I was blundering around in muddy waters. I was likely to end up totally out of my depth and covered in something very unpleasant.

Bill returned with two, apparently normal, mini fluorescent bulbs, "I'll just test the Master Link, if you'll plug them into your desk lights." Having done so, I followed Bill to the working monitor. Perfect! Apart from the distortion for the fisheye lens, my desk was crystal clear. Removing the bulbs headed I for the Central.

Antonio was in Reception. He was not his usual calm self, but was near to tearing out his black hair.

The parti-chef had taken his cards, the e-mail was acting stupid, there was a party of Japanese arriving in an hour and the Texan was due at any moment. It was hell for him, but just what I wanted. The porter led me to the service quarters.

He was one of the most morose men I have ever met; blessed with only one speed and nothing could shake him out of it. He also had very limited imagination and no curiosity. He didn't see through my lies that I had two experimental lamps to try out. 'To find out if they saved money', I said.

He grunted, "That's all they ever think of, money, money, money. Never a thought for the workers, never ask us what we want. Do this, do that . . ."

Thankfully he left me in the service area and departed, still reciting his monologue, still plodding at the same, bovine pace. I blessed my lucky stars I didn't have to work with him day after day. I also thanked providence for the ease of getting hold of the pass key as I headed for the first floor and room 102. This was the room reserved for Al, the hopeful descendant of Roger de Clinton. I fitted the device in the overhead light and quickly departed. Just in time. As I headed for the staff stairs, the gravelly growl of the drawling American Southern accent rumbled menacingly from the ascending lift.

One down, one to go. I rushed to the staff locker room.

As a precaution I'd taken a genuine mini lamp, so I wasn't worried as I used the step ladder to replace a tungsten bulb with the real one. It was quiet as expected, but I was reaching for the second lamp when a door closed and a surly voice call out, "And what might you be doing?"

The ladder wobbled as I jumped, startled, "Don't ever do that again," I snapped. "You nearly had me off."

"Well?"

"Well what?"

"Well, you haven't said what you might be doing."

"I might be flying to the moon, but I'm not."

"Clever beggar are you?"

"Not very! I just can't stand people who throw their weight around. Especially when they don't know what they are talking about." I looked down from my lofty perch. "You could start by telling me what you're doing here."

As I spoke I was desperately trying to place his accent; he had a vague, nasal North American whine, but there was a sense of both Lancashire and Yorkshire idioms.

"I'm George Brown, head Restaurant Waiter. And you still haven't told me who you think you are skulking about in the staff locker room."

I plugged in the lamp and descended the ladder. He whined on, "Can't be too careful after the attack. Never know who's about here." He sniffed his disapproval. I folded the ladder.

"I'm Bert Fradley, a friend of Antonio's. He might tell you what I am doing. But so as there isn't any mistake, I'll tell you as well. I'm conducting an experiment to save lighting costs, which just might make your job more secure."

He seemed to lose some of his bluster, but none of his truculence, "Nobody tells anyone anything round here! There've been some thefts and then this attack and I don't like it."

Replacing the ladder I said, "Well, now you know. I'll be back from time to time to see how things are, so we might meet again. Cheerio."

Out in Reception Antonio was at last calming down. The Texan was installed; the Japanese seekers after Samuel Johnson were due in half an hour. The Dining Room was nearly ready and there was a new parti-chef arriving tomorrow. I simply waved as I left. He made no attempt to come across, for which I was glad.

Entering the nondescript door to my own quiet world, Bill was watching the split screen monitor. He was intently watching the left hand half. This showed the staff locker room. I was as fascinated as Bill as we saw the dark features of George Brown scowl at the bulbs. What was remarkable was that he had climbed the ladder to examine them at close quarters.

Bill spoke first, "I was sweating for a minute, but he removed the real one first and seemed to be satisfied. He's looked at ours, but hasn't touched it thank goodness. I heard your encounter loud and clear. A very suspicious character is our Mr Brown."

"What do you make of his accent, Bill?"

"As phoney as Snow White's apple. And as good for your health." He sat back as Brown climbed back down the ladder, "I've a recording, so I'll run it through the analyser later, but I'll bet next month's wages he's a Bostonian. Whoever taught him that accent ought to give him his money back." He strolled to the window. "Now there's a coincidence! Ace Computers are here as well. It looks as if we're going to have a party."

Chapter 18 Application.

Bill came into the office the next morning, his face clouded, "What the heck are they up to this time?" He threw the copy of the Citizen on my desk.

"Look at the planning applications. Just look!"

Rather bemused and not particularly interested in new housing estates or car parks, I was about to give it back when an item stopped me. With growing unease I re-read the end item. 'Telecommunications array for British Telecom for radiotelemetry transmission, to be mounted on the East steeple of the Cathedral. Also temporary mobile office for the duration of the construction, to be sited at the rear of the Angel Croft Hotel car park. The siting of the temporary building not to exceed six months. Proposed plans for the above may be viewed at the Planning Authority offices or at the Cathedral Coffee shop.'

That old nasty feeling started creeping up my spine again. My mind was clicking as fast as a mainframe. I was making connections with the DEMOLISH project, covert audio devices attached to my jacket, the presence of Liza, the unexplained assault and the Texan. It was mind-numbing; I just looked at Bill for a whole minute without speaking. He did not need to hear what I was thinking; long hours together and an uncanny closeness of thought had made us almost telepathic. Neither of us spoke, but I could feel the same chill creeping into Bill's mind. And neither of us liked what we felt.

It was with a dry throat that I spoke, "What the devil have they landed us with this time?"

Bill shook his head, "I wish to God I knew!"

This shook me as much as the planning application, Bill was a man who took his Christian faith seriously. When he said what he did, it was no idle use of God's name.

I rose, "I think I'm going to the Cathedral Coffee shop this morning, coming? My turn to pay."

This brought a wry smile to his face, "It must be serious! How can I refuse?"

We locked up and went.

The coffee shop was heaving with the curious and outraged. The plan was set out in the sunny Green Room. Comments ranged from "So what - only as bad as a weather cock!" to "It's tantamount to blasphemy! Christ threw out the dealers. What is the Dean thinking of!"

I did prick up my ears at one comment, "They say it's worth £30,000 a year in fees! That'll cover a few of the running costs."

Bill and I sat, or rather were squashed and jostled, as we sipped the coffee. It was no better and no worse than the usual café standard. Bill left half of his, but then, his taste was for a Turkish consistency. I had long since given up talking of 'a slice of coffee'. Equally he had never tried to push it on me, thank goodness. The displayed plan itself was simple. It was the usual mobile 'phone mast, standard sized and placed just below the actual tip of the spire. It should be all but invisible up there once the newness had worn off. What nobody had noticed was the one unusual part. There was a single tube on the South side. It was about, as far as I could tell from the scale, 2.20 metres high and .015 metres diameter. The only aerial I knew like that was DEMOLISH.

We were subdued and silent as we returned to the office. We were even more silent as Bill checked the integrity as usual. This time the Radiation light blinked at one second intervals. Someone had tried to force an entry, but had not succeeded. Silently we ran back the monitor memory. We learned nothing. The figure was in a dark anorak with the hood over his or her head. We ran it three times and both agreed it was likely to be a man. My fortress was under attack, there was the feeling of being under siege.

I understood the apprehension of Warwick facing the Parliamentarians, but, unlike him, I didn't even know who the enemy was.

We achieved little that day, beyond knowing that our first line of defence was still secure. We did receive the first rapid burst from the AV 4 in the staff locker room at the Central. All it showed was the staff doing their normal and legal things in the room.

There was some horseplay between the young waitress with dyed yellow hair and one of the kitchen porters, but it was neither serious nor important. The view in room 102 was totally boring; the Texan had unpacked and gone out. We also packed up and went home.

As I was about to lock up I stopped. Reflected in the glass of the door, I saw the fat man stroll past; he glanced at my back and carried on strolling. I re-entered the office and put in my 'hearing aid' before I re-locked the door and walked to the car park. The footsteps of my 'tail' clearly follow me as far as the pedestrian entrance; he then turned another way.

Chapter 19 Innocent?

Liza was due to return in four days' time, so I set my mind to the computer capacity of the mobile phone I was enhancing. It was not easy. The capability of the new toys is increasing rapidly and I find it hard to cram even the newest micro chips into the diminishing space. Inwardly I sighed for the days of Bakelite GPO systems. But it was no good pining; I had a living to make. My latest effort was to have the power of 1000 GHz with the ability to operate single handed or even by voice control - it wouldn't be very convincing to play with the keyboard in the street. The pressure control in the sides was very sensitive and needed careful use, but I was nearly there. Too tired that second day to go home to cook, I went to the Bearpit. I'm being honest when I say that Annie was a definite magnet to me; her cheerful smile and open nature were a breath of clean, fresh air to my stifled brain. It came as a bit of a shock to see her looking less than perky. She was somewhat wilted, her eyes a little puffy, hair a bit lank.

She did grin at my question, "Boss been working you to death?"

After she gave a quick glance towards Jim at the other end of the bar her reply was soft and lifeless, "Might as well, I've got tomorrow off and nowhere to go! I'm a mite homesick, I s'pose. I look forward to my rest period and then don't know what to do with it." She had that Labrador puppy look of pathetic suffering, the look that ensures the dog its position as a family pet. She turned my old heart all right.

"A pretty young girl like you! There are so many places to go and to see. There's Doctor Johnson's Birthday Celebrations for a start. All the Japanese are here for that. Then there's the Dungeons, then . . ."

The horror-struck expression on her innocent features made me stop. I laughed at the woebegone look that followed as she realised that I'd been fooling.

Suddenly contrite I said, "Only kidding. But surely you've someone." As she slowly and sorrowfully shook her head, I spoke rashly, without thinking, "What if I give you a ride in my Jag?"

Her eyes opened wide, "You mean that gorgeous, white, soft top sedan? Wow! Now that *would* be just dandy." She looked sad, "I bet you're just foolin' with little me. You don't mean it?" She finished on such a pathetic, appealing note of hope that I just could not refuse; no man could.

"What time can you be ready tomorrow?" I heard myself ask.

She rapidly lost her careworn look, "Day break!" and laughed at my expression.

Realistically, however, I was in the Duke's car park at 8.30 am. Annie came happily tripping out of the staff door, her smile as sunny as the weather. I felt as if I was playing truant from school, her gaiety was infectious. She slid into the small passenger seat, before I could go round to open the door for her.

The weather was one of those days that we dream of in England; the sort that we assure ourselves were the normal state of things in our youth. The air was already warming, despite the still low angle of the rising sun. There had been a slight mistiness on the Minster Pool as I entered the old town. Wispy, cirrus clouds glided like feathers high in a sky of deepest blue. It was the kind of day that sceptics always say, "It won't last." As long as it lasted until evening, I didn't care. Annie was in no doubt that it was going to last, she had on a pale yellow, sleeveless dress with a scooped neckline that highlighted her young skin. It was held at her waist by a slim belt of white leather, she'd carried a dainty, white hand-bag in her left hand and a picnic basket in her right.

I looked at her squashed in the restricted space and said, grinning, "Better put that basket in the boot, there isn't room for you both."

As I walked round the car, she seemed puzzled, then her eyes opened in her innocent way, "Oh, you mean the trunk!"

She laughed again as I said firmly, "No, I don't. You're in England now." Settling myself again behind the big wheel I said expansively, "Now where do you want to go?"

She flashed her white teeth, her cheeks crinkled in a fascinating way, "Anywhere in the world. On a day like this anywhere at all!"

"Well, there's King's Bromley show, or there's Drayton Manor," I hesitated as she began to look bewildered. A wicked thought emerged. I continued, "Shall I start at Burntwood Park?"

She just smiled, waved her arms in the air and said, "Let's just go."

I set off into the thickening traffic and weaved my way until I stopped in Church Road. She looked round as I stopped, I pointed. "There you are, Burntwood Park."

She stared at the inoffensive, minuscule piece of greenery, *"That? Is that it?"*

I laughed, "Burntwood Park, the smallest park in England - officially!" She swiped at me with her tiny bag. "You're foolin' with me aren't you?"

Laughing manically I let in the clutch and squealed away. "All right, I am!" I chuckled at her false pout. She was as fresh as the day and was making me do silly things. I was beginning to enjoy the day out.

The wind whipped her hair back round her face; she could not keep it out of her eyes, so I stopped the car,

"Haven't you brought a head scarf?" She shook her head in reply, so I gave her my handkerchief, which just fitted under her chin in a tiny knot.

She grinned at me, "OK! Let 'er roll!" We both laughed as I set off again.

Out in the country, my heart was lighter than it had been for years. We called for a coffee at one of the craft outlets and looked for a proper head scarf.

We wandered slowly round; she laughed at the joke shop, shuddered at the prices of the hand-made furniture, was surprised by a shop selling American fabrics and finally found a square of bright material, which made a serviceable headscarf. This looked as if it was straight out of a 1952 Motoring magazine so we set off again.

It was going to be a crazy day, so I headed for Drayton Manor. I was slightly high that day and it just seemed right to do those mad things I did years ago.

Her eyes popped as we entered, "Gee! A Theme Park. That's fantastic!" We joined the crowd already queuing. I paid for us both, despite her protests, and we entered that Magic Kingdom.

When I look back from the following events, it all seems so silly and childish - which I suppose it was. It was made the way it was by Annie's sheer delight in life, the enjoyment of simple thrills and fun. It all seems now so sad, such a waste; but while it lasted it was wonderful.

She shrieked and clung to me in the Haunting, screamed deafeningly as we experienced the Apocalypse, only to insist we do it again. She got wet in the canyon and buried her head in my chest on the Stormforce. We had a break for the picnic she'd brought; the sunshine was hot, but not scorching as the spreading, cirri cloud had slowly thickened. Never did ham sandwiches taste so good. After I had been given a half hour respite, we went round it all again, ate ice creams and doughnuts - she scoffed at the size of them, but still ate them. We weren't quite thrown out at closing time, but we had a very full time of it. I still felt like a truant schoolboy, tired, shaken and overfull, but totally content.

I really do think that Annie enjoyed that day, genuinely and as a breathing space before the future that we could not see. The day passed in complete forgetfulness of DEMOLISH, AV 4 s, micro chips and even, I found myself guiltily aware, of Liza. Annie was like a teenager, intent on living each day to its fullest extent.

She unselfconsciously put her head on my arm as we drove back. I took the quiet way through the country, eager to hold on to that time. She roused herself as we neared a country inn, "I don't know about you, but I'm famished." I must have seemed reluctant for she kissed me ever so lightly on the cheek and said, "Oh, go on, I'll pay this time." I protested that it was my treat, but she insisted, so we had a traditional English, pub meal in a noisy, smoky room.

I saw one or two cast a funny look in our direction. It wasn't so surprising; Annie would stand out anywhere. Her grin threatened to split her face in two and her chatter went on brightly all the time.

It was growing cool as we left, so I turned up the heater and drove slowly. She leaned back, a blissful peace on her features, her hair wafting attractively over her face from time to time.

There was with a real sense of disappointment when I left her at the Duke. She was just as reluctant to go in, to finish the day off. She had a sort of dreamy, contented tiredness about her that spoke louder than any words. We stood facing each other for what seemed an age, until she quickly reached up to me and kissed me lightly and briefly on the lips. Before I had time to think much or even respond, she'd turned and run easily to the staff door. She paused there long enough to blow a kiss and disappeared.

I slowly and thoughtfully drove home in a haze of elation and fatigue. It had certainly been a day to remember. At home I could no more go straight to bed than fly; so I played The Miraculous Mandarin. As I listened to the power and force of the strident passage of the murderous attack on the mysterious figure, the attack in the Central came to mind. I wondered about Liza's part in it all. I was unsure if I was cast in the role of the victim or as an innocent observer. Who was the enticer? In a fit of rising doubts I stopped the intense thudding of the attack and put on Whispers of Creation.

I listened to the gentle, flowing notes washing over me and felt myself relax. I could feel once again the uncomplicated effect of Annie, her way of living life as it was. After the music faded away I sat for nearly an hour, letting my thoughts swirl round. I was no nearer an answer then than I'd been two hours earlier. I went to bed, to sense the still lingering, exotic perfume of Liza's and I slept disturbed by dreams both vivid and formless.

Chapter 20 Changes.

The following day was cooler, the cloud having thickened overnight. The Medieval Market was not going to be blessed with yesterday's warmth. It was the usual English summer day that slowly turned damp and then wet. The market was not a great success. The only satisfaction I had that day was the receipt of the first advance of the DEMOLISH project; even that annoyed me, the invoice was for a 'Transmatter'. With all the modern spell check systems, I felt there was no need for it at all.

Feeling grumpy I ran to the Bearpit, to find it uncomfortably full because of the rain. Annie was behind the bar, she waved to me when she saw me, her smile the complete antidote to the English weather. Managing to force a way to the counter I placed my order. Annie was back to her usual bubbly self, "My! We timed it right yesterday." She wrinkled that pretty nose, "I wouldn't like to be out today!"

As I nodded in the drone of the hubbub, she almost shouted to be heard, "The usual?" I shook my head, "No. Ham salad today, I ate far too much and it starts to show if I'm not careful." She laughed at this, but I was not sure if it was me or the idea that caused the merriment. I jerked a thumb towards my corner, she nodded.

As I reached it I was regaled by the growling bass of Al Clinton. He'd been tucked into the hidden recess. I suppose I should have expected *someone* to be there, but it was another on the debit side for that day.

"Boy, you do have a lot of weather in this country."

Resisting the temptation to respond with the time-honoured joke, I merely shrugged.

Aloysius was made of sterner stuff. "What do you think of the chances of finding any traces of my forebears at

King's Bromley? I hear they have records back to the 1300s and that old Roger was resident there at one time." I pondered how I could tactfully say '*Not a hope in hell.*' Instead I said, "You never know! You might just be lucky!"

With the din, I didn't think he caught the underlying sarcasm. He nodded, "On a different tack, I'm wondering how your tests of the new, low-consumption lights are going ..." My skin tingled as he went on, "I'm hoping to cut costs in my plant and save the world at the same time ..." I waited and he carried on as I showed no signs of replying, "That light in my room is a dandy, it's neat and compact, but great at night. I might be able to put a big order your way if it's OK!"

Before I could start to prevaricate, Annie arrived with my salad. I started to get out my wallet, but she laid a warm hand on mine. The touch was enough to balance the nasty tingle from the Texan's remarks, "It's on the house today, my treat." She leaned nearer, I caught a whiff of a light scent, it reminded me of lily of the valley, "Could I be very naughty and ask if there's a chance for next week, I'd be ever so grateful. Yesterday was so wonderful."

The Texan's interested attention was tangible as I said, "Sure, why not. Weather permitting of course."

Her dazzling reply was uplifting, "Now, that's something to hope for."

She wiggled away through the throng as Clinton tried to look uninterested. He restricted himself to, "Nice girl."

I tried to sound off-hand, "We only had a day at the theme park." I looked him in the eye, "She's a kid at heart, she loved it, but I couldn't stand too much of it at my age. I just felt sorry for her, lonely kid in a strange country."

His expression was bland, but I felt a grin lurking, "Now what about those lights?"

"Not really conclusive. I need more data. Glad that the light aspect is all right and not troubling you."

"Absolutely no way. By the way do you have any feedback?"

Trying to read something into this exchange and failing, I knew I would be hopeless as a poker player. But I just knew that he would be very good, "If you like I'll call on you to talk."

He nodded in acceptance, "Look forward to it. Say, why don't you and the little lady come to dinner tonight?"

I shook my head, "She'll be behind the bar here."

He waved a huge paw of a hand, "No, the other one, Letty or something."

"Liza? She's not here."

"Ok, just you then?" As I nodded, it felt as if the world was out of control again. This was a feeling I had experienced too much lately, and it was totally unsettling.

Back at the office Bill was hopping about, "Come and look at this." 'This' turned out to be the burst of data gathered by the device in the staff room. Most of it was simply people coming in, opening or closing lockers and leaving. There was one session of heavy kissing by the porter and the flighty waitress, which was broken up by another staff member. But it was the shot at 3.31 pm that shook us. There on the screen was the hooded figure that had tried to enter our workplace. What's more, he was forcing open locker after locker and removing some items. We never saw his face at any time.

Turning to Bill I said, "I can't understand it, it's as if he... "I stopped.

Bill finished it for me, "As if he knows."

Stunned I sat, "But there's no-one who does. Only Antonio." I racked my brain. Something about that figure had been familiar all along, something in the way he moved, the way he held his head, "It can't be!"

Bill was grave, "What was it Holmes said? 'When you have eliminated all possible alternatives, then whatever is left, no matter how improbable, is the answer'."

I looked at Bill in despair, "What the hell is going on?"

The dinner was not as arduous as I had expected, Clinton was almost apologetic at the talk of business, "I'm always being told off by my sister for jumping in with both feet. I won't say a word if you like."

This floored my carefully prepared fabrication. It was obvious to me that Aloysius Clinton the Third also knew what was happening. I had to remove the AV 4 immediately before something happened to it. The same had to be done with the one in the staff room. Neither had the slightest chance of telling me what I needed to know, "I'm sorry if I gave you the wrong impression this afternoon," I said easily, "But they are ..." lowering my voice for effect I confided, "they are experimental and could be embarrassing in the wrong hands. I was about to say that I want to replace it with another and examine the original for wear and faults."

He leaned forward, "As a businessman, I quite understand. Industrial espionage is big business over the pond." He sat up, "What say we go up straight after dinner?"

I hesitated, stuck firmly on my own deviousness. In the end, deciding to cut my losses I said, "Why not indeed?"

The rest of the meal wasn't very enjoyable, especially as Antonio was edgy and finally came to me as Clinton excused himself and went to the toilet. He poured out his woes to my reluctant ear, I hinted that I had little to tell him, but he scurried away as Aloysius returned. The rest of the evening was spent in removing the bulbs and replacing them with normal ones. I sweated a bit as Clinton weighed the unit with a thoughtful frown, but he gave no indication of his thoughts as he handed it back to me.

He didn't notice that I stuck my own grey blob on the ceiling fitting while he was hefting the unit. I only hoped that something would come of it, more than the AV 4 had given me so far. We shook hands, I promised to contact him later.

He spoke chilling words as I was leaving, "Gonna be 'round a spell. This Roger is hard tracking down. But I'll get there, never surer. If Aloysius gets on the trail, he allus gets there."

Somehow that didn't reassure me at all.

Chapter 21 Problems.

Even less assured I returned to the office the following morning. Jostling among the crowds, the fat man was there once again. I was fed up to the back teeth with this uncertainty. It seemed that everything was false or had double meanings; that is except for dear sweet Annie. That day of pure pleasure still stood out in my mind as one of the few things I could rely on. That and of course, dear, old, reliable Bill. But he was not his usual self either. The body language, as he sat in the visitor's chair, was of frustration and tension. His face was set in a scowl as he read the Citizen. "How do they do it?"

"Do what?" I snapped back.

"Get round the councillors."

"What *are* you talking about?"

"This Telecom mast, that's what!" We stared at each other until I walked over and picked up the paper. In the list of cases to be heard this month, was the application for the mast on the Cathedral. Bill was very annoyed, "It took me two months even to have my extension put on the list and another two months to have the result. Whose palm has been greased for this one?"

I stared, "You can't believe that! I can't see our worthy locals standing for that."

"Perhaps not. But it's damned queer all the same. You just watch, it'll all be done in weeks."

I was not really concerned with our council representatives, but even I knew to my cost, the speed, or total lack of it, that was the normal procedure in the Planning Dept. Those words spoken at the outset of the project I was completing came back to me, '*This is big! It comes from No. 10, not Horseguards.*'

And with them, unasked for, came an intense feeling of unease. If this *was* part of the scheme as we believed, then there would be no delays, one way or another. As there was nothing I could do anyway, I turned to a matter nearer at hand, "Bill, has there been any activity on the scanners just now?" He rose and went to the control desk, "Nope! Not a sausage. Why?"

"I've just seen that fat man again outside. There are just too many things I don't get. I shan't be sorry when this is all over and done."

Thinking of the steady, almost boring life pre-Liza, I sighed for the lost peace and quiet. Bill knew too and sighed as well. In a tired voice he muttered, "There's a funny e-mail in the bag, I think it must be from Ms Vancyk."

He switched the screen to the incoming icon. It popped up: - 'To AF ex LV. 28th del. MTF.' I grunted. "It's a bit late to cancel the monthly buyer's visit on the 28th, but I'm getting totally brassed off with this lot. More to follow. Huh!" I flopped in the leather chair behind my desk, "What say we shut up shop for two weeks? The project is in their hands, the buyer's visit has been cancelled and I'm bushed."

A lifted eyebrow was all the reply, but he was not going to look gift horses in the mouth. "Have I time for a coffee first?" We both laughed out loud.

I smiled at him, "It's Friday today. Let's clear up, shut down and secure and be off this afternoon." Bill's grin brought back some of his old self. We were done by three pm, some sort of record. The sun had come out again by then.

Bill was going out of the door as I locked the safe and waved to him, "See you in two weeks." and he was gone.

The 'phone rang just as I reached for the door handle. I hesitated, cursed and picked it up. The voice was quiet, "Mr Fradley? You won't know me, but my name is Teddy Wilson. We have a mutual friend, Liza Vancyk?"

He went on as I stood rooted to the spot, "I must see you on a matter of great importance as soon as you can spare the time."

My mind was racing, what was happening now?

"Are you sure you have the right number," I cleared my dry throat, "Liza who did you say?" His voice hardened and chilled me, "I have seen Miss Vancyk with you, so don't try to deny it. Believe me this is no trick. It really is vital that I see you now. I'll be in the Cathedral Coffee shop in ten minutes. Be there!" The line went dead. A quick check on the trace revealed it was a payphone. Sweating I stood and breathed deeply. Slipping my 'hearing aid' in I locked up. The awful sinking feeling of the night before had returned. It was all going out of control again.

As I stood in the Georgian doorway of the coffee shop, my eyes adjusted to the low light filtered through the tall windows. Impervious to the intricacy of the sun-cast patterns on the floor, I jumped as a hand touched my shoulder. A cultured, soft voice spoke closely, "So glad you could come!"

The fat man was right behind me, one hand bunched casually in his jacket pocket, "Over there near the showcase." My 'hearing aid' gave no warning clicks or hums. He did not seem to be armed or wired. But I was still far from easy as we sat on the hard chairs.

"Would you like a tea or coffee?"

Might as well get something I thought, "White coffee, two sugars!"

For a fat man he moved swiftly and lightly, in no time at all there was the standard café, brown liquid in front of me. I sipped it distrustfully, "Now what's this all about?"

He looked at me as if he could see through the façade, "What I say must never be repeated to another soul until I say so." I leaned back in, what I hoped was nonchalance, "Can't say until I know, can I?"

"What do you know of Ley Lines?"

"What?" I almost shouted in disbelief.

"Don't say 'what' it's rude. *Ley Lines*," he repeated testily, "the forces of spiritual and cosmic power that govern places and people!" Nonplussed didn't even begin to describe my confusion. I said nothing as my mind tried to equate this crackpot with his statement that he knew Liza. He looked aggrieved, "It's not a game, Mr Fradley. This is a serious subject. And it concerns our mutual friend, Liza."

I sat up at that. He knew he'd hit the target, "Yes, Liza Vancyk. Perhaps I should enlarge on that?"

Angry now I retorted, "I think you'd better." Feeling more sure of myself I went on the attack, "And I want it all, I'm sick of your lurking about my office. Don't bother to deny it, I've seen you."

His next words floored me, "I am very much afraid for Liza's life, Mr Fradley."

He knew he had taken my breath away, he went on, "Yes, her life! I knew her from Staffs Poly. She was a lonely girl." A picture of Liza looking lost flashed across my mind.

"She was brilliant in electronics, but easily misled by, well, boys, to be blunt. That is, boys who were really men of the unscrupulous kind. She'd been sheltered all her life and was not prepared for the pressures of sexual harassment." Guiltily I thought of Liza, naked in my bed as he finished, "I took a fatherly interest in her, although she was nothing to do with my Department; I'm in Medieval Studies, by the way."

My whirling thoughts were slowly settling; was he trying to warn me or claim a prior right to Liza? If he was, he was in for a rude shock. Really angry now, tiredness was sapping my patience, "Come to the point! I like Liza and I warn you that if you are after her you will have ..."

His bellowing laugh stopped me in full flow and also conversation in the café. He wiped his eyes, "You young people." I winced. Was I young?

"All you think of is love and entanglements. You flatter me, young man, if you think that Liza would look on me in that way. Mind you I would find the idea very pleasurable." He changed to a serious tone, "This *is* life and death, real death. The permanent kind!" He had my attention and knew it.

"I said that Liza was brilliant, that isn't doing her the justice she deserves. For her thesis, she was working on a very powerful communication system that had her tutor very excited. He was secretive about it to a fanatical degree and helped her to set up a mock up in the Physics Lab." Feeling very insecure I waited. Teddy quietly continued, "He was so excited that he was told off for neglecting other students."

He paused, "One of them was another Hungarian, Stefan Islic."

It was time to stop right now, so I stood up, "Thank you for the coffee, don't think I am ungrateful, but I think you'd better come up to my office. This is going to take a long time."

Unlocking the office door, I automatically checked the integrity and set the Radiation Seal. His eyes were alert and missed little. He sat in the visitor's chair across my desk, his bulk straining the framework., "I assure you, Mr Fradley, that I am 'clean' as you might say," The term used by cheap, thriller writers did little to assure me, "There is, however, have one thing that you should see." He drew out his calculator and laid it on the desk. In reality it was a rather crude meter, it had been put together in an amateurish way, it was probably a 'mock up' done at the Poly. As I looked, he repeated his question, "What do you know of Ley Lines?"

"Nothing at all." I paused and added hesitantly, "I vaguely remember a book in my book club list, by John Timpson, if my memory is right."

He snorted, "That clown! All he could do was make some cheap and snide remarks on something that he knew nothing about." *Like most people, including me, I thought.*

"In 1920, Alfred Watkins, a retired businessman, noticed something odd about the alignment of ancient sites; barrows, pagan sacrificial sites, high places and standing stones. They all seemed to be connected by straight lines. Being a practical man, Alfred assumed that they had a physical reason and purpose; he thought they were tracks linking the sites. Since then others have tried to prove or refute his ideas. No-one has done either." He pointed to his meter, "Until now. This was made for me by Liza as part of her efforts and it has led me to understand enough to set me on a mission." There was silence as we looked at the rather battered and rough object.

"This proves that the Ley Lines *do* exist. What's more, I believe I know what they are."

I coughed nervously, "You say that Liza was working on this with you? What happened to the research results?"

"They were destroyed."

"Destroyed? By who?" I stared at him.

"By *whom* dear boy. By Liza."

"Why? What for? I thought she graduated with honours."

"She did, but it was all a bit of a mystery. There was a hint of outside interference." My mind went back to recalled phrases, '*No. 10, not Horseguards.*'; '*my planning permission took months.* 'I said nothing.

"Anyway, she literally blew it up, wrecked the Physics Lab in the process. The whole matter was hushed up and forgotten by most people after she left." His tone was sombre, "Except for me. And Stefan."

The uneasy feeling was back again, "Do you still keep in touch with them?"

"Stefan is believed to be dead somewhere in GRU or KGB torture rooms, no-one knows for sure. You do know that her parents were killed by them at the same time?" Uncertain where it was leading, I nodded.

"She was a very vulnerable person - mentally and emotionally. Stefan was envious of her and I think he wanted to bring her down. He could be ruthless if he wanted and he hunted her down as a tiger would hunt a gazelle."

The clock slowly and relentlessly ticked our lives away as he went on, "It was a great sadness to me to see her pulled down as she moved in with him. That and the death of her parents have left a horrible scar that may never heal."

This was part of the wall between Liza and me.

He sighed, "It used to be so much simpler in my days. A girl just would not go to bed with anyone she barely knew." Inwardly I recalled that night when she lay in my bed. It was as unreal as a half-forgotten dream.

"Anyway, I have discovered that the Ley Lines are in fact electromagnetic force lines at the very extreme end of the spectrum. They are about 43 kilometres wavelength and extend for far further than anyone believed possible." As he was talking, my mind was struggling with the immensity of the conception. Something suddenly clicked. Reaching for a calculator, I stopped him. I was right! The DEMOLISH project was a harmonic of the wavelength he had just described.

"How did the Physics Lab blow up?" I asked worriedly.

He started at my tone, "I don't know, I told you it was all hushed up. All I know is that there was nothing left to salvage afterwards. It is lucky that Liza was outside the Lab; she was stunned, but unhurt. It was funny at the time. I often wonder how she operated from the quad, but I suppose it was remote control."

I was afraid of this vagueness more than I showed. It all began to take on a hideous and dangerous character, "Let me see that meter." I spoke to cover my fears.

It was very crude and simple, but as I pressed the power button, the needle shot up to the end of the scale. "Very interesting!" remarked Teddy.

"What level do you expect to find?" I asked him.

"That is a high reading, higher than I would expect." He looked round with interest, "Just what do you make, Mr Fradley?"

"Money." This was my stock answer to such queries.

"Don't we all?" He smirked as he stood to leave. His eyes actively noted the monitors, screens, workbench and parts bins as I escorted him out. "It must be interesting - making money."

Still holding the meter I stopped him, "Would you like me to, er, tidy this up for you?" His hand started to reach out for it, but he changed his mind.

With a shrug, he left it with me, "Why not, I don't suppose it will come to any harm?" He gave me the number of his hotel; I promised to call him later. We shook hands and I let him out.

I set to work immediately; I had to find out what Liza had got herself into. The first priority was to make my own meter to track this force line for myself. It was 1 am before I wearily put down the last test probe and stretched, stiff as a board, but I now had two meters. They were in my standard digital communications watch for speed of assembly. It was in essence quite easy, but it left me totally bushed.

As I left I double checked the locking process; a single slip would be disastrous, especially with so much at stake and the unknown agencies at work. I drove home to fall exhausted into a dead sleep, glad that I'd given Bill the time off. There was no pressure to interfere with my search.

Chapter 22 More Questions.

On the Sunday, I went into the city centre, to check the Ley Line detector watch. As I mingled with the crowd of visitors to the Dr Samuel Johnson event there were accents from the world over; many Japanese, but also French, German and others that I wasn't sure of. As I'd already set the power on the watch, all I had to do was to give a double squeeze of my fist to open the meter icon. The digital display was clear and rock steady, it was in the quadrant that Liza had marked Green edging to the Red. I walked up the pedestrianised Dam Street until nearly at Cathedral Close. At this point the display went mad; the figures ran rapidly up until 'E' blinked rapidly. I hastily switched it off in concern. Round to Gaia Lane I tried again. This time there was the steady reading of the safe level. Retracing my steps to Beacon Park I followed the path towards the Western By-Pass. There was the same high reading as in Dam Street. Worried, I turned it off and headed back to the office.

As it was a Sunday I took five minutes to open up. It was a necessary evil, but it was frustrating.

Dismantling the watches I added an extra resistance to the function, it would come on automatically if there was a surge and the LCD had a warning icon that it was in operation. Locking up again took a further five minutes. By this time it was nearly lunch time. The second test run worked perfectly. The strength of the EMF was higher by a factor of four in a straight line right through the Cathedral, roughly South West, but fading slowly the further I went. Satisfied and hungry I squashed into the Duke of Cumberland. Annie spotted me at once, her open, welcoming face cheered me no end. It was almost like coming home.

I stopped myself. She was not for me; she had all the world at her feet.

"Hi! This is a surprise. Run out of food at home?"

"No, just can't keep away from work, been testing a new meter."

She did not appear to know what I had in mind so just accepted it at face value, "Now don't you go working too hard. What would you like; the special today is Coq au vin, it smells delish."

"Just a sandwich thanks, I eat lightly at midday."

"Be with you in a mo'" She put her head near mine, to whisper, "I've got next Wednesday off, any chance . . .?"

What could I do? If I hadn't liked her, perhaps I could have said no. "I look forward to it."

She dashed off, face aglow. It was the fastest service anywhere; she was back before I could settle down, "Gee, I do appreciate this, where to this time?" She giggled, "As long as it isn't that Burned wood Park."

"Burntwood Park! If it's nice I thought I'd take you on the canal on a small boat. Bring a picnic and a drink."

"I'll pray for sunshine," and she wiggled off between the crush. Guiltily I thought she had a nice wiggle. I shut it out of my mind and ate the sandwich.

I'd just finished and was thinking of escaping the noisy crowd, when Antonio squeezed into my corner, he was worried, "Was there any joy from those eyes of yours?"

I shook my head sadly, "We had some lovely pictures, but the thief was wearing a hood and we couldn't see anything; to be truthful, we weren't even sure if it was a man or woman." Was I wrong; was I looking for something not there, or was there the slightest trace of relief?

"Anyway, it's all irrelevant now;" he laughed ironically, "the Union of all people are pressing for a proper security camera to be installed. At least it's out of my hands."

Making my excuses I left then. I needed the fresh air.

Early Monday morning I rang Teddy Wilson's hotel. The receptionist was chilly, "Do you mean *Professor* Wilson?" When I agreed that I did, she crowed, "Hold while I try to connect you!"

He answered swiftly, "Wilson."

"Bert Fradley here. Could we meet at the Coffee shop again *professor*?"

"Eleven?"

"Fine, see you then,"

"'Bye."

Stick that in your supercilious pipe and smoke it madam.

At our meeting he was taken aback by the watch, he seemed unable to accept that it was true. As I related my test there was a gleam of excitement, "I can't wait to try it..." We left the coffee half drunk and went out. I didn't tell him of the duplicate. Some things were best kept under wraps.

It took him a few moments to get used to the double squeeze to turn from time to meter, but his face was that of a little boy at Christmas.

"By the way," I warned, "never squeeze it *three* times or attempt to open it."

"Why?"

"Believe me," I hesitated momentarily, "you just don't want to know."

He looked at the watch as if it was a poisonous spider. But he still put it on his wrist with a gesture of satisfaction and determination, "What do I owe you, my boy?"

I let the 'my boy' pass without remark waving away any attempt to pay and just accepting his delighted, fulsome praise, "It's a hobby sideline of mine, no trouble at all." He did promise to keep me up to date with progress, thought it might go as far as Bridgnorth. He was eager to trace the extent of his theory; I was eager to return home to the quiet of The Orchard.

Chapter 23 Relaxation.

My 'garden' is always a peaceful, rustic retreat, but it was beginning to rival the Amazonian rain forest, so I decided to attack the under (and over) growth tomorrow. This is an event of infrequent happening and not to be undertaken lightly. I needed a good night's sleep first. But I also hoped for rain to dodge the struggle.

The next day the clamour of birds fighting over the wildlife of my jungle woke me. As I opened the curtains the sun warmed my naked body. There were one or two fluffy clouds, but no rain. I was committed. At the end of four hours of hot, hard hacking and slashing, I needed a shower and something cool and lingering. My efforts on the growth had made the garden grow in size, but it now looked like a collapsed haystack. On the whole I preferred it as it had been. The thought I might postpone the mopping up until Wednesday tempted me, until I remembered Annie. There was no respite; it just had to be done today.

"You're just too good-hearted for your own good, Bert. It'll get you into trouble one of these days!"

Bill had said this often. That was to be true much sooner than I expected.

Wednesday dawned as noisily as Tuesday. Annie must have said her prayers persuasively; the day promised to be hot. The chilled bottle of white wine went into the insulated bag; I grabbed some fruit and went to meet her.

The day was wonderful, but there was a lightness in my heart that was not entirely caused by the weather. Playing a Chopin Étude I burbled steadily along. I was happy, but half afraid of the reason. Having to choose between two women was not something I relished. Unsuccessfully I reminded myself of Annie's youth and tried to think of Liza. It came as a shock to realise that all this had happened in two months. It sobered me for a while. The mood lasted precisely as long as it took me to meet Annie. She was stunning! She was wearing a sun dress with the tiniest straps and, for me, a too low neckline. It was made more tantalising by the total absence of any necklace. She swung elegant legs into the footwell, revealing an intriguing glimpse of shapely limbs.

She asked the name of the Étude; I'm ashamed to say that I couldn't recall it, but she said she liked it.

She seemed surprised that I was going near to Drayton again, but I drove past and turned into the comfortably untidy boatyard where my hired boat waited. We quickly stowed the picnic, rug and her bag into the small, open launch and whiffled along the dappled water towards Fradley Junction.

"Say! It's just like a little car. It's cute," she enthused.

We passed along the backs of the houses, Annie was intrigued to see boats moored along the gardens, "Just like Florida," she murmured with a wistful sigh.

"A bit colder," I retorted.

She smiled back, "Not today, it's just perfect." We gently swished along for an hour; she was smiling and silent as the scenery unfolded. The gentleness of the English canalside is very soothing. Ahead I spotted a fallow field, probably a Euro 'lay-by subsidy'. Steering to the bank, I hopped out and moored. It was surprisingly quiet, no passing boats, and no sound of cars.

Annie flopped down on the rug I laid out, "This is heaven, I could die here." It had intended it to be a brief stop, but she refused, "I *like* it here, please let's stay for ever." Annie was so excited she bubbled; she kept up a flow of chatter that I half listened to and made only short replies.

"My Mom and Pop run a Motel, well really more of an overnight stop, in South Pennsylvania, near Williamsport. It's too small for us all, but I met so many interesting people that I wanted to see the world."

She gazed around at the open country, "In so many ways it's like here, but so much bigger." As I breathed deeply, eyes shut against the sun, I thought, *everything in America is bigger*; I've learned that from the tourists.

"Pop was very unhappy about it all," her drawled 'all' was appealing, "only five per cent of Americans ever leave the US of A, did you know that?"

"No!" I mumbled back, "I didn't know that." What I did know was that I was feeling relaxed in the heat: Annie seemed to be in a talkative mood.

As we lay side by side on the sun-warmed bank, she chattered on, "I bet you're having a hard time with all those Japanese imports, they're having an effect on our car industry. You being in electronics and all." There was a pause, "What do you make, Mr Fradley? Is it something exciting?"

My mind was racing, although my face was immobile. It was not the Japanese that was my problem. It was the Finns! Nokia was making things that had been in the realm of science fiction only ten years ago.

No-one had foreseen the explosion of communications with the coming of mobile 'phones. And there were some amazing things in the research laboratories of the many manufacturers. I was finding it both hard and easy. It was easy to obtain micro parts: it was getting tougher to keep ahead in the field of data transmission. I had been utterly gutted when one of my inventions, the transmission of data through a handshake, had suddenly appeared in a Japanese PDA.

"Money," I replied through half opened lips.

She nudged me playfully, "Don't tease! Come on, what do you do?"

"You don't want to hear about boring work," I opened one eye to squint at her pretty face.

She sat up, "If you don't tell me I'll ... I'll tickle you until you do."

Hands up in surrender, I conceded, "All right! But you won't be impressed." Pausing for effect, I admitted, "I make microwave detectors." It was not an absolute lie; I had a few in the office to cover eventualities.

Her tone showed her disappointment, "Oh! I had you down as one of those mysterious secret agents."

There was a silence except for a droning insect.

I prayed that my face did not reveal the shock that gave me, "No such luck."

My eyes stayed shut as she drawled on, "How much do they cost, I'd like one for the folks back home, something to show off."

"£220 plus Vat, and postage," I lied.

"Gee! How do you sell them at that price?" She sounded decidedly shocked.

"I've a contract with a Government Health Protection Agency, they take a regular supply." Once again it was not an outright lie, but the word health can cover a wide field.

"Do they pay you a lot?"

"It keeps the wolf from the door." I hoped that I had managed to keep a few wolves of one sort or another away over the years.

She sighed and lay back, contemplating; "Now that's a thought. Keeping the wolf from the door." As I lay beginning to bake in the sun, I wondered at her questions. Was there more to it than appeared on the surface, or was I being paranoid about everybody?

We stayed for five hours in the end and only left as I was worried we would be too late for the boatyard, but she sprung another surprise on me after we had been there for three hours.

It was a scorcher and I was feeling red, despite the cream I had lathered on. Annie sat up and fanned herself, "Boy, I'm hot! Do you think anyone would mind if I took a dip?" I must have blinked in surprise, for she went on, "I won't if it isn't allowed."

Not sure what to say, I said with some hesitation, "It's not that, there's no problem as long as you keep out of the way of any boats, but , I mean ..." She laughed at my reddening face and undid the zip at the back of her dress to step out of it in a pale yellow, one piece swim suit. She giggled, slipped off her shoes and dived smoothly into the canal. She stood up in the middle, "It's not deep at all!"

"I never said it was," I called back.

She swam with a powerful crawl for about fifteen minutes, before we heard the plonking of a single cylinder diesel in the distance.

"Annie!" I called, "Boat coming." She swiftly swam back and I helped her on to the steep bank. She stumbled and put her arms round my neck, dampness ran excitingly down my chest. We stood for seconds, but it felt an age. She dropped her arms and sat on the rug, glistening, tanned and anything but girlish. I can still picture her sitting there, vibrant, alive and totally seductive.

"I didn't bring a towel; you can use the rug if you want."

She lay back, "I'll dry off in no time in this sun, you'll see!"

As a traditional narrow boat thumped past she sat up. We waved at the old boy at the tiller, his dog lying on the bows. He replied with a single, effortless wave and went slowly on his peaceful way.

She was entranced, "All that painting! It must have taken hours."

"It does," I replied, "It's a labour of love to those who do it."

All was still and at peace as she lay back in the sun again. She turned with a gentle sigh from time to time to dry off; but by the time I was getting anxious, she sat up and slipped on the skimpy sundress. Giving her hair a shake, she rubbed it to fluff it up and smiled.

I was treated to a contented and satisfied glance, "I haven't been so rested for years, this reminds me of a swimming hole near my home. Thank you for another wonderful day." She gave me a kiss on the cheek and started to load the launch.

The sail back to the boatyard was over too quickly; Annie sang to herself as we bumbled back past the peaceful gardens and moored boats. She sang some Country and Western tune, like 'Billy Joe', it was sung as if she knew it from first hand.

I drove, I was never sure if it should have been 'navigated' or 'drove' a launch, in silence for some minutes afterwards, but she was equally reflective. It was me who broke the mood, "Are you a C & W fan?"

She seemed to rise from a shallow sleep, "Sorry, I was dreaming. What did you say?"

"Are you a C & W fan - do you like Country and Western?"

"Not really," she smiled back, "I was just thinking of a friend I once had." Her voice tailed away sadly, but she sat up and continued a little too brightly, "But I do like it, the songs seem to be about real people, their hopes and dreams, lives and loves." She sighed, "Do you like music, Mr Fradley?"

"Please call me Bert, everyone else does. Yes, I like music, but I prefer Chopin. His music has a timeless brilliance, there is something fresh each time I listen." I turned to look at her face, which showed the remains of a vanishing frown, "By the way what's your name? I can't just call you Annie."

This time there was a definite grimace, "Schwartz. Some distant German origin I think. I hate it really." She had every right to do so, *Schwartz*. It seemed to me that so many Americans have awful names.

I tried to be gallant, "I shall definitely call you Annie, it suits you. How about changing your name to Annie Smith, or Brown or," laughingly, "Annie Gunn?"

She stiffened at that. It was a mistake, so I hurried on, "Or Chopin. He wrote such wonderful music. I'm sure you'll like it." She just looked at me blank-faced as I floundered, "It's very different from C & W, in that the feelings come from emotions rather than words, but there's a depth that shouldn't be ignored."

I turned to look ahead, not wanting to see her face as she pondered the next question, "If you don't have anything else to do, you could come to my cottage and hear some of it. But only if you're not tied up."

She laughed out loud and sent a moorhen skittering away over the placid water, "Tied up! I like that." She laughed again, "It's so easy to get things wrong between American and English language. Yes." I sensed her looking closely at me, "I would really like to come to your cottage to hear your Chopin, as long as I can bring some of my own CDs."

"Certainly. By the way, would you like a cold ham salad for dinner? It's too nice to go to a bar tonight. I made one this morning ready for me, but it can stretch to two?"

"Why not? It'll keep my figure right. I eat too much in the hotel. It's awful the way the chef is always nibbling."

"Right!" I said as we came under the last bridge, "You can eat my salad and I'll listen to your discs."

As we arrived old Clive was not quite hopping from one foot to the other, but was certainly ready to head for the 'Boot and Shoe'. The 'Shoe' stemmed from the days of horse drawn narrow boats as the trade moved between the Potteries and Coventry or London. Anyway, he was wasting no time; he followed us to lock the gate as we left. I wondered, as I sat on the sun-warmed leather and savoured the hum of the straight six engine, whether I wasn't being just a bit unwise. Annie was young and fresh, she made me feel younger, but was I getting too involved? The idea was dismissed; she was just a happy-go-lucky girl, who would simply go on her way in a few months.

I'd only met her weeks ago and that was no time at all to know her. In fact, I realised I knew very little about her and what I did know seemed to be a conundrum. There was some hidden depth below the light-hearted exterior. The line of thought was shattered as the remembered face of Liza came unbidden into my mind. Shockingly, I suddenly ached for her and nearly cancelled the evening there and then. It was only the thought of disappointing sweet Annie that I didn't.

We stopped briefly at the Duke, for Annie to pick up her CDs; she came with a case of them and a red jacket over her shoulders.

"There won't be time to play all those!" I protested.

"I know that,' she giggled, "they were all agog where I was going. I refused to say. They'll all be rubbernecking to see. You'll do my reputation no good at all."

I sat motionless, still shocked over my feelings about Liza, "If you'd rather not."

She squeezed my arm, "No way! I'm starving, if you're not."

"OK! On your own head be it." And I drove off with a squeal of tyres, imagining the whole population of Lichfield watching.

She hummed another tune as we weaved along the lanes, the sun was still high, but the shadows were lengthening as I bumped along my own track through the orchard.

Annie gasped with delight as she saw the low, tiled roof, the part timbered front and the friendly circle of trees round the patch of meadow I had razed yesterday, "It's beautiful! Wow! I love it."

Parking the Jag in front of the barn I reminded her, "Mustn't be too late taking you back, tonight." She had a funny, enigmatic expression, simply picked up her CD case, handbag and jacket to follow me in the low door. Inside, I pointed out the bathroom and the dining room, before I went to the kitchen to remove my cling-filmed salad from the 'fridge.

It reminded me of the time I'd shown Liza the bathroom and I felt the flutter of my heart as I remembered her closeness, her scent, now faded from my dressing gown. By the time Annie had returned I'd done all the preparation, except for the drink.

"How do you like your coffee, or tea, I forgot to ask?"

She laughed, "Back home, I always drink coffee black, but I've gotten used to your tea. Whatever you're having is fine." So I made black coffee. She was impressed, "That's good!"

We munched the salad, demolished the ham and finished a Pavlova, before we fell into my sofa. I made a mental note to restock my larder. Annie wasn't pretending when she said she was starving. And thankfully there were no more questions to disturb the atmosphere.

The rest of the evening was simply music. Patsy Cline and Box Car Willie alternated with Chopin's nocturne E and a prelude. I confess that I was bored by long sessions of Box Car Willie; he was too predictable and repetitious.

But Annie was transported, singing alongside him in a soft, crooning voice. To be honest her voice was to me better to listen to than the pseudo-country professionalism of Willie. Also being honest, she did not find the pleasure I did in Chopin.

It was getting dark outside as I pointed out the time, so we wriggled out of my sofa. At the low door, she surprised me by giving me a hug, quickly, but firmly.

She let go immediately and went to the car without a word, remaining apparently deep in thought as I wended our way back to town. Her parting was brief, a quick, perfunctory kiss on the cheek and she was gone.

Driving home slowly, soothed by the reassuring purr from the straight six engine, I began thinking of Liza, her face not as distinct in my memory.

I also thought of Annie. She seemed to be a great kid, nothing more. So I'd been deeply disturbed to feel a small gun in her handbag as I had handed it to her outside the hotel.

Chapter 24 The Farm.

Another glorious morning woke me early. From experience of the brightness, it was unlikely to last all day, so I rose, showered and did my ten minute routine that was necessary to combat my sedentary work life.

It was a good time to polish the Jag and put it in the barn out of the sun. I was wringing out the final chamois leather when the 'phone rang. There was a voice I did not recognise, but sounded faintly familiar, "Sorry to disturb you Mr Fradley, this is the CID. We've found a piece of electronic equipment that has us puzzled. Could you spare the time to look at it for us?"

This disturbed me. I'd thought I was unknown in the city. To be called by the police as an expert was distinctly unsettling.

"Are you sure you have the right person, er, who is that, by the way?"

The voice was suave, "Sorry. Should have said. Inspector Newman. Yes, I was advised to approach you by the Home Office. This is ticklish. Definitely something odd here."

There was something odd, very odd. But I was foolishly intrigued enough to want some answers, "Shall I come to the Central Station?"

The voice was placatory, "No, the item is where we found it. Can you come to Harrison's Farm as soon as possible?"

Harrison's Farm wasn't far, a gloomy, isolated, half-ruined old property that was in the middle of a large copse. I knew it because I'd considered it as a new home once. But I didn't like the dark, neglected wood surrounding it; there was a shifty feel about it as if it had a nasty, hidden past, "I will be there in ten minutes, if that's soon enough?"

"That will be absolutely top hole, sir, just perfect."

I should have known then. But curiosity has always been one of my failings.

So I garaged the Jag and went in the Rover with my 'hearing aid' and small tool kit.

I drove slowly along the overgrown track. Obviously no-one else had liked it enough to buy the place either. Weeds sprouted through the uneven cobbles in the yard where I parked. There was no sign of a car, but the front door was open. As I emerged gingerly from the car, the voice I'd heard on the 'phone wafted from the dark opening, "In here Mr Fradley, sir. It's a bit dark, mind your head."

Peering into the gloom I discerned a rain-coated figure looking down at a shiny, grey box in the middle of the floor. I slowly approached the object, which did not seem to have any wiring externally. The figure did not turn, but pointed down, "What do you make of that?"

My mind was racing, but not fast enough. Alarm bells were ringing, but what was wrong?

"Just there, sir." The voice was insistent, "Down there."

Putting down my tool kit I started to crouch to see in the dim light. And that was as far as I got, before I heard a flurry from the raincoat and sensed violent movement. The top of my head exploded into a searing light, which just as quickly disintegrated and vanished, leaving a black pit that I fell headlong into.

Chapter 25 The Pit.

I lay at the bottom of the pit in sooty blackness, frantically clawing at the sides, but bits kept falling off and the voice echoed, ringing round and round, A voice kept repeating hollowly, 'Down there! Down there!' Gradually a grey light permeated the blackness accompanied by an engine throbbing. I tried to speak but merely croaked.

Putting up my hand I tried to climb out of the pit and felt cold stone flags.

What were flags doing lining the sides of the pit?

Except that the flags were not in the pit, they were on the floor. And I was lying on them. The throbbing engine faded. It was my head that was throbbing. An attempt to sit up made me cry with the pain, a star of blinding light burst in my eyes. I lay still until it turned to grey. The stones were cold, hard and unyielding under my face. I pushed against the gritty surface and my head shrieked at me. Taking a deep breath I persisted, agonisingly until I sat with my head bent, beaten and aching. There was blood on my hand from my forehead. I stared at it. This was my blood, what was I doing here? Wincing in pain again the memory came back, flooding, accusing and terrifying. In fear of what I might find, I reached for the back of my head. That was a mistake. There was a large, tender lump that bitterly resented being touched. I grimaced and groaned with the agony.

But the deepest pain was that I'd allowed this to happen.

Slowly as the pain subsided, I began to think I might live again. The greyness lifted as light filtered through the two doors. Two doors? Concentrate. There was only one door. My vision settled and the two images merged into the open door I had entered. The light that forced away the blackness was glaring; it was bright and sunny out there.

Suddenly I had to get out of this room, so I tried to stand, but didn't make it, and crawled to the blessed light and freedom. As I reached the door I felt wonderful warmth from the sun, but my eyes rebelled and refused to bear the dazzle. My head hung down and I waited.

How long it was, I don't know, but gradually the headache grew worse and my sight became better. I forced my jelly-like legs to raise me from the floor and leaned gratefully against the warm wall. My sight was clearing now; my head was throbbing in deep, insistent waves that made me nauseous.

I looked at my watch; it was nine-o-clock. The past hour had vanished.

My Rover had also vanished from the weed-strewn yard. Cursing my stupidity, I also began to feel vicious and cursed the 'Inspector', which made me feel better. It was the rage at my assailant that finally got me moving. Stumbling and shuffling trough the knee-high weeds along the tree-lined track I eventually reached the road. There was nothing in sight in either direction. The pounding in my head was becoming worse, so I started to hobble to the village on my left.

The throbbing in my head sounded worse, until I heard a raucous horn from behind and realised that the noise was outside my head. Turning painfully I saw an ancient, dark red Bedford half-truck approaching. It groaned to a halt, ticking over unevenly and smokily. An old man in open-necked, checked shirt and stained corduroy trousers climbed out.

He rubbed his bristly chin, "What's 'appened to you like?"

He started forward as I wobbled alarmingly, "'Ey up duck, you'd best come an' sit down." I waved feebly, but allowed him to half-lift me into the cab. He drove a little way and turned towards an ugly, modern bungalow surrounded with a hedge so neat it looked engineered. A fat, bustling woman came out as he stopped.

Between them they assisted me into the kitchen, which was obviously their main living area, and started bringing me back to real life. After the ministrations of tea and plasters, they both were pleased with the result of their efforts. I was feeling the places where he'd clouted on the head, where my nose and forehead had hit the flags and was decidedly delicate. I managed to duck too much detail, but asked them to contact Bill, who arrived in a lather of worry. He also brought Sheila, who nodded approvingly at the repair work by the old couple. After offering, and being firmly refused, to compensate the couple for their help, Bill helped me to the car.

He was even more worried when I told him that my keys were gone along with the Rover. Grim-faced we went to the office, but were relieved to see the door closed. I creaked up the stairs and sat pale-faced with pain and shock as Bill ran the monitor recordings to see what had happened.

The security breach, integrity light was flashing in triple sets, showing that there had been a nearly successful attempt at entry. The intruder had managed to unlock the two deadlocks, but was repelled by the double digital locks of my own. Sheila made me a welcome cup of good coffee as we looked at the 'Inspector', wearing a motorcycle helmet and leathers, carry out his efforts for nearly fifteen minutes before admitting defeat. I groaned as I thought of the cost of replacing the locks, resetting the digitals and new car locks. Sheila misunderstood and told me I ought to be in hospital or at least bed. As I just couldn't argue then I agreed to go home. The thought of home suddenly hit me. Had my home been invaded as well?

The thought made me feel violated, dirty. Sheila was worried at the way I jumped up until I told her why. Both of them shared my feelings, so we rushed to lock up and went rapidly to The Orchard.

Bill stopped before we were within eye-shot of the cottage.

We listened, but heard nothing, so we approached slowly. The Rover was on the drive, the driver's door open. We sat for a full minute, but still nothing happened, so we got out of the car and waited tensed for action.

Still nothing happened, so I stumbled to the Rover to look inside. It all looked normal. I left the door open as Bill circled the house, but found nothing. We started to relax.

He tried the cottage doors, they were locked. We wondered if the keys were in the Rover, so he reached for the handle, but something made me call out to stop him. On my directions he fished around in my shed and brought out a piece of rope, tied it to the car door handle and went away as far as he could. Bill told Sheila and me to shelter behind their car, he lay down and pulled hard to slam the door shut.

There was a whumf as the car interior filled with gas. I began to shake and lay face down until Sheila came to see if I was alright. Bill came and knelt beside me, "I think we'd better call for some help from the firm, don't you?" Not daring to think what else I might find, I nodded.

Bill and Sheila were tremendous. They bundled me into their car and went to their modern house. From there Bill organised 'the firm' to check out the office, the Rover and the cottage. The surprising thing was that there was only superficial damage to the car interior and no entry to the cottage. It was clear that my security systems had worked, which was a relief in one way.

They cleaned the car of the gas, which was taken away for analysis, changed the locks on that, the office and the cottage, checked for any electronic activity and declared all to be clean. It was more worrying to me that I'd allowed it to happen in the first place. Sheila ordered me to bed with a hot drink. Her comforting, protective bossiness soothed more than anything else.

Chapter 26 Undercurrents.

That night as I sipped Horlicks prior to retiring to my solitary bed, I felt the loneliness of my life. The attack had triggered off what had been slowly growing. The need to share thoughts, fears and ambitions, not to mention good music was surging through me. It was no good deluding myself; I wanted a warm, soft body for mutuality of comfort and satisfaction. I was experiencing a spiritual, mental and sexual need as I'd not done before. Liza and Annie had momentarily given me an extra companionable dimension to my life. They had also woken my suppressed and confused male libido and it was beginning to make me unsettled. I went to bed in a sombre mood, dreaming of Liza and Annie chatting about me. I was dumb and unable to butt in. It was not conducive to rest. The dawn came to find me tossing and mentally fogged.

Some inner instinct, or maybe just habit, made me eager to go to the office. At the back of my mind, vaguely just out of reach, there was a gnawing doubt, almost a fear that I'd missed something important.

Bill showed no surprise at my intention. We looked at each other with a sheepish grin, he spoke first, "Can't you keep away either?"

At the office Bill opened the terminal and whistled. I looked at the screen he was studying. We both looked at it puzzled. There were several messages about hotel bookings, orders for dinners and directives to the Manager. They were all for the Central.

"Bill, what are you doing hacking into the Central's e-mail?"

"I was about to ask you the same."

"Didn't you instigate this then?"

"Nope!"

A chilling fog of uncertainty crept into my brain.

"Who the hell did, then?"

Bill scrolled down the list, said nothing, but pointed.

The message read: - "From acchemicals@langley.va.com

To

central.hotel@btopenworld.co.uk

Personal to A Clinton, Central Hotel, Lichfield, England.

Regret to inform, leak more severe than anticipated, action required urgently to limit damage. Should we close feeder plant? Advise. Klausky, C E O"

We stared at each other as the words Langley, Va sank in.

We spoke together, "CIA!"

Bill scrolled further. I looked at the screen.

"From central.hotel@btopenworld.co.uk

To acchemicals@langley.va.com

V Klausky, C E O. EXECUTE! Keep informed. Contract here nearing conclusion. Associate is optimistic. A Clinton."

My leather chair creaked comfortingly under me, "Bill, this is looking serious. I think it's time to call HG for more than a spring clean."

"Already done! I can only assume that someone has set this up for our benefit. No-one else knows this terminal. It has to be someone who has access to it at times." He did not need to say it, but it was clear that there was only one person in that category. There was only one person with inside knowledge, ability and the nerve.

LIZA!

My world was crumbling around me, I heard again Annie's voice, "*Just what do you do?*"

"Bill," I said heavily, "I hate to say it, but we'd better carry out a full search.'

He nodded. It was clear that he was wondering just how far he could trust me. So I told him of the outings with Annie, especially her blatant pumping of yesterday. I bored him with all the details because I had to earn his trust. Also, two minds are better than one.

By focusing on two viewpoints in the past we usually arrived at the correct diagnosis. It had always worked before and I hoped it was to work now.

"It's all linked with this transmission device of DEMOLISH," he mused. "I think that we're going to be very careful about what we say to our buyers, when they deign to appear. Someone is taking liberties and it's all one-sided. I'm prepared to stay all day if you want."

Undoing my collar another button I croaked, "Let's get to it. You check the e-mail for viruses; I'll start with the integrity of the lines." We worked without a break for four hours and stopped as the clock in the square chimed one. My head was thumping again. I stretched and looked over to Bill, "Time for the inner man; I'm skipping the Bearpit, for the time being. Fancy something plastic in the Three Spires?"

"How about a delivered pizza instead, that way we don't need to go out and lock up. We'd save near half an hour." We did just that and carried on until three.

Finally Bill stood, stretching his long frame, "I think that's all. If there is anything, then I can't find it." We compared notes and tallied what we had.

There was a complete list of the Central's e-mail. Apart from the two Clinton items, there were a fair number of Japanese bookings. There was confirmation of the union request for the security cameras and an order to our friends at Ace computers to fit them. I could see nothing that warranted the hacking into the terminal. We had some audio feedback from Clinton's room, but there was only one possible thing of value. At the approximate time of the first e-mail from 'A C Chemicals' he had uttered one loud expletive and slammed out of the door. Perhaps the 'leak' was the reason for it.

It was little enough for the effort put in, but at least there had been no breach of security or integrity and we could find no viruses or clandestine monitoring.

In that respect, no news was definitely good news.

Reaching for the red 'phone I pushed the scrambler button. I went through the checks in a fit of impatience, until D's voice barked his usual uncivil greeting, "Ball!" One of these days I shall give myself the satisfaction of barking back, "And ball to you too!"

In the meantime I must eat, so I simply said, "Arraye."

His voice softened a little, not much, but enough to sound half-way human.

"Trouble?" He never did waste words.

"Could be big." Enough to hint, vague enough to need further information. It is silly really, but I bait him, just for the hell of it.

"Well?"

"I need an AV 3 in the staff locker room of the Central here, soonest. Ace has a job. Channel three."

"Need? Or want?"

"*Need.* Repeat, soonest."

"Will do. More?"

"Negative."

The line went dead. Bill winked at me, "Let's have a coffee while we wait."

I was just finishing the last mouthful as the black 'phone rang. Picking it up I held it at arm's length as the squawking went on for many seconds. I put it to my ear to catch the final tirade, "....and what the bloody hell do you mean by setting D on my back? I'm up to my arms in sh..." I interrupted, "Language, language! You might upset someone's finer senses."

"There'd bloody better not be! You think I'm sitting here on my big fat ..."

I interrupted again, "My heart bleeds for you, you poor, underpaid, overworked, unappreciated and delicate old sod. Now you've had your say, listen to mine. This is serious! There's a class A1 + project here that looks like going pear-shaped."

He calmed momentarily as I went on, "You're not the only one unappreciated. Someone's just tried to beat my brains out and another's using me and I don't like it. What's more, there's one above D, or even C, who won't like it if it does."

There was a long silence as he chewed this snippet over, "Is it right?"

"Too true." My voice dropped to a confidential tone, "The truth is that right now I don't know who's who and I can't find my Debrett's. I *need* to find out for myself and quick."

"All very well, but where am I supposed to put it? Stick it up...?"

I was getting fed up with him, "You can stick it where the hell you like, but do it!" There was a hiatus. Calmer I went on, "With all those cameras, no-one's going to query a mere junction box, now are they?"

There was a rude word remarkably like Clinton's and the line went dead.

Bill was almost rolling round the floor, helpless with laughter. He finally sat down and wiped his eyes, "If Disney could see this lot, he would die of jealousy."

So it was that I got my eye into the place that was to reveal some of the answers to the unknown factors of the whole business. Bill went home a happy man as I set up the computer to examine the logging of the e-mail from the

Central. I also scrolled the complete list again without spotting anything new. There was still that niggle that there was something staring me in the face and I didn't recognise it.

Unable to face anyone, especially Annie that night, I locked up the fort and went home. I was very jumpy all the way there, but there was no sign of anyone taking any interest.

I treble checked the new locks and microwaved a frozen beefburger. That tells you how far gone I was that day.

True to my instructions my AV 3 came on line promptly at 9.30 am the following day. The prospect was not a happy one, it was not as sensitive as the AV4 and could suffer from the position it had to be placed, but it was all I could fall back on at short notice. I decided to stay in the office that day, watching and waiting. There was this gut feeling that things would happen quickly or not at all.

And that was how it turned out to be.

My monitor showed the technicians putting the final adjustments to the very prominent security cameras and I watched the room from the two viewpoints. The cameras were overlapping; my split screen was able to show all three angles - the two obvious ones and my own discreet one. Nothing in that room was hidden.

I watched all morning, sipped coffee and ate digestive biscuits right through until the three-o-clock shift came and went. For another half an hour nothing happened. Just as I was beginning to need to answer the call of nature, the door opened and the familiar figure of Antonio walked in.

He pointed a remote gadget at the cameras, they went blank. Peering closely at the scene I automatically started the recording to review later. There was no haste and no furtiveness in his actions as he locked the door behind him. He went to the corner and opened the last locker, to remove a jemmy. He went to one locker and with one quick action had it open. Rummaging around, took out a wallet, an envelope of A

4 size and a small cloth bound roll. He checked the wallet and replaced it in the locker. Next he opened the envelope, extracted some papers and photographed them with a pen-sized camera, before replacing them. The roll of cloth he weighed carefully and unwrapped it. It was an automatic pistol.

I was too far away to see what make, but it gleamed with that oily sheen that showed it was cared for. He seemed to be undecided, but finally wrapped it back in the cloth and replaced it also in the locker. He jemmied the door shut, shook the handle and smiled. The mini-camera went in his pocket, the jemmy back in the locker. He secured the locker, unlocked the hall door, clicked the remote device and went round the lockers before going out of the door again.

I stared at the security camera screens; they were back on view as if they had never been off. By zooming in on one of them, I was able to see the name on the door he had attacked.

It was GEORGE BROWN.

Running the recording showed it was exactly the same as I remembered it. It was all very interesting. I left the screen and went to the archive monitor. It took a few moments, but I picked up the images of the attempted assault on my workshop and the AV 4 record of the hooded figure in the locker room.

The niggle had been right. They were all Antonio.

But. They were not the 'Inspector', nor the man in the motorcycle outfit.

Returning to the surveillance of the Central's locker room I saw nothing of the image in front of me. I would have given a lot to see what he'd photographed and was also desperate to know why. As a habit more than expecting anything useful, I set the activity recorders and locked up carefully. I blessed that cantankerous old devil for being efficient in installing the AV 3. Tomorrow would have been too late.

The red 'phone rang. Apprehensively I picked it up and listened.

I felt positively frozen as the man in question spoke quietly in a sombre tone I'd never heard him use, "Thought you ought to know. That gas in your car is Sarin. We've sent a sample to Tokyo for comparison. Just thought you ought to be warned. Bye."

Visions of the Tokyo Metro disaster seared my mind. Sarin!

I began to feel vicious. I wasn't going to take it lying down. I had a few tricks of my own to use. Later, going to the Frog Lane car park I was also wearing my 'hearing aid'.

It was no surprise to hear footsteps trail me as far as the entrance. It was a relief that they then went a different way. It was time I started putting some odds on my side.

My security was intact on the Rover, so I started off going twice round the Bowling Green Pub and doubling back at the Friary. As far as I could make out no-one was obviously following. I stopped at the village pub and again at the track through my orchard, but there was nothing. The thought of another frozen meal repelled me, so I found relaxation in making a Hungarian Goulash. I grimaced as it struck me. Thoughts of Liza always popped up in the most unexpected places.

Chapter 27 Suspicions

The holiday was truly dead, Bill was as jumpy as me; he shared my conviction about Antonio, but was amazed as I said I wasn't having him tailed. He was very uneasy but I pointed out that he was almost always in the Central and had so far shown no threat to me. Not like some other unknown person had.

It was late as I saw Bill off. Not in the mood for making my own meals I went to the Bearpit again and realised that I was hungry as the old familiar scents reached me. Annie's open smiling face released a different longing. This uncertainty was ruining my peace of mind. I would just put on a brave face and carry on as if nothing was amiss - in fact up to now I had little firm evidence of much. It was also rather ludicrous when I thought of it, the CIA using e-mail to contact an agent. I began to feel better about the Texan.

His grating voice reached me before I was aware of his presence; it was then that I thought, '*Speak of the devil.*'

"Albert Fradley the Fourth. Where have you been hiding yourself? I've not seen you for days."

"Oh! I've been about . . .," smiling at Annie as she brought my Steak and Ale pie. "For one thing I've been cruising with this charming young lady."

Annie's smile was a little less than her usual as I said that. She looked at me in an uncertain way, "I did wonder if you were avoiding me as well. I'm glad to see that you're back again." She looked carefully, "What's happened to your face?"

"I was just careless. Didn't look where I was going."

Neither of them believed me, but they let it pass. I grimaced at them both in turn, "I do have to work you know, I won't be able to come here if I don't, and it's been busy lately" There was an expectant pause, they said nothing, waiting, "I've been taking stock prior to working on a new contract for the Government. I 'm afraid it's all at a ticklish stage right now, so I can't tell you about it yet."

Was I being paranoid again or was there the flicker of mutual knowledge?

I switched the subject, "Would you like something to eat, Mr Clinton? I can recommend this pie - it might be small by American standards, but what it lacks in size is more than made up for in quality!"

He wrinkled his nose, "Tempting. But what about this BSE or CID disease?"

"CJD." I corrected, "No problem there, this is local beef, no chance of any contamination - we even know the grass it eats. You can rest assured that there's absolutely no risk here. Right Annie?"

She nodded as Aloysius spoke firmly, "In that case I'll have one too Annie. By the way, call me Al. This formality of Mr Clinton isn't my way."

I spoke in what I hoped was a nonchalant tone, "How's the family tree going?"

He shrugged, "Coming to a halt through some clumsy goon. My lap top got busted day before yesterday. I was fuming, but no-body owned up to it. I've got a new one coming tomorrow from the States. It has all my back-up material, so I can pick it up then, but I'm running into a fence in the 1500 s. The records were pretty sketchy then."

If I didn't stop open-mouthed, then I surprised myself. They say the mind has massive resources that we don't use to the full. Mine clicked into hyperdrive. There had been one mysterious item on the sound recorded from Al's room, that had been of little interest at the time, it was simply a sort of scratching noise between the sounds of the door opening and closing. There had been the e-mail to him and the dismissal of it as a means of the CIA contacting an agent. It was obvious that the swear word he uttered shortly afterwards was the discovery of the tampering with the lap top.

A lap top could be a very accommodating device in the right hands. No matter what the risk, I had to get a new AV 4 into his room. My mind also clicked into retrieval mode at a speed that astonished me.

Casually I said, "Have you been to Eccleshall?"

His blank expression was all the answer I needed. This was my opportunity to give him a scent to follow tomorrow. I needed that time to set up my bug, "Yes, Eccleshall, it's the other side of Stafford. It might seem strange but the Bishops of Lichfield were also over Stafford and lived in a castle next to the Holy Trinity at Eccleshall - at least until 1860 something, I can't remember the exact date."

At the mention of the word 'castle' his eyes lit up, so I went on, "It still has its moat and bridge, but it's now in private hands, so you might not be able to get in."

I looked at his interested eyes, as he was trying to hide his thoughts, "Of course, you could try to *buy* it," I laughed. He was hooked, so I gave him a little slack to run, "You'll probably find the church records available in any case."

"Now there's a thing! There was me thinking it was all going to fizzle out, I was just at the end of my rope and you come up with this."

We both looked up as Annie approached with the pie for Al, "My, my Mr Clinton, you look like the cat that ate the canary."

We both laughed; I began to feel like my old self.

The next day I was in the office at the crack of dawn; as I watched the Central's door and listened to the sounds in Clinton's room, I also glanced at the staff room monitor from time to time. For an hour nothing much happened. I was beginning to sweat. Was he going to take the bait? It was 8.34 am when I heard what I was praying for. Over the speaker, I heard Al, as I'd started thinking of him, call for a cab to be available all day.

Bill was in time to see my grin as he arrived, "You must have had a good night. Felix couldn't hold a light to you."

"If you must know I had a rotten night. I've been here since six."

His brows shot skywards, "Six? I give up! Why don't you sell that grotty cottage and save yourself money. You might as well live here."

"They wouldn't give me planning permission," I sniffed.

Bill bellowed with glee, "Thank heavens for that! What is all this anyway, not more to do with DEMOLISH?"

"I really don't know what *is* going on here, so I'm making a few steps to try to find out. Everyone and everything is making me suspicious; it's getting to me as nothing has before." Appealingly I looked at him, "Apart from you, I just don't know who's real and who's playing a part."

Turning to the screen I was in time to see Al enter a taxi and drive away, "One out of the way."

Going to the outdoor clothes locker I pulled out a boiler suit and cap.

Bill was clearly puzzled, "Digging for diamonds?" Our private joke, referring to the Seven Dwarves, wasn't able to suppress my high feelings.

I took up the AV 4 and my detector from my desk, "See you in an hour; I'll have a coffee when I come back. I'll need it. I'm just going to see a man about a bug."

Feeling as inconspicuous as Santa Claus I crossed the lane to the staff entrance of the Central. No-one challenged me as I picked up a short ladder and headed for the staff room. I stopped to glance at the AV 3 under the security camera; it

158

seemed to be just a small junction box set in the armoured cables.

Whistling tunelessly - I can't whistle any other way - I wandered along to room 102.

There was a pile of linen on the floor outside 104, so there was a bare ten minutes to do what I wanted. My hand shook a little as I tried the first of my SWIPE cards in the lock. The light remained red. I was sweating as the light went green at the fourth card and slipped in. The chambermaid came out of 104 and went into 103.

Bolting the inner lock I stood looking around. There was nothing immediately to cause a problem, so I activated the detector. It showed the presence of four bugs. I tried again – same. One I traced to the rear of the large picture on the wall opposite the bed; it was about the size of a sugar cube. I blinked. I'd thought that the standard GRU pattern had long gone. The second was mine on the light fitting. The third was hard to find, but it was clever; it was in the light pull for the overbed switch. The fourth was the one in my hand. Wasting no more time I put the AV 4 in place of the bulb overhead and was going down the stairs, whistling as the maid came out of 103. I nodded to her and went through the staff door into the yard, returned the ladder and went back to my office.

The coffee was ready as I entered. Bill lifted an inquisitive eye, "OK?"

Flopping down I threw the cap aside. It was clammy in the boiler suit; my palms were uncomfortably damp and sticky. My head had started to throb again.

"I am not suited to this any more," I moaned rather than spoke, Bill ignored me. I struggled up and removed the boiler suit, "If I look like trying it again, lock me up and throw away the key."

All Bill said was "Ha!"

As it was Saturday afternoon, I gave Bill the time off and threw caution to the winds. The Jag needed a good warm up, so I headed for the A 51 and Tamworth. The day was dry, but with those wispy cirrus that are not a good omen.

I drove fast in the early morning light traffic and headed east. Skirting the shopping and industrial estates I just headed where the fancy took me.

After an hour, my feelings were more relaxed, the six cylinders of the engine were purring like the big cat it was and all was well with the world. There is nothing so therapeutic to me as simply wafting along in the open air, hood down, CD of Chopin playing and the enjoyment of power on tap, waiting to be unleashed. It isn't often I floor the accelerator, partly out of respect for the car, partly for the security of having plenty in reserve. Bill said it's a sign of old age creeping on: I think of it as controlled use of latent power. Much as a black belt karate expert doesn't go around beating up all and sundry, but is serene in the knowledge that he has the ability to deal with life's problems.

I stopped for a coffee at one of the many tea shops and sat admiring the sleek lines of the Jag. If only people could be so reliable and dependable. By now there were many more vehicles about and I felt it time to return home, especially as the cloud was thickening as I expected. Having warmed up the Jag and calmed myself I felt ready to tackle the world again.

It was habit more than positive thought that took me to the office. There was a niggling doubt about the AV 4 in Clinton's room that kept me from returning home. The thought crossed my mind that Bill wasn't far short of the truth hinting that I spent too much time there. If I was honest to myself, I had to admit that my bachelor existence was beginning to feel less than complete, my thoughts drifted back to LIza and Annie. I was fond of Annie, there was no doubt, but she seemed to be another Sheila, rather more cute, but still

160

ultimately lacking some depth of attraction. Not so with Liza. I had never felt as I did when I first saw her. The trouble was when was I to see her again? She was so elusive both to meet and to understand. Anyway, I knew so little about her. Apart from the almost sensual and spiritual meshing of our minds that transcended words, I hadn't had any real indication that she saw me as anything more than a good friend or mere mechanic.

It was with these thoughts unsettling my peace of mind that I drove to my usual place in the car park. Putting up the hood I went to the office. Despite the increasing cloud, there was a good crowd around the streets, already there was a queue of Japanese at the door of the TIC.

Opening the e-mail I dumped the usual unwanted mass of hopeful circulars. It was always an irritant that so much time was spent on throwing things away. At least it wasn't mounds of paper.

The live view of Al's room was static. I was just about to turn on the recording when he entered holding a Securicor parcel. Turning on the coffee pot I watched. As he unwrapped it to reveal a lap top computer, I poured my coffee and settled down to observe. He went to the drinks cabinet and poured out a Coke. Surprisingly, he gave it a shake prior to opening, which made it fizzy. He put it near the big picture. Clever! The fizz would blanket any meaningful sounds for the KGB bug. He went to the bathroom and came back with a damp face cloth that he wrapped round the light pull.

I began to sweat as I thought of the grey blob on the light fitting and my precious AV 4 overhead. I needn't have worried; he proceeded to pick up a Time magazine. Taking out a folding microscope he looked closely at one page. He then went to the lap top and removed from the base a slim bundle of wires that opened out like a circular fan to become a dish on a tripod. He placed it on the window sill and pressed a button on the keyboard. The dish swept back and forth, up and down until it settled, pointing up at a steep angle.

He sat down at the computer and rattled along at an impressive typing speed, before sitting back and waiting. My radio detector dutifully recorded a ten second burst of high-speed transmission. Later, our computer revealed it as a GOV/DOS code. The screen was static for another minute, but then became a blur as the LCD tried to keep pace with the inflow of data.

When it ceased, Al pressed a single button and closed it all down again. He picked up the face cloth, returned it to the bathroom, picked up the Coke and the Time magazine and settled down in the easy chair to read. It was impressive; he was a cool customer all right.

I was also rather relieved. My initial guess was right. The CIA was here.

The niggling thought was why? I wasn't too happy about his failing to spot my bugs.

As I drank my cooling coffee I pondered.

Wandering to the window I noted it had started to rain lightly. The shoppers and tourists scurried to shelter, the illegal traders gloomily packed up.

I stopped dead.

It struck me like a ton of bricks! Al hadn't failed to spot the bugs.

He knew someone would be watching. It was all for my benefit.

This was his way of telling me that we were on the same side. But it didn't tell me why he was here. That was to be a lot more difficult to discover.

Just before I was about to leave, the red 'phone rang again. It was Black Harry. I hadn't realised that he was so close to D. This time he was in a sadistic, gleeful mood, He was even more obnoxious than usual and positively oozed obscenity as he sniggered, "Japan's confirmed what I suspected." He paused as I sweated, "Practically identical. You seem to have upset some really nasty people this time, you clever, little egghead." Laughing like a drain he slammed down the handset before I could rise out of my shock to swear back at him.

The maelstrom of field activities was sucking me in again.

My shock had metamorphosised into a gritty chutzpah that made me dangerous. Up to now I'd always drawn back from actually using my armoury. Not any more.

Chapter 28 Food for Thought.

As I wasn't going to learn anything useful from watching Al, I turned to the messages from HG. One made me go warm. Liza was due on Monday at 10 am for a briefing and progress report on DEMOLISH. My pulse quickened, my forehead throbbed. She was coming. It upset all my calmness, so carefully built up that morning. After failing to settle I opted for my other therapy. Shutting up shop I went to the delicatessen and bought the ingredients for leek soup, duck en croute and my own special trifle. The Jag bore me swiftly to The Orchard where I shut myself in the kitchen and spent my time enjoying doing something I really knew all about.

Back in the office early again on Monday I felt better. My totally lazy day on Sunday was both untypical and refreshing. It would do me good to do it more often. I'd been pleasantly surprised by the change of the weather to a balmy, warm, soporific sort of day. Not in the mood for battling with the Sunday drivers and tourists, I sat in my meadow, read the Citizen, never a demanding process, and sipped a cool Cinzano and lemonade. My thoughts must have drifted to Annie and Liza again as I sipped the cool drink; the one like Coke, the other like the cool drink I held. One was light and attractive: the other was deeper, but not easy to become familiar with. Idly I wondered if I was not being dazzled by Liza. Was I chasing an elusive shadow? Could I find the peace I had begun to need in Annie's youth and vivacity? Musing and smelling the drying grasses of my earlier trimming efforts I dozed gently off.

Later I remembered that day as a parched, desert traveller remembers a blessed oasis.

Monday was the day that Liza swept into my office and back into my life as a freshening breeze tells a yachtsman there's is a lively time ahead.

Foolishly, I thought I could cope. She'd discarded the business suit for a light summer frock of floral cotton. It was not the High Street replicas sold by the thousand, but was, as usual, an example of the subtle art of classic simplicity. I have always admired the genius of the ancient Greeks in that field, the way that the soft folds of the garment hid and emphasised at the same time. As always she made me feel scruffy and unkempt. But I was glad to see her. Her smile seemed to be genuine; her hand shake was firm and sincere. She laid down her document case, "Lovely morning. It's a pleasure to be out."

She looked at my battered face, "I heard. I'm glad it wasn't worse."

I grinned, "I'll live! You're a little early this month. Anything special?"

There was a twinkle in her eyes, "Could be. I'm here to observe the Planning Application for the BT mast. If all goes well, we start work next week."

I gaped at that, "I knew there was more to it than just a mobile 'phone mast! But why the Cathedral? Surely you want something not so obvious."

She laughed, displaying her white teeth in that warm, red mouth. She was so desirable as she went on, "Where's the best place to hide a log? In a wood yard. There are some other reasons as well, but those are technical." She picked up her case, "Are you interested in the workings of local democracy?"

Not really I admitted to myself, but the idea was becoming interesting as I thought of sitting alongside Liza. I restricted myself to one word, "Very."

The room was stuffy already as we took our seats. The pile of papers before each councillor seemed daunting; it looked as if they would be there until midnight. The meeting was called to order and the first application, a resiting of the cold store at the Central was passed with the rider that it was to be in local materials. As it was hidden behind a ten foot wall, I thought it was an unnecessary provision, but the architect was clearly pleased.

They quickly worked down the extensions and shop fronts, following the Planning Officer's recommendations in the main. It soon became clear to me who was the awkward customer who could founder the scheme we had come to support.

Councillor Heathcote was not being told what to do by any Planning Officer and had an objection to almost everything. Even in this short time I could sense the battle lines drawn between him and the Chair, Mrs Duval. I was uncertain of others, who saw the obvious snags, but were fair. There was a solid support for the Planning Officer and most schemes were approved or rejected as he advised.

There was a stir as the item we wanted to hear was announced. "1964/04, Aerial Array for British Telecom for short wave radio transmission." It was followed by a buzz until Mrs Duval banged her gavel for silence. The Planning Officer stood, "You have all had the plans and my recommendation in this matter." He cleared his throat, "There has been some emotional and acrimonious criticism of this application ..." there was an uprising of voices until the banging of the gavel restored peace.

He continued, "You must put all those consideration from your mind, including the nature of the building involved. The Cathedral is, in planning terms, just another Listed Structure. I have had long discussions with BT on this matter and the plan has been modified to meet my proposals and requirements."

He paused to fix Heathcote with an icy stare, "I have no hesitation in recommending approval of this application as described in the latest, amended drawings you hold. The effect on the Cathedral will be minimal, almost invisible from the ground and will be undertaken at the same time as necessary repairs."

He cleared his throat and peered over his half-moon spectacles, "I have inserted a condition that the required temporary building will be removed in one month." He sat to a general murmur.

Mrs Duval spoke firmly, "As we have a full list, I will ask for brief comments before we vote. Councillor Heathcote?"

He rose to glare at those around him, "This is not really about planning, it's about legalised vandalism." There was another burst of shouts, "Good for you," "Rubbish!" and "Trust 'im", before the gavel was wielded with vigour, "This is not a bearpit!"

I grinned to myself as Mrs Duval glared round, "There must be no further interruptions ... Councillor Heathcote."

He resumed, "We are told that we must bend before the great god of progress, that we need to move with the times, that there's just a bit of this, a bit of that and before you know it we've swept all the old away!" He glared at the Planning Officer, who was studying the ceiling intently. Several reporters were scribbling away. "This is destroying our heritage by erosion of pure commerce. This is selling our birth right for a mess of mobile 'phones. We're going to have our beautiful, old Cathedral desecrated by the mammon of power, and for what? So that the teenagers of our town can spend more time with that carbuncle of today glued to their ears. In the interests of sanity and preserving our city from more erosion, I beg you to reject this application." He sat to the cheers of a group of older people on our left.

Mrs Duval went red and pounded the table until the din subsided, "If there is a repeat of this behaviour I will clear the room."

Silence descended, "Now can I have those in favour?" There was a flurry of raised hands.

"Now those against?" There were three hands raised. "The application is approved!"

There was an immediate outcry from the crowd on our left, followed by the repeated shouting and pounding gavel from Mrs Duval.

As quiet descended, she roared, thoroughly aroused and red in the face, "I will not tolerate this behaviour. This meeting is adjourned for ten minutes and will reconvene 'in camera'."

As we trooped out, I glanced at Heathcote's face which was grim and glowering. Liza seemed almost elated and was certainly not downcast.

Later a reporter told me that the rest of the applications were so savaged by Heathcote that one developer swore to never build here again. He also said that there was a hint that the Planning Officer had been told that, if he knew what was good for him, he'd better approve the application and quickly. He refused to say where the pressure came from, but it certainly wasn't from Mrs Duval.

Liza and I had a long and leisurely French lunch. The warmth, her company and the wine induced a most pleasant state of lethargy. To round off this extraordinary day, she sat back, gazed at me in a most disturbing fashion, "That was lovely, I feel wonderful."

'*You look wonderful*', I thought.

She smiled in a way that was intriguing, and dropped her bombshell, "I've a whole week now until the team arrive and start erection. The scaffolding will take almost that long to put up. Would you mind my company for a few days?"

I wondered if the blow had knocked me silly.

She went on, "It's been so hectic over the past months and I'll have so much to do next week. I need a break, would you do that?" Looking at that smile, and that slim body clothed in the subtle lines of her dress, I was disbelieving my own ears.

Would I? *'Try to stop me'*, I thought.

* * *

Bill was hard at his newest idea as I arrived back. His greeting was not very cordial; in fact it was almost exasperated. His notion of incorporating a transceiver into the fabric of a garment, in this case a sweater, was meeting several unexpected snags.

He was very cynical about the planning permission so quickly granted to BT, "Typical! It took me months to get permission for my conservatory, and then it was festooned with conditions: - local stone, a certain colour, not to ..."

I interrupted. I had heard it all before, "I suppose it shows that we have some weight behind us, that's all I was about to say."

We eyed each other warily, I spoke first, "Liza's here for the next two weeks at least. She's waiting for the scaffolders to finish before the installation of the transmitter."

Bill just grimaced. We had accepted the obvious that the BT array was simply a cover for the project. We had accepted it, but it was clear we were not being told everything. It was a potentially explosive situation in our minds; we hadn't the faintest idea then, how really dangerous it was.

Glowing at the prospect of Liza for a week, I accidentally rubbed Bill up the wrong way, "Could you hold the fort for one or two days next week? I thought I'd show

Liza some of our fair county; she hasn't had chance to see much with all this dashing about."

His sarcasm was bitter, "Sure thing, keep the home fires burning and all that. You have to take the executive decisions. I just have to do as I'm told."

"Don't be so touchy, Bill I..."

He jumped up, "Please sir, can I go to lunch?"

"Don't be so ..." I stared aghast, "Do you mean you haven't had it yet?"

"No, I ruddy well haven't! I was expecting you back hours ago, but I suppose that Liza is more important than the job."

My face showed my concern, "Oh, hell. I'm sorry. I took it for granted."

"Well, I haven't eaten yet. Oh, blast it! I'm sorry, I've been battling all morning, one step forward, two back. It's all my fault, I wanted to get somewhere and I haven't."

In the ensuing silence the creaking hide of my chair sounded intrusive, "Bill, I'm worried. Everything's going out of control, it's all happening too fast." He nodded as I assured him, "I'll see you back her in no less than an hour. I'll just look at the records of the staff room eye."

With that he left.

To my eye the sweater he was struggling with had begun to look quite promising, so didn't think his ill-temper was justified. I opened the program controlling the recorded views in the staff room. Skimming through the usual activity I came to a shot of Antonio. To be sure I ran it three times; it was clear that he was spying on George Brown to an exceptional degree. After he opened the locker with a key, he photographed a paper and relocked the cabinet. He also called someone on a mobile before he restarted the security cameras. The conversation was almost inaudible, "Not yet. There's some activity, but not conclusive. Will call again Monday."

I was eaten up with curiosity to know who he was calling. Could I persuade Horseguards to patch in to his number? I wondered, but doubted it; they had refused before and would probably do so again.

Bill returned in a better mood and almost seemed to be anxious to please. The upshot was that I was going to take the next four days off and leave him to work uninterrupted on the sweater. I would look in once in the early morning to check the recordings, but nothing else was to be done unless he called me. It was not ideal, I felt as if I was going AWOL, but it was less disastrous than it had been an hour ago. Why, oh why was life so complicated? I was being torn in two again.

Chapter 29 Trust.

Early Tuesday morning, there was nothing on the scans, so I drove to Liza's hotel in the Rover. It was a warm morning that made me feel good, weather affects me more than I care to admit. With the sunroof open and the player soothing me with Chopin I'd lost the guilty feeling of yesterday and was looking forward to meeting her. That anticipation was not misplaced; she had on a pale yellow dress with tiny cap sleeves that showed off her slender neck and the golden tan of her arms. She had no jewellery, no rings, bracelets, just a gold watch of slim design. Readily agreeing to use the Rover as I suggested, we pretended we were tourists. We started in the city to explore the exhibitions and the old parts, particularly the Cathedral Close.

We spent a pleasant morning wandering round the old buildings. She was impressed by the state of preservation of the houses, but seemed to be very interested in the Cathedral layout. It puzzled me a little, but I put it down to the forthcoming developments. I didn't know then, how true that was. We lunched again on French fare and limited the wine to one glass. I was enjoying just being with her, looking at her and feeling her presence. We didn't touch, even by as much as finger tips, but I felt as if I didn't need to; the feelings between us were more a meeting of like spirits than physical contact, it seemed as if she was beginning to feel as I was. It was a magical morning; the future began to beckon enticingly. Like all fantasies it couldn't last.

It was at her suggestion that we dodged the crowds and sauntered by the Minster Pool to Beacon Park. We sat on a shady seat with a vista of sweeping grass and ancient trees listening to the distant traffic hum. It was very peaceful and pleasant.

Liza sighed, "This is just what I need. I've been so involved with talk and discussion that I needed to say nothing. Not been boring you am I?"

"We both have been so, as you put it, involved. It may sound silly, but I think that I can sense what you feel without your saying it." I turned to her, to look into those deep, dark eyes.

There was the merest shadow of a cloud, but it passed quickly and she smiled at my seriousness, "I've felt that way ever since I first saw you when that big American nearly floored you in the Duke of Cumberland. Don't ask me to explain it, I can't. I just felt that somehow I could trust you completely." She sounded so sad, "In my life that's something that I rarely find, if at all."

"Do you remember that too? I'll never forget it."

Turning away so that I couldn't see her reaction I said, "Do you believe in love at first sight? I've always been sceptical, until then. It wasn't the Texan that knocked me for six."

I paused, thought, *'What the hell'*, and burned my boats, "I fell in love with you then and have never stopped since. You've affected me like no-one else and I can't imagine they ever will." Not daring to turn my head to see what effect I had on her I sat still, staring blindly into space.

Unexpectedly her hand crept into contact with mine and I turned. My breath caught as a tear trickled down from one closed eyelid. There was trembling at the corners of her mouth, face warmed with a peachiness on both cheeks. Her eyes opened as I dropped her hand, "I'm so sorry, I shouldn't have said that."

She grasped my hand fiercely, "I'm so glad you did. I wasn't sure that you felt as I did. I had my doubts, were you simply being nice to a buyer? When I stayed, I wasn't sure how you saw me." Her eyes glinted sharply, "I thought I was

174

in love; I wondered if you saw me as I saw you, or just as a passing friend."

Squeezing my hand hard, she paused and went on, "I lost my love and my parents; been hurt and betrayed; I've been so afraid of loving someone else that I still can't let anyone into my life. If you do love me, I can try. I will try and might succeed, will you help me?"

I gripped her hand in return, "I can wait for whatever you give me. Yes." We sat hand in hand, saying little, but in some way we didn't need to, everything important had been said.

Later we wandered to a restaurant, early enough to beat the later rush. The old building was fascinating to Liza, although she was not too happy at the designer's foibles in the ornate style. We settled into a corner to watch the world arrive. I had their fresh fish of the day course; Liza dined heartily on a steak that was much too rare for me. It must have been obvious, but the waiter left us alone for a longer time than normal. The time simply flew in a way that I wouldn't have believed, but we still left before the real rush reached its peak.

As we strolled side by side, Liza spoke of her life in the Magyar, her fond memories of riding; the family; the dancing and the hot blood of the courting males; the suffering under Stalin and Khrushchev. I'd known little of any of this, but she made it live so that I could almost see it in my mind.

I also began to feel her love of the drive of Bartok's music, linked to the Gypsy dances and folklore of his native Hungary. "He must have been a very sad man to leave his country. Do you think he ever found peace in America?" Liza looked sadly at me, "I know from his works that he never did, that in the end, he just let go." She turned away quickly, but I felt the yearning of her melancholy state radiate from her.

I was tempted more than I thought I could bear, to hold her, to give her the love I felt, the assurance that I wanted her to understand, that her loneliness was past. But I was still held back by something.

Even in those days when I did not know her as well as I did later, I knew not to rush her private battle.

It would be resolved sooner than either of us thought.

She stopped and turned to me almost shyly, "Don't say yes unless you really want to, but I would like to go to the NEC tomorrow night." I smiled my assent.

"They have the Hungarian State Dance Group there. I wasn't sure if I could make it so I didn't book ..." She trailed off wistfully.

I would have gone to a lecture on the merits of Egyptian Mummification techniques to be with her, I simply said, "If we can get tickets, I'd love to!"

She brightened; her dimpled smile flipped my heart all over again as the clock tolled ten.

"What time were you thinking of going to your hotel?" I queried, "I'm only asking because I've a day planned for tomorrow if it's fine."

She spoke in a soft tone, "In that case I think we'd better go now; with all that good food and wine, I feel rather dopey." The memory of Bill's words made me grin, but I just nodded and walked with her to the hotel. We did not kiss but just held hands. We parted with the briefest of waves, but I was in a blissful mood of expectation. I'd begun to live. I was yearning to share everything with her, just her and no-one else. Annie didn't get a look in; I had felt the first stirrings of desire to hold and caress Liza. It was just a matter of time before the barrier fell and she was able to give herself with no restraint. Or so I thought.

* * *

Wednesday was not promising at all, as I drove in the Rover along the A5192. There were spots on the windscreen, I cursed the English weather, its fickleness affects me a lot. By the time I arrived at the hotel, there was a steady drizzle. The only optimistic note was that Liza waved two tickets for the NEC at me. I glowered at the weather, "That's the trouble of trying to arrange a day in the sun in England. Now I don't know what to do."

She smiled and I felt as if the sun had come out, "Let's just drive anywhere. I feel free today." Her smile was as serene as I had ever seen her. She persuaded me to simply drive aimlessly around until midday. It sounds silly, but the weather didn't matter at all. We enjoyed just being together until we stopped for food at a sleepy café that was all brass and old beams. We had a sandwich and coffee for lunch, before we set off for the hotel. At the hotel door, I made as if to go, but she said, "Come on up, I want to change and you may as well sit in comfort." I felt a catch in my breath as I followed her up to her room.

It was not very large, but there were two easy chairs. I flopped into one as Liza took off her Mac. She headed for the bathroom, "I want a shower, but won't be long, help yourself to a drink, if you like."

As I was to drive to Birmingham soon and didn't want any trouble I had an orange juice. My mind wandered as I waited, I flushed gently thinking of Liza in the shower, just on the other side of the door.

Deliberately I started to think of the project. That calmed me down. It also raised a number of questions that I had no answers to. I was wondering about the backing from on high; the undoubted influence on the Planning Officer, the speed at which the scaffolding was going up, the interest of Antonio, my assailant and the Texan amongst other things, when the bathroom door opened and Liza came out. The robe she wore was generous by hotel standards and was long on her, but she made little effort to keep her legs covered as she moved. This made my eyes open as I saw her legs to just above the knee. It was not intentional, I am sure, but the effect on me was electric. I've seen women in Paris and elsewhere touting for illicit business, who deliberately reveal more; they had the opposite effect on me than their desired one. Not one of them caused my heart to thump as Liza did in that robe, her hair in the towel turban.

In the way that I was becoming used to, she sensed my emotion. There was a slight heightening of the colour in her cheeks. She gave me a provocative lift of her eyebrows and turned her back. Picking her outfit from the wardrobe, she gave me a wicked wink and returned to the bathroom. Gulping some orange I ran my fingers through my hair, wincing as I touched the still tender lump. My palms went warm; I rubbed them on my handkerchief, aware of my heartbeats sounding like a drum. I stood and looked out of the window at the rain as keeping my thoughts firmly on the drive to the NEC; it was going to need my concentration - all of it.

She came out in a black, full skirt and a white blouse with puffed sleeves and scooped neckline, embroidered in bright, flamboyant patterns. With her black hair, creamy skin and a touch more make up than usual, she looked wonderful. She was no meek, soft and cuddly female; she was a woman who was alive, vibrant, who sparked with an inner passion. At that moment, I could have seized her and met her fire for fire. Sheer sexual power rose within me.

"That's gorgeous! It really suits you," I said lamely. She laughed; face turned upwards, teeth and eyes flashing, cheeks glowing. The air between us was as volatile as an unstable bomb.

We dined at the Central, where she caused a minor sensation, particularly among some Japanese tourists. All was high spirits until she suddenly seemed to stop breathing, her face a mask of something like shock. It was so fleeting that I was not sure. Turning I saw the back of George Brown as he went into the staff door.

I muttered, "Are you all right?"

Her reply was distant and uncertain, "Yes, yes ... nothing. I must have just done too much that's all."

We both knew she was lying.

Chapter 30 Betrayal.

The journey to the NEC was quiet. The drive through the spray took all my concentration, Liza was again in her own world of thoughts that did not include me; this roller coaster of emotions was terrible.

The show was splendid. There was reluctance for the audience to allow the perspiring dancers to stop. The sheer exuberance and force of the fiery dances lifted us all to fever pitch. The orchestra played as one possessed; never before and never since have I been so transported by a show. Liza was lifted out of her mood to stand with the audience as we shouted ourselves hoarse. Afterwards, she made an excuse that she needed the ladies' and was gone for half an hour. I was getting frantic when she appeared talking rapidly with one of the dancers. As it was Hungarian, I had no idea what was said, but it made her turn to a cold anger that I had not seen in her before. I was worried that she was upset, but she reassured me she was not. As before, we both knew that it wasn't true, but rising between us again was that wall of silence that shut me out. The drive back was if anything more silent than the journey out. A whirlwind of thoughts battered me. The heat of passion had raised me to the heights as I'd experienced the fire of Liza's homeland music and then I had been firmly shut out of a situation that she would tackle alone. The most awful feeling persisted that it was of the utmost danger and I was powerless.

Our parting at her hotel was brief and soulless; she held my hand in a cool, detached way and spoke in subdued tones, "Thank you for taking me, it was very moving. I'm sorry I wasn't better company, I, I've a headache. I'll call you tomorrow."

She wasn't the only one with a headache.

Why had she bothered with the pretence; she knew as well as me that neither of us was fooled. Instead I said, "Call the office, I'll be there early, some work to catch up on." I cursed inwardly. Now I was joining in the game of deceit.

Thursday dawned with the birds singing as if their hearts were overflowing. I woke from a troubled sleep feeling irritable and confused, anxious for some facts, something solid that I could either fight or accept. In one way I hated the day that Liza had entered my life.

Up to then I had been happy enough, I had a good business, in some ways the ideal business, I sold things that people wanted and wanted badly enough to let me go at my own speed. I was anonymous enough to have a quiet, simple life; I enjoyed my music and my culinary efforts. It had seemed to be so complete.

Now I was totally confused, my peace was gone for good, I'd been given a taste of paradise and now it was all lost. Things could never be the same again, but my old life had turned to dust in my hands. I felt bitter and betrayed. For once I breakfasted at home. By my standards it was enormous; I had corn flakes, toast from my own bread, marmalade from the church stall for roof repairs, and a good, ground coffee. It satisfied me a little, but left a deep gnawing hunger for the Liza I had briefly met and loved. And I did still love her. I wanted to take her away from all this double life, the things that made her switch so abruptly, that put the chasm of unspoken meanings between us. But there was no escaping the fact that her presence was becoming addictive. I yearned for her touch, her release from the pent-up emotions she kept shut away.

As it was such a glorious morning I lowered the hood on the Jag and drove swiftly through the sleepy villages to the city, passing two lumbering farm tractors. The increasing size of these monsters, complete with an array of spikes and cutters always made me treat them with the greatest respect in our narrow lanes. Parking in the nearly empty car park I walked briskly to the office. There I felt safe and secure.

I settled down to clear the usual clutter of paper and electronic mail. It took me an hour to deal with the accumulation of bumf; I sat back with a coffee to sustain me and mused. I was more settled, but still wanted solid facts. Rerunning the recordings of the staff room surveillance camera and the spy in Al's room told me nothing. Al was meticulous in his habits, he was tidy to a degree that I would never achieve, indeed I didn't want to have. Tidiness is all well and good, but I don't let it dictate to me. My thoughts turned to Liza. She was tidy, but not to the degree that Al was. I believed that she was very organised in everything, she was never late and seemed to know exactly where and what was going on, always in control. Until last night. Then she had been upset by something deep in her life, something that threw her completely. I wondered again what it was and why she had to face it alone. Was I a hindrance? Was I incompetent? It never crossed my mind that she was protecting me. All I felt was that I should be protecting her.

My 'hearing aid' was handy, I picked it up intending to insist that she was going to wear it from now on; it was only a little thing, but it had saved more than one life in the field. Mine was tuned to two sounds; footsteps and the mechanism of a fire arm. The awareness of a follower and the split second's warning of the squeezing of a trigger made all the difference; or so I was told.

It hadn't been my experience to need it and I'd no intention of doing so. I went to the stores and found another. She would be told, yes, I thought then I could tell her, to wear it as some advantage. I was shaken out of my thoughts, jumping slightly as the 'phone rang.

It was Liza. I held my breath.

She sounded more like the lively woman I was falling for, the woman I was starting to need. "What have you in mind today, Bert?"

"Well, nothing really. I did wonder about day at a race course."

She interrupted, "Can we have a quiet day, somewhere away from cars and people, I can order a packed lunch for two so we can sit and talk in peace." My mouth went dry, it sounded so serious. I swallowed and said casually, "If that's what you want, fine. When will you be ready?"

"Give me an hour. Can we go in the Jag?"

"It's ready and waiting like me," I laughed. There was a hint of a sigh as she put down the 'phone. Slowly replacing the receiver I wondered. What was she up to now?

Liza was in a quieter mood than usual as I drove to Chasewater. She was not silent by any means, but she said things that were non-committal in themselves, the sort of thing that strangers or distant friends would say. As we passed a Japanese tour bus heading for Wall and the Roman site I remarked that these must be the biggest culture vultures in the world; this amused her and she waved at the rows of smiling faces. She smiled at me as we whizzed past, "You'll now be in forty Japanese holiday albums. They all took your photo as you zoomed by." For once that day there was a genuine smile of mirth, but it didn't stay for long and she lapsed back into her preoccupied state.

Being midweek, it was quiet near the boat club; it looked as if we might find a quiet spot after all. I took out the travel rug, put up the hood and locked the car. Liza took our picnic and we set off along one of the paths winding through the shrubs to an area popular with bird watchers.

I detest the term 'twitchers' and still refuse to use it. It annoys me how people insist on fracturing the English language, manufacturing new words where there is a perfectly good word already. I *will not* say something is 'horrendous' or 'ginormous'. Anyway, we strolled in the warm air and I spotted a half-hidden glade, away from the water, but still with a glimpse of a view. It promised to be sunny, so I was careful to site the rug in the dappled shade.

Liza sat gracefully down on the rug, her legs curled demurely beneath her print skirt. With that and her short sleeved, green blouse, she looked sweet and delicate.

It was more her air of being absorbed in her own thoughts that made her seem so feminine and almost helpless than the clothing, but there was no mistaking her overall sense of being bruised by events. I was recovering from my own bruising and regaining my self-confidence. Whatever the cause, I was fighting the desire to hold her tight, to reassure her that we were two not one who could face the difficulty whatever it was.

It was hard to fight this instinctive move as I was sure that there was still a reticence that I could not so easily overcome.

We sat in this reflective quiet for an hour, softly and occasionally talking of the birds on the water, the small number of passers-by and the occasional cyclist swishing by, intent on getting round the route as fast as possible. It was as I was about to suggest opening the packed lunch that Liza spoke of the cause of her pensive mood, "I'm not very good company, I'm afraid, but I've been given a shock."

"You are excellent company," I countered, "I want nothing else but your company, no matter whether or not you want to talk. " The remark petered out as an opening if she wished to take it. To my relief, she did.

"As you saw, at the dance show the other night, I met a man from my home country." She looked to the water and let her eyes see something that was in her mind, "It really shook me and I don't know how to take it in." I waited as the inner struggle subsided and the cause came near to the surface. It was a tense moment; this was to be a test of me and my reaction.

"You remember how I told you that I lost my parents due to their returning to Hungary after they'd been given a message that it would be safe to return?" There was an anguish on her face that wrenched my heart in pain. I could almost feel the hurt radiating from her as she fought the surge of remembered pain.

I dared not breathe or move as I endured the agony. One wrong move and the spell would be broken, possibly for ever.

I sat without breathing; the very air seemed to have stopped moving. But not quite everything. In my hearing aid I heard quiet footsteps in the shrubs not far away. I put them down to a bird watcher. Liza seemed to pull herself together and spoke firmly, "It always seemed to be wrong, somehow, that they were arrested so soon after their arrival. They had been so popular with the townspeople. I thought they would be safe now under the new regime and the opening up to the West."

She faced me and I felt her need, for someone to trust, reach out to me as the sun warms a face. Crabwise I shuffled nearer to her and held one hand in mine, it was trembling and cold.

I wondered if she was ready for the intimacy of an embrace as she went on, "Igor recognised me from all those years ago, he couldn't believe his eyes, he was very sorry for me and he told me. . ."

I never did hear what he said. I was suddenly intensely aware of a sound in my hearing aid that turned my blood to ice. It nearly made me freeze, but thank God I didn't.

The sound was of the first pressure of an automatic being readied to fire. And it was very, very close.

I flung myself over Liza and pressed her body to the ground, her face an inch from mine. It was a picture of astonishment that would have been comic in another situation. Pressing my lips on hers was the easiest way to silence her protests. As the split seconds dragged by, we both stiffened as we heard a plop followed immediately by a thud in the tree trunk behind Liza.

We knew what that was and we lay totally still. There was a soft footfall and I heard the first pressure being taken up again, I tensed for the tearing of the bullet in my back.

Then all Hades was let loose, I heard two more footfalls, but this time they were running fast. A shriek and a giggle broke the quiet together with the sound of someone crashing through a bush. In my hearing aid I heard the click of a safety catch going on and the sound of stealthy footfalls edging away. The next thing I heard was a flood of Japanese as two young tourists burst through the bush behind us and stopped with a look of embarrassment. The young lady put a hand to her mouth and giggled, red-faced: the young man bowed and said, "So solly! Velly solly." and they both backed away bowing. I lay for what seemed an age, my face so close to Liza's and yet so far.

She was in my arms, I had just kissed her, we were apparently in an intimate embrace but we were separated by a mental barrier. It was as if we were in different rooms. Liza wriggled, "Please Bert, I think there's a lump in the ground just here." Rolling away this time I really did blush. She sat up and straightened her blouse as I turned away. Looking back I saw her shake her hair and smooth it back into some sort of order. I listened for footfalls, but there wasn't a movement within the range. We both started to talk at the same time. I stopped and waved Liza to speak first, she hesitated but then spoke with eyes fixed on mine, "I think I owe you my life if I interpret your actions right."

"It was in both our best interests," I went on hurriedly, "not that it wasn't pleasant." It sounded lame even to me.

But I saw a brief flicker of amusement at the corners of her lips, "It was certainly unexpected; I didn't take you for the madly impulsive type." She wriggled to a more comfortable sitting position, momentarily displaying more of her lovely legs than was good for my state of mind then. She sat, demure again, legs tucked under her skirt, "How did you know?"

Removing the ear piece I handed it to her, she examined it with interest. I rubbed it with my handkerchief to clean it, "Put it in your ear and close your eyes."

She opened her eyes fractionally, but did so.

Silently I stood up and crept round to the rear of her position and back to the front. She opened her eyes with a look of wonder, "I see!"

Giving it back to me, I replaced it in my own ear, "I have one for you in the office; we can go and pick it up on the way back."

Standing up she hugged herself and shivered, "We'd better adjourn to a place less open." She swung round, "But in a way it was the Japanese, who saved us wasn't it?" I nodded, but both knew that the other's thoughts were racing along speculative lines with the speed of light.

It was certainly good fortune that they had arrived when they did; or was it?

My speculation came to a halt as Liza laughed, "It was a drastic way to get a kiss; for a second there I thought ... well, I thought you were mad with lust." The look on her face was once more a kaleidoscope of emotions chasing one another in rapid succession. I was not too sure, but I felt that one was a wistful, lost, pensive sign of regret. Pulling her roughly to me I kissed her. But there was no response; the kiss was simply taken by me because there was no defence put up. There was no defence and no resistance; equally there was no reaction, no life or feeling. The shield was back in place and I was firmly shut out.

I didn't even ask what Igor had said. Whatever it was, it had gone back into the privacy of her mind and it would stay there, possibly for ever.

We made our way back to the car with a sense of walking on eggs. The day was still wonderful, warm, sunny and full of happy people, but there was an arctic chilliness both between us and in us that killed all closeness. This second attempt had made me feel so vulnerable and so angry. I dirtied my fawn slacks by peering under and inside the Jag, before we settled into the red leather seats. Liza said nothing until we were well on the way back to my cottage.

By now it was well past our lunch time and we were, at least I was, ravenous, "I'd like to have the lunch at home if you'd join me. If not I can turn off here and take you back to your hotel."

She gave a firm shake of her black hair, "Right now, I want to just sit quietly." Emotions swirled and eddied in my heart, sitting quietly was not at all what I wanted, but nothing would make her do what she didn't want to. My self-control was severely strained as she wrestled with her own private devil.

Chapter 31 Further Complications.

Lunch was a strained affair; there was no enjoyment of the rolls and cakes. Not that there was anything wrong with them: it was the events that had ruined the day. I tried once to get her to open up about the Hungarian and the information, but she remained vague and told me nothing. It was still eating away at her, but she wasn't letting anything out, or in. In the end, I played several CDs of Chopin and cooked a simple meal of baked potatoes with a cheese sauce. Liza seemed to recover slowly after that, but sat snuggled in my sofa, saying little and still withdrawn into herself.

It was starting to grow dim as I realised how late it was getting. I helped her out of the sofa and she did an unexpected thing. She stood on tip toe, put her arms round my neck and kissed me warmly for seemingly an age. It took me by surprise, and I was slow responding, but I gently put my arms round her waist, holding her to me. For a few blissful moments her tenderness and softness warmed me from the lips down to my toes; I did not want it to end, but she let go and drew away with a sigh, "Poor Bert, it hasn't been much of a day, has it?"

I cleared my throat, "I wouldn't quite say that." I smiled at her serious face, still close to mine, "Two kisses is a start, and two hugs as well."

There was a sadness in her eyes as she spoke so quietly that I hardly heard it, "If only." She straightened up and said clearly, "Could you give me that ear piece you said you had for me, I have the feeling it might come in handy."

Seizing her hand harder than I meant to I spoke harshly, "Just what is happening? Who was that? For pity's sake tell me. I'm not used to all this business."

I tried to correct myself, it was my business, "I'm simply a technician; I don't like someone sniping away at me;

or you either. I told you I love you and I want you. I want you alive and sharing everything with me, not cold in some hole in the ground."

There was a pain in her look that made me let go of her. She turned away, there was a catch in her voice, "Please, let's go. You know full well that it can't be; that I can't tell you."

I drove savagely back to the office and fitted her with the 'aid', demonstrating the range and operating system, she learned quickly. She looked at me in the clutter of my workroom. Somehow she was smaller and more vulnerable than I'd ever seen her.

Without warning she leaned forward suddenly and kissed me quickly on my mouth, but drew back before I had the time to react, "Believe me; I now know your feelings about me. I'm still not sure how I feel about you. I sometimes think . . ., I sometimes wish . . but there is something that I have to do. Trust me. And," she turned to the door, "try to forget me, for your own good."

* * *

On the Saturday an early 'phone call surprised me, Liza ask me to meet her in the shopping centre at 8.30. I asked if she was well, but, apart from her rather stilted words, she gave no clue as to her feelings. I dressed unhurriedly; there was plenty of time before the appointment. The danger was becoming all too real, despite the lack of someone solid to identify. As I felt too vulnerable in the Jag, I took the Rover and drove with a frequent glance at the possibility of someone following. There was nothing out of the ordinary, but I was still jumpy as I arrived at my usual spot. As I locked the car, I listened carefully, but there was no stealthy footfall.

I found Liza gazing closely at the fruit and veg display. She did not turn at my approach, but spoke softly, "I heard you in good time, even though it's so busy." She turned to dimple her cheeks at me, "You know your stuff all right."

I smirked inwardly. Praise is music to my ears; not having a mother for years left me with a hunger for approval, which Father couldn't give, "I like to think I do! Anyway, I don't need any courgettes today, and in any case," I pointed, "those are not organic, they taste of wet paper."

She did laugh at this, albeit with a brittleness that made it sound forced, "I was hoping you might invite me to dinner; purely on business of course."

I scowled at the offending vegetables, "So much for my animal charm."

She turned to face me, her expression serious and inscrutable, "Now isn't the right time for going into that. I told you last night. For your own good forget me and I meant it." Before I could speak, she took my arm and walked into the store, "I can't ask you to my place, but I can cook! Can I impinge on your hospitality and use your kitchen to prove it?"

I did not know what to say. Taken by surprise and uncertain where she was leading me, I was becoming totally mixed up and confused, "If that's what you want, then all right."

She gathered together a small load of fresh, organic vegetables, but thankfully avoided the cooked meat counter. Instead she bought some local pork. So far I could not fault her choice. By then it was nearly 10.30 so we headed for the nearest coffee shop.

As we were about to enter, I stiffened as I heard Al Clinton's dreaded voice, "Bert, you old son of a gun, there you are. Bin looking for you all over; can I corral you for a mo'?"

He stopped as Liza turned, "Beg pardon ma'am, I do apologise. Didn't know you were together. Some other time perhaps?"

Liza flashed a smile, "Not at all, we were only going to have a coffee, would you like to join us?"

Al beamed, "So long as I pay. If you *don't* mind, I'd be delighted. Did you know that Bert here has set me on the right path and I'm so excited?" Over the coffee, Colombian for us, the tasteless, decaffeinated variety for Al, he enthused over his trip to Eccleshall.

It wasn't surprising to hear that he'd talked his way into the castle with his hopes of tracing his link to Roger, "The old guy was real taken up. He was as excited as I was that there might be a link to the past." He pointed a thick finger at me, "I suppose you know that old Roger was quite a guy, he was well in with that Empress Maud; in fact it's rumoured that he was more a politician than a bishop, always poking his finger into somebody else's pie." He laughed at his own thoughts, "Just wait 'till I get back home and tell the guys! Me, the latest in the line of wangling Brits." He was certainly a wangler. He seemed to have a way of getting his own way by one means or another. All in all, the coffee break turned into an hour of swapping information about what history I could recall and what Al had ferreted out. Liza did not say much, but she wasn't bored; I wouldn't say fascinated, but she had a keen look in her eye and an apt word that showed genuine interest.

Finally Al looked at his watch in disbelief, "Hey! I sure am sorry. I've taken all your morning; I'll just mosey along and leave you young folk to yourselves." He squashed my hand in a grip that would have dented solid steel, "I'm mighty grateful to you, I sure am. If there's ever any chance of you crossing the pond, let me know and I'll arrange something special for you."

As we went back to the crowded street, Liza was actually grinning broadly, "He's as tactful as a bulldozer, but I like him. He almost restored my faith in humanity; he seems to be a genuine character."

I looked quizzically at her, but there was no sign of sarcasm or duplicity. I thought of the bugs in his room and thought whether or not *she* was being straight. As I took the shopping from her she linked my arm, much as any other couple in that busy place. I was getting accustomed to her presence: if only it wasn't so fraught with doubts and uncertainties. Would I ever find the real Liza under all those layers of impenetrable shell?

We wandered round the Arcade and the centre shops, Liza seemed to be less tense than earlier, but did not buy much, simply wandered and looked. We had a sandwich and coffee for lunch. Liza ate sparingly and afterwards wandered a little listlessly.

It was clear that she was not as relaxed as I had thought, so I said, "This shopping is getting heavy. What about going to the cottage and starting that meal you promised?" She seemed to be somewhat startled at this, almost as if I had suggested it, "Yes, OK! I'm getting a bit tired of this strolling by now. You should have said if it was heavy, I could carry it as well." Shifting the bag to my other hand I said, "It's no problem really, but I find wandering to be very tiring. If we hurry I can make you some tea or coffee at home." The sound of 'home' was pleasant and had a domestic ring to it. I was getting hooked! I needed to take stock of this situation before it went too far.

The Rover was still secure, operating the remote control I stowed the shopping in the boot. As Liza sat in the passenger seat, I casually asked if she had any idea of dessert. She was horror struck, "I totally forgot! I'd better go and get something quickly. Wait, I shan't be long."

"Don't bother," I chuckled, "I've a sherry trifle in the 'fridge, waiting to be eaten up, I've been eating out too much lately and I wouldn't like to waste it." She was suitably crestfallen and sat back without another word.

We arrived back home in quick time, at least it seemed so at the time, Liza had recovered some of her life and chatted of the tiny flat she had in Ditton. It was in a new development, overlooking the Thames, so it was easy to maintain. The down side was that it was expensive, but at least the security was reasonable and the access to Central London was good, due to the high number of business commuters. It all sounded very soulless and sterile. She didn't seem to treat it as a home, but somewhere to hide out when not on the move.

I formed the impression that she was often away, that she was restless in nature and employment. It made my own snug world feel very reassuring.

My home security system showed that there had been no intruders.

So, driving up the part hidden track, I was happier in my mind. We unpacked and Liza set about her cooking. If someone hangs about when I'm cooking it puts me off, so I left her to it once she had sorted out where things were. I was in need of something to lift me out of the sense of tension, so I played "The Firebird." It might seem strange, but I find the force and power of it is far better than any serenade in taking away outside influences. Liza popped her head round the door, "It'll be ready in twenty minutes!"

Happily I nodded in reply.

It was one of the best meals that I've had. It could be because I didn't prepare it: it could be because it was the first meal that Liza had made. But I think it was mostly due to a subtle shift in my whole existence.

Up to then, I had been in command of my life; I'd courted a few women, but found little to excite me. The impact of my mother's asperity had lasted a long time; no-one had been able to draw me into their inner life so I'd dropped the idea. Now, I'd been well and truly smitten by someone I wanted to be with a lot. This meal was a hint of what might be if Liza wanted it as much as I did. The slightly heady atmosphere of her being alone in *my* kitchen had an almost risqué attraction. If only I was sure of Liza's intentions, especially in my direction. The truth was that I was afraid of being dropped again as I had been when my Mother walked out. I couldn't face a second time.

The clock struck nine as we finished the meal.

I was ready to settle back and let the night lead where it may, but Liza stood and apologised, "I have to be in the control hut tomorrow early, so if you wouldn't mind, I'd like to return now."

It did sound like genuine remorse and she refused my attempts to stay for a while at least. I was astonished when she told me the time of the meeting.

I exploded, "Six?"

She smiled weakly, "Yes. And if it's all right, I will be busy nearly all week setting up a final trial for the top brass."

Chapter 32 Intrusion.

It might have been the bright, almost aggressively fine weather, or it might have been a sense of apprehension. Whatever it was, I was awake by five the next morning and couldn't settle, so I was driving through the deserted streets of Lichfield at 5.58. As I was locking the car there was a sudden, single clap of thunder. The pigeons, rooks and starlings rose in an offended, fluttering, clamouring rush. Amazed I looked round. There was no cloud within sight. For once the sky was clear and blue. I was uneasy, but there seemed to be no repeat, nothing else happened, so I started for the office. But something made me change my mind. Walking to the rear of the Angel Croft car park I stopped. There was a steady, muted growl from a generator, there were lights in the temporary hut and Liza's car was there. There was a temporary trench across the street and along the Close to the Cathedral. Wondering, I turned and went back to the office.

The morning went quickly checking the recorded goings-on in the staff room and Al's room at the Central. There was nothing remarkable, except for George Brown being evasive about his locker; he kept his back to the security cameras or the door masking the contents. Even the AV 4 was not much use in seeing inside the personal space. It made me itch to find out. By lunch time I was hungry; the effects of Liza's dinner having well and truly worn off; my scanty breakfast not helping matters either. As much from habit as conscious thought I headed for the Bearpit. I felt guilty as I was met by Annie's smile. She had a child-like, slightly hurt look, the sort that makes me want to console someone. Looking back, I can see that it was just what was intended.

I'm not too good at hiding my feelings, so I smiled at Annie as she looked lost and lonely. She could put the screws on my emotions so easily, but she *was* great to look at.

Anyway, to cut a long story short, I agreed to show her some more of the country on her day off, next Wednesday. After all, I reasoned, Liza was going to be busy all week. And there was nothing between us. Besides, it might do Liza good to see that she wasn't the only pebble - especially such a good looking pebble as Annie. She rewarded me with her dazzling smile that nearly had my heart turning somersaults. I chided myself, '*Watch it, don't start something you might regret.*'

Relaxing later, full of Waldorf salad and basking in Annie's warmth, I saw Teddy come in and look round. When he saw me his eyes opened and he weaved his way through the thinning crowd, "Just the man I want to see." He flopped down and wiped a damp forehead.

He was clearly excited. He spoke in a stage whisper, that nearly everyone in the bar could hear, "I think we had better go to your office, dear boy, I've got something I must tell you." He winked broadly and sat back. I was more than a bit cross. I'd spent a lot of time cultivating the aura of a quiet, dull, small businessman and a very low profile. In thirty seconds he had blown it to the winds. The best move was to cut it short. *Now!* So I also spoke in a stage whisper, "If it's about that Japanese copy, then I think you might be right. Sony have been after my microwave for months." I gave him an equally broad wink as I nearly laughed at the consternation on his chubby features. To save my own face breaking into merriment, I hurried him out of the door. As I did, I saw Annie's face show a puzzled expression.

In the office, I turned on Teddy, "Please don't ever do that again." He had the grace to look sheepish. "I don't want *anyone* to look too closely at me and my business. You never know who might be listening."

His desire to speak cut me short, "I am really sorry, but the most amazing thing."

I motioned him to sit, "OK. Tell me about it."

He undid the watch I'd given him and laid it on the desk, "This is the most wonderful thing. It's proved to me, if not to my sceptics, that the Ley lines are real," He sensed that I wasn't too impressed, for he hurried on, "I've been able to confirm the existence of a powerful line through the Cathedral, straight down the aisle, through Beacon Park and beyond." He paused for effect. His next words shook me rigid.

"I traced the line from there to Onibury Church, Heath House, Abingdon Burford, Bridgnorth and as far as St Davids. The force of the field varies; it's strongest in the apse, weakening as you go through the park and strengthens again every 23 kilometres. It is, as I suspected, some form of ultra long wavelength that seems to extend to infinity. The most astonishing thing is that at six this morning, I heard a clap of thunder, I looked at the meter and," he spoke softly, "it went off the scale for a full minute."

Now sometimes I am not too quick on the uptake, but at this my mind went into hyperdrive. It was like a computer clicking and fitting things together. The wave length was a harmonic of the DEMOLISH project; the time was when Liza was 'working', the puzzle of the aerials on the three spires became obvious.

The carrier wave and the modulator wave relationship was now crystal clear. Liza was at the bottom of it all. Liza was possibly the Principal. It was no wonder she was jumpy and tight-lipped. If, as I suspected, this came from the top, the very top, it was no wonder that someone had heard of it and wanted to steal it - even to the extent of trying to kill for it.

Teddy must have sensed at least some of this; he rose and came to me, "I say, are you all right? You're as white as a sheet. Can I get you something?"

His fussing acted better than any tonic or brandy; I shook my head as he sat uncertainly, "Are you sure?"

By now I was feeling life come back to my shocked frame, "Professor, you mustn't breath a word of this to anyone unless I agree, do you understand?"

It was his turn to look shaken, "What do you mean? I thought that this was a scientific discovery, something that I had to share." He frowned suspiciously, "What do you know that I don't?"

Sorely tempted to tell him I was afraid for his health if I did, I had to think fast. As I could not see his being able to keep quiet, I tried to look sincere, "Tell me what the importance of Lichfield Cathedral is before I tell you what I know."

He seemed to distrust me, "Why?"

"Partly because I'm involved with the instrumentation you use in this experiment and partly because I do know something else that might and might not be connected. I think the BT array might have set up an unexpected effect."

This seemed to satisfy him, "The significance is that there has been building on the site for as long as people have lived here. There was certainly some church here before 660. There has been rebuilding and changes, including the 13th century rebuilding. This, to me, indicates a site of special properties, known from the dawn of man. When it is linked with the other sites, hill forts and ancient holy places, it is obvious that there *is* something there." He paused, "I've also discovered a weaker line from Aconbury, Credenhill to Ipswich that crosses the St Davids line here in the centre of the Aisle. This is the very centre of a powerful natural force." He paused, "What happened to make it surge so strongly at six?"

Inwardly my thoughts was in disorder, outwardly I was pondering. Teddy waited until I spoke as if thinking aloud, "Could the sunrise have some effect on the field, especially if the BT engineers were testing at the same time."

He thought, but was doubtful, "Could be."

"You've given me a lot to think about for now. I admit that I don't have the answers right now, but I have your number and I'll call you when I know more. I should have some news by the weekend."

I spoke confidentially, "In the meantime, keep mum. You know how people can steal your thunder (I winced at the pun) and you deserve the credit for all the hard work you've put in." We shook hands and he left. Flopping in my creaky, leather chair I hoped Liza knew what forces she was unleashing.

She rang to say that the first test was successful, but there was a lot of fine tuning to be done in readiness for the 'Top Brass'. In her apology there was a definite lift to her voice, a brightness of some thrilling tone that was responsible for my admonition to take care. She *was* excited and paid little heed to my words.

I was not happy. In fact I was miserable if the truth is known. Once again I was dumped by a woman without a proper explanation, she was doing something perilous and I couldn't prevent it. It was in that same mood of rebellion that I met Annie on the following Wednesday.

Chapter 33 Distraction.

If ever there was someone to lift my mood of dejection on that day, it was Annie Schwartz. The only word for her was breathtaking. She was gorgeous. And she flaunted it. She caused a minor stir as she sashayed across the car park to the Jag. The sunshine that I was beginning to associate with her helped, as well as her undoubted innocent, good looks. But the stunning part was the dress she wore, or to be more accurate, that graced her figure. It was not skimpy, not too short, nor too low in the neck. It was a floaty creation of pale, muted colours; pinks, yellows, blues and greys. They all formed a mist of gossamer that almost shimmered and glowed as a summer cloud. It was not tantalising, but it was a hint of mystery and a living thing at the same time.

She was out to impress me, to tempt even, and I liked it. Annie saw that look of astonishment and candid admiration in my eyes and gave me the most dazzling, warm smile ever. It was a fantastic start to the day, with the promise of more. I said the totally unnecessary words, "My word, you do look lovely."

She dimpled charmingly, "Why thank you. I hoped you'd like it." She giggled shyly, "It cost a fortune, but it was worth it." With a contented sigh she sank back into the red leather seat and her clean scent mingled with the heavier tang of sun-warmed, good English hide. It was in a dream-like state that I drove out of the city and headed for the country. Making absolutely sure that there were no followers I twisted and turned round the familiar villages. The network of narrow lanes was tailor made for eluding any tracker.

Annie chatted on about her folks back home, the rising cost of fuel, now nearly $1.10 a US gallon, Presidential manoeuvring, crime, robbery, pilfering. Only half listening, replying with monosyllables I concentrated on driving.

That was until she said something that shook me, "Do you know that cuddly Professor, Teddy Wilson? He was mugged last night near the Stowe. He's all right 'though, apart from a sore head and scratched wrist. He lost his watch and his wallet, credit cards and such. I wouldn't have thought there would have been much crime here. It just goes to show. " Her voice trailed off as she pondered the ways of the world.

My head started to throb again. The loss of the watch was in itself no great problem. But I had that awful feeling that it was the thief's target, that the wallet was simply window dressing to disguise the main purpose. This put a stop to my euphoric mood. In Annie's company, however, it soon reappeared. She admired all the churches and half-timbered houses along the way.

She was captivated by the 'Olde Tea Shoppe' that I used for our coffee break; she insisted on paying for it, but let me buy filled rolls and cool drinks for the lunch.

Later as we sat on soft, dried-out grass near sparkling water, a breeze teased our warm skin and I was at ease for the first time in weeks, if not months. She did not even mind that I dozed off for a while as the gentle sounds of water, birds and Annie's quiet chatter lulled me wonderfully.

I woke with a start at shrieks, but relaxed as I saw two children playing at the water's edge. England has no rivals in my book on such a day, no wonder Browning wrote wistfully of England, 'now that April's there.' The time passed all too quickly. I thought that there were worse prospects than being 'impressed' if not actually wooed by Annie. Sure that she was out for something, but *not* sure if it was me or my knowledge she was after, I just let it waft along and enjoyed the experience. When I finally sat up it was nearly four.

The effects of the lunch were wearing off, so I suggested afternoon tea back at the café. She leaned back and looked at me from beneath lowered lids, "Can I be very wicked and have tea at your cute cottage? I simply love it and I'm just a bit too hot here."

She laughed lightly, "That's something from me, who moaned I would never be warm when I first came." Perhaps she *was* after me after all, but I felt I could handle it.

A bit of the rebellious mood rose within me. Why not? I was still free to do whatever I wanted, "If you don't mind English tea and just my company, we can. So long as you don't have to be back for work or anything."

She smiled a contentedly, "Not 'till ten tomorrow morning. And I feel so, well, so safe with you. I'd drink the worst English coffee for that." I wasn't sure that I liked that, but let it pass. She sighed again as we bumped along the track and the cottage emerged from the bushes and old trees, "Gee, it's almost like coming home. I love it."

We had tea and pieces of a rather stale sandwich cake under the shade of the old pear tree, Annie sighed again comfortably, "Much better than that 'Oldee Shopeee'," she mimicked. We both laughed. It felt good.

She spoke in a dreamy voice, "You know Bert, I don't believe you!"

I opened my eyes wide; she was leaning back, eyes closed.

"Why don't you believe me?"

Opening one eye she said, "'Cos I think you're a fraud, a very sweet fraud, but definitely a fraud."

I wasn't so much at ease now, "How do you make that out?"

She sat up and leaned towards me, confidentially, "Because! I don't believe a word of this tale of you making microwave detectors; in fact *I* think you're a spy or an agent, like - like Indiana Jones."

I tried to look hurt, "Not like James Bond?"

"Oh, no. Not James Bond. He's no gentleman, he's too ruthless. No. You're too kind. I could never fall for him." She left the words unsaid.

"Well, I'm sorry to disappoint you, but I'm not. And I do make detectors. They *do* operate on high frequencies, you can call them microwaves, and that is all I'm going to tell you, my little, curious girl. For all I know you're a Russian spy sent to entice me." There was a minute movement of shock, but it passed so quickly that it might not have been there at all.

I stood up, "I think I'd better take you back to civilisation for some dinner."

She stood, looking disappointed, "Not yet surely, I don't want a dinner. Haven't you got something in the 'fridge, even a wilted lettuce leaf? I don't want to go just yet."

How could I refuse? "All I've got is some cold ham and the remains of a Waldorf and some potato in mayonnaise."

She brightened up, "Now that sounds just great." She lowered her eyes, "I am sorry I said what I did just now, about not trusting you and all." She raised her face to look me straight in the eye. "I'm not a Russian spy, or any other spy I can tell you." We both let the matter drop at that.

We ate *al fresco*, the light meal was surprisingly fresh, but Annie shivered as the sun dipped behind the trees, so I ushered her indoors. As I put my hand on her back to guide her to the door of the kitchen, I could feel that she was wearing very little, if anything, under that dress. Whatever else she had on; she was not wearing a bra'. Putting the tray on the side I told her to sit in the sofa, but she stood in the doorway, "Could I ask you to play one of my discs on your Hi-Fi?"

I groaned at the thought of Box Car Willie, "Yes, if you want to."

She rummaged in her bag or 'purse' as she insisted on calling it, and passed me a CD.

I glanced at it, "Oh. It's not Box Car Willie."

She smiled, "I heard it in the Duke's staff room the other day. I like it. I hope you will too."

"Show of Hands," I mused, "Where do they get the names from?"

It was refreshingly different. It would never be my first choice, but the instrumental variety and ability were above the average, at one point I was definitely impressed. The lyrics were undemanding, and light.

All in all, it was a pleasant surprise.

Annie was very pleased and after about an hour, she snuggled down, her head on my shoulder, her arm round mine in an intimate way. I was very aware of her softness under that misty inconsequence of a dress and the lack of underwear beneath it. If I had been so inclined it could so easily have drifted further.

Time to stop it. I clenched my left fist for five seconds and relaxed.

The 'phone rang, "Damn!" I muttered struggling out of the sofa and Annie's clinging hold. I picked it up and heard the dialling tone, "Yes!" I barked. Annie watched me. I waited and then snapped, "You can't mean it!" I turned my back to Annie, "Not now. Can't it wait till tomorrow?" I hoped I sounded suitably annoyed, "This is most inconvenient! Oh, well, I suppose if I must." Turning I saw Annie's questioning face, I turned my eyes to the ceiling, "I'll be there in half an hour," and slammed down the 'phone, "I'm sorry, but I've to go to the office, someone was seen skulking about."

She pouted with disappointment.

I shrugged resignedly, "They think he might have been trying to break in. What with this mugging and thefts." Annie uncoiled herself out of the sofa and wiggled her way to me; she put her arms round my neck and moulded herself to me.

Now I know that certain cheap fiction stories for women use that word freely, but there was really no other word to describe it. She kissed me softly, warmly and moistly. I felt her from my knees to my mouth. For a split second I was tempted to call her bluff, to cancel the 'emergency', but I managed to keep my head.

Gently lifting her arms from my neck I smiled at her, "You'd better not do that too often, or I might forget that you trust me."

We drove back with little chatter from Annie; I was still wrestling with my own thoughts as I escorted her to the door. She gave me a brief kiss, then hesitated, "I've forgotten my CD, it can stay till next time." She turned and was gone.

For appearance's sake I went to the office. For something to do I ran the recordings. Antonio was once again using his mobile, I could just make out his voice, "I'll call again tomorrow, same time." George Brown was a little careless with his use of his locker door as a screen. In there he had Night Vision binoculars and a watch that looked familiar. I was not 100% sure, but it looked like the one I'd given to Teddy Wilson.

Chapter 34 Casualties.

I hate visiting hospitals, but it was imperative to see Teddy. Fortunately I was known through Bill's wife and allowed to see him, despite the reservations of the Staff Nurse, "I don't know what you expect, but he has been rather savagely beaten. He's better today, but he'll be here for a week at least." She paused, "I'd like to be allowed to perform on animals like the one who did this." She walked stiffly away.

Despite her warning I was still shocked by the bandage-swathed figure that was barely recognisable as Teddy. He was squinting at a paper with one eye, the other was covered with a thick bandage; his left arm was also well wrapped and clearly very uncomfortable. He let the paper fall as he saw me approach; his voice was weak, but firm, "What a surprise! Take a pew. Sorry about the make-up," he waved his good arm, "Some blasted layabout felt he had more right to my wallet than I did." He wheezed and coughed, "I've got bruises I can't show you and a cracked rib that's the very devil."

I interrupted, "Just keep as quiet as possible, that's the only way, not that I've ever had personal experience thank heaven." Pulling over a chair I put some grapes on the locker, "Someone certainly went over you with a vengeance."

He grinned very lopsidedly, but it turned to a grimace of pain as he moved, "I would like to meet him face to face, it wouldn't be all one sided then."

"Have the police any clue?"

"Not really. It is a sort of one-off. Not the usual crime they are used to. I'll tell you what I told them, which is very little. I had grown fond of that Indian restaurant and was used to taking a short cut through Beacon Park; not too late, perhaps ten. Any way, I'd no worries, but I felt, rather than heard, something."

He groaned at the memory, "Then I was cracked over the head and had the legs kicked from under me. He booted me in the chest and I must have passed out, for the next thing I felt was the gravel hurting my face. I was lying face down, jacket pockets ripped, wallet and watch gone. He wasn't gentle about it either," he held up his left arm. "Sorry about your watch, old boy, it was very useful, almost essential in my investigations." his voice tailed away as something hurt him again.

Patting his good arm I reassured him, "No problem, I assure you, I still have another one." I paused, "*When* you're fit to use it. I don't suppose you saw him?"

He shook his head and winced, "Not a hope! Beggar came from behind. There was just one daft thing, and it wasn't the Indian food, there was a faint whiff of garlic." We chatted on about his tracing of the Ley line and his speculation of its size and changing strength. I left him as he started to get enthusiastic causing his rib to hurt. Deep in thought I returned to the office. I did little practical work, trying to make sense of the events. There were so few hard facts to go on. I was in a fog and I hate fogs. Being very unsociable I brought in a sandwich for lunch and ate in a fruitless review of the jumbled happenings. It was only intuition, but I was sure that the watch was the reason that Teddy was now *hors de combat* and I would very much like to know who the perpetrator was. George Brown was in there somewhere, but where? Baffled and muddle-headed, I gave up and went home to sleep uneasily.

It was for many reasons, one of them being the accidental playing of Annie's CD of Show of Hands' folk tunes that made me itch for some company. I rose late on Saturday, drank coffee, ate some bland cereal and paced like a caged animal. After I'd tried to settle, I gave up and went to the office in search of facts.

It gave me confidence to hear what people thought was said in private.

My reserved parking spot was taken by an unauthorised intruder, so more time was wasted before I finally got to my desk. Being in a foul mood I was not at all fit to wade calmly through the masses of information. When the 'phone rang I snarled at it. A Saturday call was rare, my ordinary 'phone isn't much used even at busy times. My mood switched to icy fear as I heard Bill's carefully calm voice, "I don't know if the news has reached you yet?" I nearly panicked, *LIZA! Has someone attacked her?*

"What news?"

"There's a body." My heart felt as if it had stopped, "They found it in Beacon Park." He drew a deep breath, "There's been no formal identification, but Sheila says it's Annie."

My heart raced, not knowing whether to cry or laugh, it was not Liza! But Annie *dead*? I had just been playing her record. Annie of the bubbly personality; Annie, full of life and fun; Annie who had wrapped herself round me and into a corner of my life. It couldn't be true. The day had turned to winter, despite the sun outside. What was going on? First me, Teddy and now Annie.

Bill's worried voice intruded, "Hello, are you all right?"

"Yes, yes, I'm still here. This is terrible." I hesitated, "There's no doubt?"

The reply was short and final, "None!" He went on, "Shall I come in?"

Stupidly I nodded and said, "I would very much appreciate it. Very much." As I put down the 'phone, it started to hit me.

This was real, this was no remote control, Annie; lovely, lively Annie had been killed. I suddenly noticed the answerphone was flashing. Automatically I pressed the PLAY button. Annie's happy voice made me jump as she chirped at me, "I hope this is all right calling you like this, I couldn't reach you at home. Anyway, I've been listening and I know who beat up the Prof. I want a bit of evidence and then I'll go to the police. Must go now. See you soon ...mmmwwhh!" There was the sound of a kiss and the message ended.

Stunned I sat for minutes, then replayed the message and cursed the girl. Didn't she realise this was no game? Didn't she think that she might get into deep water? I thought of her brightness and nearly wept; it was too late, but she'd begun to grow on me. If I'd been with the killer just then, I would have cheerfully smashed every bone in his body and enjoyed it. I was in a turmoil of regrets and rage as Bill came in and made a coffee. For once his strong brew was needed; it calmed my mood to a simmering fury.

"Sheila rang just as I came out. Do you want the details?"

I nodded; might as well have it all at once.

"She was strangled by a very powerful grip *after* she'd been hit from behind; the injuries were at the back of the knees." Something wrinkled into my brain at that. "She didn't stand a chance; whoever did it was ruthless and efficient. He tried to make it look as if she had been sexually attacked, but she hadn't. The police surgeon was definite about it and unsure of the reason." Bill looked at my stricken face, "Are you all right?"

Without another word I replayed the message.

It was Bill's turn to go pale, "This is worse than I thought. It's turning sinister." He stood up and strode around the room, "It all comes back to the project, doesn't it?" He sat down and stared me squarely in the eye, "It's time they told us the truth, starting with Liza."

We both shot up in surprise as the door bell rang - double ring - pause - double ring. There in the monitor was the black hair of the lady herself. She came in with a pale face and brittle, hard features. She wasted no time, "I see you've heard." Her voice was tired and defeated sounding. There were lines that I hadn't seen before.

I said one word, "Yes," and waited.

"I don't know any more than you about this. It's shaken the whole town, there's talk of patrols, some paedophile was beaten up and it's like a mortuary in the shops. I have my own suspicions, but there's nothing definite."

Jumping up, I glowered at her, "What is going on at HG? What are you up to? What are you going to do about it? Wait till we're all picked off one by one?"

I was furious and breathing heavily as Bill gently led me to sit down, "We'd better pool resources instead of recriminations." He made some more coffee and we sat facing in a triangle, Bill was careful to have a three-way conference.

Liza was very pale and seemed ready to drop. I played Annie's message, "Listen to this!"

There was a flicker of some emotion as she heard the kiss at the end, but she was even more upset as it ended, "The poor, silly girl. Didn't she realise what she was getting into?" She put down her cup and buried her head in her hands, "Why couldn't she wait? Why?" She looked up. I was shocked to see tears running down her cheeks. She brushed them aside and made an effort to control her feelings, "It might sound stupid, but I liked that girl, what I knew of her." She caught my eye and held it, "She didn't need to go off alone. It 's too late now; but if she'd only waited."

Bill spoke for all of us, "If only! But she didn't and now she's paid the penalty. A drastic lesson to us all." He growled at Liza, "Now what *do* you know?"

Liza's face went blank. I had met that look too often; we were not going to get anything that she didn't want us to know.

I was angry enough to shock her, "Is this project *worth* killing people for?"

It did get to her a bit, but not enough to break the barrier, "This project is more than you can know at this stage. But! It has nothing to do with Annie. She had her own reasons for doing what she did - and now we'll never know what they were, at least from her own lips."

I tried another tack, "Just what *is* DEMOLISH anyway? The pet of some odd-ball in an ivory tower?"

She regained some of her colour in a rush, "DEMOLISH is *my* pet. It's something I've fought for, lobbied for and spent blood for. I'll tell you all about it as soon as I can, but for now, I can't say a word."

Frustrated, I glared at her. She was still fobbing me off, "You asked if it was worth killing for. The answer is that someone thinks so. He might even be Annie's killer, but he's out there, waiting."

Bill was quiet for a minute, "We seem to have misjudged you. All I want to say is that you'd better take great care of yourself. I've a nasty feeling this isn't the end of the matter."

On that ominous note he took the coffee cups to the tiny kitchenette. Liza and I sat and stared at each other. Her beauty struck me hard, even in those strained circumstances. She was a beautiful enigma to me, surprising me at every turn.

But I also wanted her for myself, to take her away from all this sordid and dangerous business. The very last thing I wanted was for her to end up on a mortuary trolley like Annie. We said nothing, but it was clear she knew exactly what was in my mind. For myself, I think I saw a longing for a way out of the mess.

She stood up, straightened her skirt, held out her hand in formal dismissal, "I've a lot of checking to do before the next test so I'll go and try to get some rest. If this test is successful, I'll have some time off next week and would welcome some company."

Bill came back at that moment, "Sheila's off nights as well, why don't you and Bert come to make a foursome? I'll check later and tell you when."

Liza looked startled, but was clearly pleased, "That would be great! Here's hoping all goes well."

When she was out of the door, I eyed Bill quizzically, "Don't you trust me with her?"

He imitated an outraged parent, "Me? Never thought anything of it!"

I nearly fell about laughing, except that it was going to take a lot to make me laugh for some time.

Pocketing the duplicate Ley detector watch I locked up. Weary, disturbed and uneasy I slowly drove home. I mooned about and finally fell into bed to dream of battling with pillows, armies of them, that I couldn't get to grips with, coming back as fast as I knocked them down.

I woke at 5 am, tossed for some minutes, then rose to see the promise of another fine day. It was Sunday.

The only sound was the birds at their morning bickering over breakfast.

Some instinctive, deep premonition, made to go to town. I was dreading something happening in my absence. If I'd only been there when Annie had called, I convinced myself that she need not have died if I had. I felt a wreck, but was driven by a fear of something unknown and intangible.

It was still not 6 am as I parked the car. I thought back to the previous Sunday and the mysterious thunder. The clock started to chime and I paused.

There was a single, heavy thud, I jumped and all the birds rose screaming as before. I stood rooted to the spot for some seconds, but then started to run to the hotel car park. The rooks were settling again as I crossed Bird Street, silent at that hour.

Racing into the wide, open space I saw lights on in the temporary hut and Liza's car parked nearby. I continued my headlong rush and hammered on the door. A face peered out of a window, before the door opened a crack and Liza slid out, closing it behind her.

I stood in amazement. Her face was radiant, tears glistened in her eyes. She was almost deliriously happy. We stood face to face, speechless, as the joy slowly ebbed from her to be replaced with the blank look I had come to dread.

She opened her mouth to speak, but before she could do so, the door was flung open and a white coated, bald-headed man stuck out his head. His flushed and shiny features were ecstatic. He yelled, "They've got it!" He saw me staring and his face seemed to collapse. With an embarrassed shrug, he snapped off the grin like a light going out and slammed the door. In that brief moment I saw banks of switches, glowing computer monitors, flickering lights and a jungle of cables on the floor.

Liza's face was contorted in an appealing, lost look, "Don't say anything Bert. You mustn't ask anything – please."

I started to speak, "What?" But was stopped by her hand on my lips, "*Please*! Not now, it's not the right time. I *will* tell you, but not now."

Turning on my heel I went. I would be wasting my time trying. Not even the hounds of hell could drag anything out of her right now. As I went to the office via the Cathedral the Dean emerged. He seemed surprised to see someone walking by, "Lovely morning. Er, you weren't coming in?" I shook my head and smiled gently. At least *he* knew where he was. He coughed apologetically, "We don't open so early usually, but lately I've found some need for quiet at this time."

He chuckled, "My wife is not so appreciative of the hour, not like John Wesley's wife. He used to rise at four and spend three hours in prayer every day. I'm not so conscientious." He started to go, but stopped, "Did you hear a bang just now? Car perhaps?"

I spoke vaguely, "Yes, there was, but it wasn't a car."

He was unsure what to say to but too diffident to enquire further. We nodded and went our separate ways, him to his peaceful, ordered world, just coming to life: me to the utter chaos and ruin of a future that was bleak and unknown.

I spent the morning going over and over the recordings, scouring the receptors for transmissions, but there was nothing in the range up to 2,000 m. Then I thought of the watch still in my pocket, I pressed the pressure pad and stared. The display was jammed. It glared at me, unblinking, accusingly "E".

After resetting it now registered 150 and stayed steady. On impulse I stuck it into my pocket and walked to the Cathedral, where people were moving in and out steadily. The display remained steady; it was 160. I wandered, seemingly looking at the decorated windows as far as the statue of the sleeping children.

The watch display had jumped to high mode and was registering 800. As I moved to the east, it flipped back to 160. Back three steps it shot back to 800. I wondered!

The high reading went straight down the aisle, heading about south west. I couldn't go too far because of the people, but the inference was that it went on and on. No wonder Teddy was excited. With a start, I realised that if I continued in the same direction I would reach the car park of the hotel.

The various pieces fell into place with an almost audible click. Whatever Liza was up to, she was using the ancient power of the Ley line as an ultra strong carrier wave.

Feeling weak in the knees, I went to the coffee shop, needing physical as well as mental rest. As I sipped the bland, brown brew my mind was made up, one way or another Liza was going to tell me. I had the feeling that she had no idea what forces she was about to unleash.

As usual, my resolutions were not to be fulfilled.

Chapter 35 Calculations.

Her hotel answered my call to say she was out. The hut too was locked and deserted. This was becoming irritating. As it was 2.30 I thought of Teddy Wilson. The watch was still in my pocket, so I bought a bunch of flowers from the supermarket and went to the hospital. Jostling with the throng of visitors I found him semi-dozing, an opened journal in front of his glazed eyes. He gave a start as I spoke to him, "Don't apologise, old boy, only too glad to talk to someone. With these painkillers and the babble of everyone talking at once, I'm almost in a trance." He seemed to come to remarkably quickly and stowed the journal in his locker, "I just can't concentrate on the squabbles of Stephen and Maud with all the racket, even if it seems there's new evidence that our own Roger de Clinton was a powerful figure trying to stop the civil war." For some reason I thought of Al. He would be interested, even if I wasn't.

"What induces you to bring cheer and comfort to me? I'm not getting any visitors yet and I'm likely to die of boredom."

Placing the flowers on the locker, I tried levity, "Sorry to say it, but I was bored too, I thought, 'Why not go and torment Teddy? He can't walk away.'" He dutifully laughed, but there was a gleam in his eye that said he wasn't fooled.

I asked him how his bruises were going, (black and blue he said) how the head was, (sore bearish) and the legs. He paused before answering, "Very sore! The doctor is not too happy; it seems that I was thumped with something big and solid. That's why I fell so heavily. Not your usual mugger's way, is it?"

"No," I said, but my mind was on the way Annie had been laid low.

A professional job, they thought.

Feeling in my pocket, I brought out the watch, "I've found the spare, you might find it useful when you're fit to leave."

His face said it all as he held out his hand.

As he took it, I casually asked, "What readings did you get on your investigations?" I went on quickly, "Just asking as I tested it to check it was working, and I got a funny reading in the Cathedral."

His hand stopped in mid air, "Now there's a thing." His hand closed on the watch, "Just suppose I ask you what you found yourself?"

"Between 160 and ..." I paused, "800!"

His face lit up, "I knew it! I knew it. Just wait till I submit my thesis. This'll shut those sceptics. Now tell me in detail where and what the readings were."

So I told him roughly where and what I'd seen. He beamed, "This has done me more good than all those pills. You've made my day, dear boy!"

"Tell me," I mused, "Just what you have found out."

He sighed, "Now how much do you know of natural earthly radiation?"

I must have looked blank for he said, "I thought not. Without being too technical, the earth has many fields of EMF - Electro Motive Force - and they vary from place to place. They are frequently observed in the higher latitudes, like the Northern Lights for instance, but there are anomalies in many others ..."

I settled back as he started to lecture. Most of it was way over my head, or perhaps out of my field, but I began to see the line he was taking, "You think that these Ley lines are forces that the ancients knew about without any instrumentation and used them to link their holy sites as a form of telepathic communication? Anyone who could use this aspect could seem to be in touch with the gods or God. It's all very interesting." This was the grossest understatement as far as I was concerned.

Liza and the project were very prominent in my thoughts.

"How far did the line go?" I asked in all innocence.

His reply was sufficient to shake my composure, but not visibly I hoped, "Well! I tried the line towards Ipswich, but it was weak. It lay at 90 degrees to the strong one and seemed to be a sort of focus. But. The line directly through the Cathedral went to Bridgnorth, Stowe, Caeo and finally St David's." He laughed at this point, "Not being the Almighty, I can't walk on water yet. It seems to go on, but that will have to wait for another occasion." As I sat trying to make sense of this as he went on, "You know a lot about electronics. You know how you generate sine waves in an oscillator, well; it seems to be the same in this case too. There are places of intense strength and these occur at regular intervals; in the case of the south west line, the peaks coincide with the sites I've already mentioned. They are about 23 kilometres apart, indicating an exceptionally long wave and low frequency. This is most unusual in that ..."

He lost me again as my mind was calculating the relationship of 23 Km and 2,875 metres. To my rough calculations it seemed to be 8:1, a classic harmonic.

I dragged my mind back to Teddy's lecture, which had now stopped as he saw my inattention, "Am I going on too much?" Trying to look interested and failing, my mind wasn't with him. I was trying to work out where the line would go if it was projected to infinity.

Shaking my head at him, I laughed, "You've given me enough to think about for now. You really have not bored me, but I was up early today and I haven't caught up yet."

I stood to leave, "I'll pop in again soon and we can continue with my education then." He had a beatific smile on his face as I left and he imagined the stir of his revelation to his peers and fellow egg heads.

I went back to the office with undue haste. It was essential to calculate and to theorise. There were two worrying aspects that quickened my fears. The first was that the 'mugging' was no casual affair; it was deliberate and well executed. It was obvious that Annie's killing was carried out by the same assassin, by the stamp in his method. He was also very ruthless and efficient. He let nothing and no-one stand in his way.

The second was that Liza was engaged in some secret activity using cosmic forces that I was sure she didn't understand. There was a third and vague fear that the two were linked in some way not yet clear to me, but there were too many coincidences to ignore. I entered the office with unquantified doubts. After an hour of thinking, checking, calculating and projecting, the doubts had turned to real fears. The projection of the Ley line was clear. I was extremely disturbed to find where it led.

Chapter 36 Invitation.

On the Monday Bill came in breezy and bright. His enjoyment of Sheila's time off nights was so clear it turned my heart. I envied him the settled and comfortable style of life he led; possibly I was more than jealous of his marriage because it was something that I felt I would never have. This was something new for me. At least it was before I met Liza and Annie. Not for the first time, nor the last, I cursed myself for a fool as I remembered the soft nearness of Annie. It was not the gut-wrenching love I had felt the first time I saw Liza, but it had many advantages that I thought I would never have with Liza.

Bill sensed the gloom and did his best to lift it; his imitation of Donald Duck getting angry with the kettle did raise a genuine laugh, "That's better, Bert, I was beginning to think I'd lost my touch."

Smiling at him, I assured him, "You're the one anchor in my life at present. There are so many things that aren't what they seem, that I feel as if I'm walking in quicksand."

He plonked down a cup of his treacly coffee, "By the way, can you and LIza make it Wednesday?"

"*I* can. I'm not sure about Liza. For one thing I've not spoken to her for days so I don't even know if she's still here." I hoped the lie was not too transparent, for some reason, I didn't want Bill to know just yet about my fears. "I'll try again later today, if she doesn't show up."

She did show up. In the early afternoon she came to the door as usual, dressed in a light blue, linen suit that was not only beautifully tailored, but oozed taste and class. It had just the right balance of femininity and practicality that was becoming my normal expectation of her.

There was no doubt of her being a very striking, woman; she also was determined to be the equal of any man, whether as a friend or enemy. Sometimes I wasn't sure into which category she put me. Today, there was a tenseness that put me in the position of being weighed in the balance. I trusted that I was not found wanting, but she gave nothing away.

Bill spoke to break the chill, "I was just saying to Bert that Sheila and I would love to have you for dinner on Wednesday if you're still here. Will you still be around then?"

Liza smiled, rather thinly I thought, "Yes, I will. And I'd be delighted to come." She turned a china doll smile to me, "I'm sure Bert will bring me, so I won't get lost on the way."

I returned the fixed smile with a casual grin, "Sure. What time do you want us then, Bill?"

"Say, seven-thirty, I usually eat earlier, but I don't want to watch the telly, so we can chat away after. It's been too long since we did entertain. I'm trying to talk Sheila into giving up the night shifts, but she feels that she can do a lot of good then. It's often in the night that emergencies occur and she can cope well. It's a thing she's good at, coping." There was an uncomfortable feeling that Bill felt that I needed coping with.

Liza sat down opposite me, "I've come to talk to you about ..."

Bill interrupted, "I'll love you and leave you if you don't need me, I've still not beaten the feedback problem on the AT 10. So if you'll excuse me?" He bowed out and shut the door behind him. It was obvious that he considered I needed someone who could cope.

Liza's voice was calm, but it had the undercurrent of stress that made her sound edgy, "I must apologise for my shortness on Sunday."

I waited, before she continued almost aggressively, "I was doing a final run. It was a critical moment."

"You've made it clear that you're working on your own and want to keep it that way," I retorted, "I respect that wish and won't interfere. However," I tried to look disinterested, "the events of the last two weeks have made me aware of elements of danger that I ..."

She jerked as if she was a puppet on a string, "Thank you for that, But I'm quite capable of looking after myself!"

"Like Annie?" I snapped back. She flinched as I pressed home the facts, "Annie obviously thought *she* could do so as well and look where it got her."

"I'm not Annie."

"Dammit I know that. I also know that I don't want to see you cold on a slab like her."

"Oh? And just how *do* you want to see me?"

My face reddened. I was lost for words to express just how I did see her. It wasn't easy to say how I did see her, beyond the trite idea of domestic bliss. If she did settle down, would she still be the Liza I wanted, or would she become less and less interesting? Would we slip into mere habit and routine that would stifle us?

She smiled a victorious smile that made me cross; cross and rash.

I blurted out, "I see you in my bed, my house, my life. I see you waking in the morning, turning out the light at night. I want you in my life, alive and safe. Annie brought all this to a head by getting herself killed. I want *you*, Liza!"

This got to her, but all it did was to put up the barrier again. She repeated maddeningly, "If only it was that simple," her voice was quiet and low.

She made an effort and sat up, "Tomorrow I've a lot of paperwork to catch up on, but Wednesday I've got nothing planned. If you have a free day I'd be glad of some company and a chance to relax before the inspection next week." There were all sorts of unspoken feelings that passed between us as she spoke.

Terrified for her safety, I wanted her to free herself of the load she carried. She was bone-weary, exhausted with the unrelenting preparations of the last three weeks; she was determined to succeed at all costs. And somewhere buried under all that there was the woman I'd fallen for - the real Liza. I was fast despairing of ever seeing her again. It was clutching at this faint hope, this brittle straw that made me swallow all the angry, unspoken words and say that there was no reason why I could not do so. We agreed to meet in my office at 9 am, to use the Jag if at all possible and go where the fancy took us.

Chapter 37 Consolidation.

Tuesday was a drag. To have the day free for both Bill and me, we needed to clear the e-mail, the paperwork for the next batch of AV 4 s for evaluation, check the newest microprocessors and up-date the software on the design program. We did it by six pm, but I was whacked. I dined at the Duke of Cumberland, but that was a mistake. All the time I was imagining Annie's brightness and soft American accent to reassure me that she was still there. But she was gone. Her ghost haunted me all through the short meal. I resolved never to go there again.

Wednesday was a glorious morning. That summer was one that I remember with nostalgia; I drove to Lichfield with the hood down, wind in my hair and a lightness creeping back into my life. Annie would never be completely gone, but she was starting to become a memory and not an accusing finger.

Liza was on time. She seemed able to gauge the exact time to be there. She was the only woman I knew who could do that. One girl friend, Jean could never be sure even of arriving on the right day! That was a lifetime ago. But Liza was, in that particular attribute, ultra-reliable. We drove aimlessly around the quieter lanes, listening to Chopin. With Liza by my side it was as pleasant as any driving is on our overcrowded roads. Liza was evasive in her answers about her progress on the project. All too soon midday came, so we picked an interesting-looking pub for a Melton Mowbray pie lunch. The pie and salad was fresh and not too filling as we had the delights of Sheila's cooking to sample later. But it seemed to give Liza a fresh burst of life; she talked again of her parents and her home village. It seemed to me that she was reaching some crisis about them in a similar way to the way that Annie's memory was fading from an agony to an ache for me.

She was looking calmly at the door when she stiffened.

I saw George Brown enter with two Japanese men in business-suits and head for the bar. He ordered something, paid and went to the Gents.

Liza rose swiftly, "Can we go now, please?" The pub used the normal practice of prepayment, so we left quickly.

Outside I pulled her to a halt, "What's the matter, you look as if you've seen a ghost."

"I was ... well, suddenly I felt shut in."

"So it wasn't George Brown then?"

"*Who?* You know him?"

"Yes, he works at the Central."

"He does? So I wasn't mistaken. Since when?"

"Let me think. About a month I think. No more. Could be less. I'm surprised you haven't seen him."

She grimaced, "I've only been there twice, remember? I did think so once, but thought I was wrong."

She glanced over her shoulder, "Can we go right now?"

I searched her face, but saw only wariness, "If that's what you want. It wouldn't be a bad idea anyway; you know what the traffic's like."

When we were in the car heading back, she seemed to relax, she asked casually, "What do you think this George was doing out here? It's a long way from the hotel."

"No idea, I suppose anyone can take a day off."

She sat pensively as the wind blew her hair forward to partly conceal her face. In the way that I was able to sense more than she wanted to say, I knew that it was a profound shock and it unsettled me. That feeling persisted until we arrived at the Huddleston's square, modern, suburban house.

Sheila Huddleston is one of those cooks who think you'll die of starvation if you're able to move at the end of a meal. I didn't have to be carried from the table, but it was a near thing.

Groaning, I refused another slice of double Gloucester and was totally unable to consume a single mint-chocolate. I sat heavily on the settee next to Liza. It was a big piece of furniture, so we were not thrown into intimate contact. Even so we were close enough to feel that we had been put into the position of a courting couple. Sheila is great, but not blessed with the ability to sense the undercurrents of caution. Liza had been charming as she chatted of her homeland; it was only me who knew that tears were springing in her eyes, unseen by Bill and Sheila. I mentioned to them that we had seen George in the pub. Bill was aware of the tension in Liza as she was hit by the memory of that encounter; Sheila just dismissed it as nothing to do with her.

Bill had us all in stitches as he told of the antics of Popeye and his nephews, Pipeye, Pupeye, Peepeye and Poopeye. He ran an early film, a tale of the boat captained by Castor (Oyle) and the boy friend Ham Gravy.

I found these rather irritating in their roughness, but I suppose for the '30s they were wonderful. Liza insisted in helping Sheila with the washing up. Sheila, bless her uncomplicated soul, saw it as an opportunity to pump Liza for information and clues of a romance. It did give me a chance to tell Bill of Liza's reaction to George. It was while I was telling him that it struck me that he had arrived at or shortly after the time that Liza had come.

Bill had noticed this too and he agreed with me that there were too many coincidences for comfort. I reminded Bill of our clandestine observations of George and Antonio. We were both in a solemn mood as Sheila and Liza emerged from the kitchen, still chatting of dresses.

Liza went to the bathroom before leaving; Sheila tugged my sleeve, "She likes you, you know." *Tell me something new*, I thought. Instead I said, "Did she say so?"

Sheila grinned, "No. But she didn't need to; it was so obvious; she was on edge all the time you were apart. I think she's very nice." She did not ask when the wedding was, but in her eyes it was just a matter of time. As Liza had said too often, "If it was so simple."

Liza descended the stairs to kiss Sheila, thank Bill for the show and left holding my arm. I was warm, full of food and good company; I had a beautiful woman on my arm and began to feel mildly optimistic. At the hotel she did kiss me, but it was brief and cool as an autumn breeze with a hint of winter. She said she would call in to see me tomorrow and was fairly at ease. She refused to commit herself further and left me feeling once again dropped.

Chapter 38 Exposure.

Liza was late coming in the morning, so I ran the recordings of the staff room hidden camera. There were several unimportant comings and goings, but I sat up and turned up the volume as Antonio came in. He went through the procedure of blocking the security cameras before speaking on his mobile. It was only just audible, but I was sure I heard right, "This is top priority. I have the specification as I said. I'll meet you at 11.30 tonight in the usual place. I *must see* you, I won't be using the rubbish bin drop, I'll hand it personally." There was a pause as he listened, "I don't like it, Beacon Park's too open. ... The one by the new bench? ... I still don't like it. ... OK! 11.30." He shut off the 'phone and re-opened the security cameras before he left.

Bill came in as I was rewinding. He was intrigued, but said, "I hope you're not thinking of going alone and doing a James Bond." It was clear to him that was just what I was thinking of doing, "Listen, this is for HG, not for you. No, listen to me for once. You were clobbered; Annie was killed in that park, The Prof: was mugged. What makes you think you'll do better? Leave it to the field agents."

Although I nodded, it wasn't what was on my mind. I was being given a chance to set clear some of the debit side. There was enough on that side to correct. Besides I would be forewarned and had my own survival devices. I would be safe enough. Liza came in as we were finishing the conversation. She looked, quizzically, but said nothing. Her light fawn, tapering jeans were much more becoming than the shapeless style of the mass produced article. She wore a small-checked shirt, tucked into the waistband, a silk scarf loosely knotted at the open neck. Her hair was tied back with a blue ribbon. The whole effect was to make her look a young, country girl without a worry in the world.

It was only as I saw the heavier make up under her eyes that I knew this was totally false.

Bill whistled, "Going riding then?"

She smiled at that, but looked seriously at me.

Trying to sense what she wanted, but finding nothing definite, I plunged in, "I thought you might like to see the splendour of Shugborough Hall, that is if you haven't been there already." She nodded her head, the pony tail flicking enticingly, "Once years ago. I was at Staffs Poly, remember? But it's such a good day I would like that. We could easily just sit in the grounds or by the canal. That would be very nice."

I went by the slow, pretty way. Liza was content to comment on the pastoral peace, the quietness as we threaded the maze of lanes. Concentrating on checking if we were followed, I was sure that we were not, but I kept an eye on the rear view mirror as we swept up to the imposing front.

It's a good thing that the National Trust runs such places, but they have lost some of the sense of grandeur that you would have from crunching the gravel at the front portico and being met by a liveried retainer. Ah, well, at least it's not a hotel, health farm or old people's home. Liza didn't spend much time in the house; it had a sense of dusty frailty, that didn't tempt me to linger in those great rooms. I had taken to wearing my 'hearing aid' all the time then. It gave me reassurance to know who was there and an edge on any follower. It remained silent except for the times we were in the staffed areas and then the footfalls were steady, pacing, not stealthy or shifty.

Outside the sun was hot, a shady tree was welcome. I scanned the open grounds before we ventured into the open. I found a cool seat with an open aspect, so we sat in a quiet, but not unfriendly silence.

Liza spoke softly, "I owe you an explanation. I've been so bound up with secrecy that I've lost the ability to see a genuine honesty when it's before me."

I let her say what she wanted at her own speed.

"The truth is, I've heard that my parents were trapped by a traitor. He sent a message to the Politburo and later joined up with the Russian Mafia. He's the most brutal and ruthless killer they have. He's been responsible for assassinating some agents in the USA and in the ex Eastern Bloc countries. He's also wanted by the FBI as well as the Japanese Ayuka and the GRU. " I must have gaped. She said firmly, "Most of all *I* want him. He was responsible for the death of my parents."

"But surely you can't mean to tackle this, this killer alone," I was horrified and made no attempt to hide it.

"The net's closing in. There's an agent from the GRU just waiting to pounce. A CIA top man is watching for him to make a move and lead us to the network." I was shaken, but I thought of Al. She went on, "There was an FBI special agent trailing him for the death of her fiancé," I held my breath as she went on calmly but sadly, "Annie paid the price of underestimating him. They don't call him 'The Vulture' for nothing."

Open mouthed I stared, "You mean. Annie was FBI?"

She nodded gravely, "She was a very successful agent - until she met The Vulture. Now I want him."

"But how will you know him? He could be anyone anywhere. Someone as successful as that isn't easily found."

She gazed round at the peaceful scene, sunlit meadows and lawns sweeping away to trees and a distant steeple, "He's here."

I looked wildly about, "Where?"

She smiled a mirthless smile, "Not here in the grounds. But in Lichfield. I know him and he knows me. I once made the mistake of trusting him."

She glowered, "Once was once too often. I used to know him as Stefan."

"The one that you ...?" I gasped as if punched in the stomach.

"Yes, The one that I lived with for a few days."

She looked around with a look of calm, "You know him as George Brown."

I couldn't believe what I was hearing. Not only about Stefan. To think of Annie, the one I thought of as sweet and naive, to be an FBI agent was the most shattering thing of all. The matter-of-fact way that Liza spoke of these fantastic and unreal revelations simply knocked the breath out of me. For some minutes the feeling persisted that this was a dream, a nightmare that would soon end and I would awake, sweating with fear, but in a normal world.

But it was no dream. I didn't wake. It was a living nightmare.

I kept thinking this was not happening, but I was denied the bliss of normality. I stared at Liza. Despairingly I gazed at the peaceful vista and went numb as the realisation crept in that this was for real.

Liza just let me battle it out in my mind. I didn't think then that I could ever be shocked so much and stay sane. It's perhaps a good thing that I didn't know the *full* story then, or I might have gone crazy.

Suddenly I could take no more. I stood. Liza started at the sudden movement. I spoke harshly, but I regretted it as her face showed pain at my words, "I just don't know what to say, I must go home and think about it. You've turned my whole world inside out. I don't know anything any more." I turned, "I'm going now. Come with me if you want to, but I need time to think."

"At the moment, I don't want to see you, the office, HG or anybody," I waved a dismissive hand as I turned my back to walk away. "The whole world's going crazy. Leave me alone." It was only as I thought about it in the future that I realised the strain that Liza and Annie and others like them live under day to day.

At that moment I just couldn't cope with it, couldn't even bear to think about it.

Liza's followed me, hesitatingly.

Hearing her footsteps falter behind me I nearly threw away my 'aid' there and then, but some basic reaction to my own work stopped me. I drove back in a blindness that was dangerous, but my familiarity with the roads and the car saw me safely back to Liza's hotel.

As she climbed out of the car and stood looking down at me, I was tempted to leap out and seize her, drag her away somewhere, anywhere away from this mad life she lived. She let her emotions show fractionally in the misery of her expression.

It was as if her heart was breaking; a tear squeezed from her eye unheeded. Grief, anguish, despair, longing and the determination of steadfast intent all flashed across her face. At that moment, as she stood seeing my withdrawal from her, she was more beautiful than I had ever seen her, but I was incapable of rational thought and couldn't bear to touch her for fear that she would clam up again. I relived the years of carping criticism, the sense of desolation as my mother slammed out of my life. My numbness turned to rage. I let in the clutch and roared off, tyres squealing in protest.

Chapter 39 Resolution

At home I sat in the car for how long I do not know, but finally climbed out and went in. Unmoving, I sat thinking until the shadows lengthened and a chilliness set in. I made an instant coffee and turned on the Hi-Fi. The simple songs of Beer and Knightley washed over me as I thought of the softness of Annie. The precious thing I'd let slip through my fingers.

The 'phone rang for a long time. I ignored it.

It rang again. I stayed unmoving. The silence when it stopped again was almost tangible. It was going dark when the growling of my stomach resurrected an animal need for food. I ate something. The taste was as nothing, but the satisfaction of my body hunger brought a new resolution to my mind. The clock chiming ten threw me into the present.

Tonight Antonio was meeting his contact.

All this duplicity filled me with fury. I was going to unmask him and close down the whole business. George would be picked up by Special Branch, Al sent packing and Liza given an ultimatum. It seemed so simple then. My own vulnerability didn't even enter into it. I've never even handled a gun, let alone used one and never want to. My anti-personal attack alarm and my own special spray were all I took for protection. One whiff of my spray and an attacker would be writhing in agony as his eyes and throat burned viciously. I was in a vicious mood and didn't feel any sense of remorse at the intention of hurting someone. I changed into my darkest clothing and took a ski mask to cover my gingery hair and pale skin. Garaging the Jag I took the Rover quietly down the lane. There was no need to be quiet there, but that was my mood as I went forward to do battle with this dark world. I parked the car in the hotel car park, thankful that the hut was in darkness.

The area was almost deserted; just one or two staff cars were near the trade entrance.

Eleven struck as I left the relative security of my tin box, to stand uncertainly in the chill of a clear night. The stars shone with an intensity that seemed to bring them within reach.

I set off for the park, stopping panic stricken for a second as I realised that I was not absolutely sure which bench Antonio was going to, but I pressed on; there was no going back, right or wrong. I crept as silently as I could along the path until I saw the bench with a waste basket by it. It was deserted. There was little cover, but the dark loom of a bush was not far away.

As quietly as possible I crouched down where I could observe, but would hopefully appear to be simply part of the bush. It was harder and harder to keep still, my left foot started to tingle and I was tempted to wriggle it, but managed to stave off cramp by flexing my toes. A figure wandered along the path, his footsteps in my 'aid' sounded too erratic to be a prowler. He was unsteady and it became clear that he was at least slightly drunk. He tripped over his own feet and swore. There was an enormous belch, he said, "Pardon! Manners!" and giggled. He wandered unsteadily away and out of sight.

He made me rue not bringing my night vision glasses. That made me regret being there at all. I began to see the folly of my actions. Becoming increasingly cold and stiff I waited as an hour passed with no sign of Antonio. Cursing myself for a fool, I heard a distinct footfall in my 'aid'. I tried to place it, but it was elusive. It was definitely stealthy. I heard two more, but they seemed to be in a different place. As I'd not used the 'aid' in action like this before the poor performance was a disappointment, it would need modifying. I strained my eyes, but there was nothing moving that I could see.

There was a quick movement to the edge of my vision, a cat streaked across the path, followed by a scuffle, then silence. Nothing was happening; I might as well go home. I started to feel foolish as well as cold and stiff.

There it was again, a furtive footfall. I froze into stillness. Then I really went cold. There was the scratching of a safety catch being removed. Wildly turning my head I tried to find the location, but it seemed to come from both front and back. I was bitterly disappointed with my 'aid'. It was no use if the direction couldn't be determined. There was another step. I was becoming frantic. Where was he?

My anxiety turned to freezing fear as I felt a cold gun-muzzle touch the back of my head and a quiet voice, "Well, Well! Dear old Bert. Got lost tonight? No. Don't turn round, just keep still and you won't be hurt." Antonio's voice had an unaccustomed hard edge. Worse, I smelled garlic. In my fright I tongue lashed myself. Fine one I was to sort out this mess.

Antonio went on, "I wasn't completely sure, but I felt you had another device in there somewhere. You fell for it nicely." He chuckled, but it made my flesh creep. Somewhere in the darkness I thought I heard another footfall, my 'aid' was worse than useless. The thought made me angry, my fear fled, "You can put that away, I'm not armed. I don't like guns." I fiddled in my pocket for the spray.

"Keep those hands out in the open, I know about you and your trick devices. Now tell me, dear old Bert, what this watch does and how it works."

I gasped, "It was you and ..."

"Tubby Teddy," he finished. "He was tougher than I gave him credit for."

Angry now I hissed, "Was Annie tougher too?"

The gun muzzle jabbed painfully, "Shut up! Now tell me all about this watch and the hut at Angel Court." He spoke sharply, "And don't think I won't use this. I want the information now and I mean to get it. One way or another."

I spoke fiercely, "Go to hell!"

"That's where you will be unless you tell me. I'll give you to the count of three and then I'll blow what brains you have all over the park."

I tensed as I detected the first pressure sounds of a trigger. Was this the end? Was it all a waste of time? I was frustrated with my 'aid'. There was no directional stability, the sound of trigger pressure was not steady; it almost sounded as if there were two. I prepared to try one desperate lunge hoping to catch him off guard.

"One, Two ..."

Desperately I threw myself sideways as I heard the creaking sound of the trigger reach the end of its travel.

Time slowed to a crawl, everything was in slow motion. Antonio's face was surprised, the gun turned towards me. My 'aid' was full of sounds. There was a tiny red spot on Antonio's forehead.

He suddenly jerked and his head fell to the side, there was a sickening, squelching sound, his silenced gun plopped twice, the bullets striking the ground inches from my upturned face. He collapsed slowly like a falling tower-block, to lie crumpled at my feet. Petrified, I heard once again the first pressure sounds of a gun. A red spot moved towards my head.

There was a sudden eruption of sound as a shot came from my left, there was a loud curse and the light went out.

Suddenly there were running footsteps in several directions. Sensing movement I turned to my left to see a matt black pistol pointed at my face, the hole like the mouth of a tunnel, I tensed for the blast and oblivion.

"Oh God! Bert!" I opened my eyes. Liza's anxious face stared me, inches away from mine.

Transfixed, I stared back. Was I in heaven - or Hades? I must be dreaming.

But she spoke relieved, "Are you all right? Say you're all right."

I croaked through a parched throat, "Liza! What, what the hell?"

She looked swiftly round and bent to kiss me. I tasted the salt of tears.

"Thank God I was in time. Oh Bert. You stupid, stupid man! What were you doing? If anything had happened, I would never forgive myself ..." She kissed me again and held me tight.

In a dream Liza whisked me towards Bird Street at a steady, but urgent walk. She was non-committal and evasive in reply to my queries. We went through the deserted lanes to the office. Because of the late hour and my semi-shocked state it took over five minutes to open up. She was silent until the security was complete.

She flopped into the visitor's chair, drained and very tired.

"Just what were you doing in the park at that time alone?"

Beginning to recover, I was shaken, but not totally addled, "What the hell were *you* doing there anyway?"

"I'm sorry; I'm not at liberty to say."

I slammed the desk top with my fist, "Don't give me that rubbish again, I'm sick of it!" I calmed as the shutters came down on her face again, "Please tell me something, I'm going crazy with all this double talk and secrecy." By now I was pleading, "Tell me before I do something even more stupid."

Her eyes revealed her conflict. When she finally spoke it was in the same tone she had used at Shugborough, flat, measured and shocking, "We've been watching Antonio for over a year. He is - was - a GRU sleeper; he came from Naples on the scent of the project. He was fed some Shop Soiled Humint to trap him and there was no doubt."

As if telling me the time she went on, "We were about to feed him some less obvious rubbish to confuse his lead and to trace the link, when he somehow got wind of the real basis. I think it was Teddy Wilson who set the idea in his mind." She uttered a dry, mirthless laugh that sounded extremely hollow.

"It was Teddy who really started me on the idea. It was ironic that he was partly responsible for its near betrayal." She mused as if weighing matters in her mind, "I received an alert that he was meeting a contact tonight and I was ordered to observe and record." She spoke as if to justify herself, "I'd no idea you'd be there as well."

I looked at her and waited, I was only given what she decided she'd give me.

"For some weeks now it had been obvious that the GRU had been infiltrated by the Russian Mafia. They saw the financial possibilities as limitless and tried to recruit him. But he got greedy and opened a contact with the Yakusa. They've at least two operatives in the area now."

She looked even more tired as she went on, "It seems that one is a maverick, the worst sort, who'll sell anybody anything if the price is right. I thought that tonight would be the breakthrough."

She sounded bitter. "It's all blown up in our faces. I couldn't see the assassin; I only just stopped him killing you." She saw my face open in wonder, "I couldn't let that happen!"

Speaking more in hope than query I whispered, "Why?"

She seemed to be struggling with emotions, "Trust me. At least until next week. I really can't - daren't - tell you any more now."

She rose to go, "I promise that if all goes well I'll tell you all of it."

Scrambling up I seized her hand, "What if this assassin's waiting for you? What if he's outside right now? I can't bear all this. I can't stand you putting your life at risk all day and night."

She was unable to hide the quiver of her lips, "I know that, but there are two jobs I must do. Nothing else can get in the way; not you, not me, not us!"

That word 'us' shook me, "D'you mean there's some hope?"

"Don't ask any more right now." She turned away. "Not now."

Outside I faintly heard the wail of a police siren. Liza turned to me again, "We must go now, I'll call you as soon as I can, but we must go."

There was an urgency that I couldn't misunderstand. In ten minutes I was well on my way home, wondering just what on earth I was doing. It all seemed to be turning into a living nightmare with no escape.

I double-checked the cottage; there was no breach, no sign of outside activity. Once more I slept fitfully and uneasily.

Chapter 40 Murder.

At the office in the morning, Bill showed me the Citizen with the headlines, "Murder in the Park". There followed an article that was lurid, speculative and had no facts, except the one correct one that Antonio Perazza had been found shot in Beacon Park. The police were 'confident of an imminent arrest', which meant they hadn't a clue. As I'm not a good liar, Bill saw through my attempted interest as a shocked resident. But as a good friend, he didn't push it. He did look worried as I was summoned to the police station later that day.

At the station I was led to a typical, cramped office and introduced to the officer leading the investigation.

The Inspector was neither Morse nor Frost; he was a balding family man with pictures of his children on the desk. He was, however, an astute and tidy man; I wished my own files were as neat.

After I was seated and given a cup of coffee, not good, but better than Bill's, he opened a drawer and took out an evidence bag, which he put on the desk in front of me.

I nearly spilled the coffee in shock. In it was the watch I'd given to Teddy. Slowly I put down the coffee, hoping that my shaking hands were not too obvious, the Inspector didn't seem to notice, "We found this in the deceased's hand." He turned it over, "I wondered if you recognised it?"

If I had been linked to a lie detector, it would have probably blown a fuse. My hands were clammy, my heart raced and I started to flush. I had to say, "Yes." But I followed it up with a question of my own, "How did you know ...?"

"Know that it was from you?" He turned it over to the face, "We keep an eye on the local industries and I know that you are Arraye Electronics."

He indicated the tiny logo on the face, "I simply wondered how The Deceased," *I hate that expression*, "came to have it in his possession." *I also hate the long winded jargon, why didn't he say 'the dead man had it'?*

"Hard to say, Inspector, I don't keep a track of all sales," I threw him a tiny morsel, "but I did give one to Professor Wilson. You may remember. He was robbed."

"Gave?" His eyebrows arched disbelievingly.

I was sweating again, "Well, sold I suppose really. He wanted accuracy and I said it was accurate."

He pressed a button on his desk and a uniformed Sergeant came in, "Would you mind taking off your right shoe and giving it to the Sergeant?"

I looked horrified, "Why?" I queried, trembling noticeably.

"Just eliminating you from our enquiries. You don't object do you?" As if in a dream I complied, even although I was petrified. *What had I done?* Then it struck me solidly, *I had been in the flower beds in the Park*, my footprints were all over it in the scuffles of last night.

Gulping the coffee I waited for the blow to fall. It was no more than five minutes. When the sergeant returned with the shoe it was in a plastic bag.

The Inspector, no longer a genial family man, but a threatening force, leaned across the desk, "And what were you doing wandering around Beacon Park in the dark last night Mr Fradley?"

I went pale and shook, my voice was a squeak, "Pardon? I - I wasn't there." It sounded ridiculous to my own ears.

"Now, don't play games with me, Mr Fradley. This isn't trampling a few flowers. I'll ask once more and the sergeant is taking notes." He glared at me, "What were you doing in Beacon Park last night?"

I swallowed. This was a nightmare, I would wake up soon. But I knew I wouldn't.

"Well, I ..." I gulped in panic. I was interrupted as the 'phone rang. The sergeant picked it up, listened, handed it apologetically to the Inspector, "For you, sir."

He took it and snapped, "Well?" His face changed, "Sorry, Sir, I was interviewing ..." He stopped and listened, there was a long period of quiet as he listened, then burst out, "But Sir, I've just ..." Ominously quiet again he listened, and then spoke softly, "Very good sir!"

Delicately replacing the receiver he looked at me as if I was a disgusting grub, "You have friends in high places Fradley. Sergeant, give <u>Mr</u> Fradley his shoe and escort him to the door." The sergeant started to open his mouth, "Now, Sergeant!" There was an almost audible click as the sergeant shut his mouth. When I'd replaced my shoe the Inspector was looking out of the window, he didn't move as I was led out to freedom.

He wasn't the only one confused by the turn of events. It hadn't been an hour since the first call summoning me to the police station. Whoever 'they' were, they moved fast. Still in a daze I returned to the office. Bill jumped up and made me sit down to a cup of his coffee.

Once again it was what I needed. More than anything else I needed an ally that I could trust, so I went over the events of last night and the police station. Well, nearly all. I left out the way Liza had hugged me in the park. Bill sensed more than I told him. He shook his head as I told him of my release from the police station, "It looks as if Horseguards have your best interests at heart. I can't think of anyone else with that pull." We both knew that what he really meant was LIza.

Feeling completely shattered I went home, took a sleeping tablet and slept solidly for twelve hours. The next morning I had a thick head and the sky was overcast, threatening rain at any time.

Bill sounded relieved when I rang and said I wasn't going in. I lazed around in my heavy dressing-gown and cooked a huge brunch of bacon, eggs, tomatoes, beans and some other things, I forget what. It tasted wonderful. It also made me feel human again. So much so that I was just wondering if after all, to go to the office when the 'phone rang. It was Bill, he sounded awful.

"I just had to call you, before someone else does. They've found George Brown in the Stowe."

I gasped, "Drowned?"

The reply made me reel, "No! He'd been shot – twice!"

Stunned, I heard Bill's voice as I nearly dropped the 'phone, "Are you all right?"

Lifting the handset to my ear I whispered, "Yes, I'm OK. This is terrible. What's happening, Bill? The world's gone mad."

All of a suddenly I had to do something, anything, "Bill, I'm coming in. I'll be there in half an hour."

He was as distressed as I had ever seen him, pacing edgily back and forth in the confinement of the lab.

"This gets worse and worse, the town's in a state of panic. I saw some guests booking out of the Central; the manager's going bananas, no wine waiter, no head waiter. The Police are crawling out of the woodwork, guests leaving and the staff threatening to leave *en masse*. And to cap it all, the Inspector's sending a man round to talk to you."

Those words were the last straw. I slumped into my chair, "What the devil do they think I've got to do with this business?" My voice was a pitiful moan that sounded pathetic. I *was* pathetic. I was in the biggest state of panic ever - bar none.

The mental slap I received from Bill snapped me out of it, "Don't be so bloody stupid!"

I stared; the shock was as unexpected as an icy douche of water. Bill had sworn at me! In all the years we had been together, he'd never once, not once, used bad language. There had been the moments of tension and frustration. He'd called me some uncomplimentary names, most of which I admit I deserved; but he was firmly and totally against profanity of any sort, especially the misuse of God or Christ. The shock did the trick. I shot up as if I'd been injected with crack or heroin.

Bill relaxed, "That's better! Now what have you been doing to attract the attentions of the CID?"

"Was I that bad, Bill?" My voice still had a tremble in it, but it was no longer the cringing tone of a coward.

"Yes! And the question still stands. We've been together for how long? Too long for there to be any secrets, at least as far as the business goes." We both thought of Liza.

I stood, looking up at Bill's height, looming over me, "Believe me, Bill, not a thing," I held up a hand as he started to talk, "I told you the truth the other night, there's nothing to add, but an occasional kiss or embrace, neither of which has the slightest bearing on the running of the business or the matter of this latest killing."

The full meaning of the word hit me; I slumped back into my chair. Killing sounds so remote until it's near to home; then it becomes truly frightening. "The Inspector's found the watch Teddy Wilson had and has linked it to me; the firm's logo."

I stared hopefully at Bill, "I don't think he knows anything. He's thrashing about in the dark, clutching at straws." The irrationality of the mixed metaphors escaped me at that moment, "He's trying to find some lead, but I think he's on a hiding for nothing. I suspect our friends at HG are behind this; I don't believe for one minute that it's drugs. If we play the innocent bystander, I think there's nothing to fear."

"We? Are you saying that I'm a suspect as well? Good grief!"

"I think he's desperate for *some* lead and is simply pushing to see what cracks. I can honestly say that I was at home all last night and nowhere near the Stowe, nor Lichfield itself for that matter. Were you at home alone, or with Sheila?"

"With Sheila all last night. She was watching some of those gardening and house decorating programmes. Were you alone?"

Bill looked worried when I nodded, but his thoughts on the matter were cut short by the ringing of the doorbell. A quick glance round revealed no sign of our clandestine activities so I let the policeman in. He was the sergeant I had seen at the Station, but this time he was in civilian clothes. To give him his due, he looked like a business caller; smart, dark-grey two piece suit, club tie and neat, brown shoes of a commendable quality, and of a normal size.

He extended a hand in greeting, showing gold cuff links in the sleeves of his immaculate pale blue shirt, "I think you will recall we've already met, Mr Fradley?"

"Yes, sergeant. By the way this is my close friend and business partner," Bill raised his eyes at this elevation in his status, "Mr Huddleston. We would both like to be present at this interview, if you don't mind."

The sergeant looked offended, "This isn't an interview, sir; this is simply a call to see if you can throw any light on the matter of the homicide of last night. We know that there was a tenuous link with the death of Mr Perazza. We are simply gathering little bits of background to fill in the complete picture so to speak."

He beamed at us in what was, to me at least, a most unsettling way. Bill's face was a good impression of a poker player with either an excellent hand or a terrible one. The word 'inscrutable' entered my mind. "Take a seat, sergeant," Bill pointed out the visitor's chair. He sat, but looked around with interest as he did so, "Never been in here before. Nice office. Do you do your assembly here?"

Bill spoke in a silky voice as I went red, "We're engaged in sensitive research with microwave detection equipment, so we don't encourage visitors." I silently seconded that as Bill went on, "I'm sure you know what lengths industrial spies will go to. For instance one of our main competitors is in Japan. And at the moment there are a lot of Japanese tourists about." I smiled at Bill's apparent sincerity, but there was a little niggle set up in my mind at the mention of Japanese. Where I had found Japanese in an unexpected place? It was there somewhere in the memory bank, but where?

The sergeant seemed to accept this; he smiled at us, "This incident of last night. It has some unusual features." I thought to myself, *I didn't want to find murder anything other than unusual.* He continued, "I'm simply talking aloud so to speak. If you think you have any knowledge that could help, we would deeply appreciate your telling us - in strict confidence of course." He settled in his chair, "The identity of the man known as George Brown has thrown up some questions in our minds."

He paused as if marshalling these questions, "Such as, he seems to have been traced by dabs, er, fingerprints that is, as one Stefan Islic, who once studied at the Staffs Poly. He left the UK in a hurry after his graduation and nothing further was heard of him. The graduates' register lost complete track of him; none of the year he was with have heard either."

He looked at me as if I might enlighten him. When I stayed silent he brought out another snippet, "His passport, allegedly a UK one, is a forgery, there is no trace on the

Passport Office database and nothing on Immigration; nothing in his supposed home town. A real mystery is our George." He sat in thought for what seemed an age.

"Then, there were the injuries; he had the backs of both legs broken by a bar or pole - perhaps a base ball bat or something similar." I began to feel my skin crawl, thinking of Teddy Wilson's attack.

He droned on as if it was a parking offence, "There was also severe and extensive bruising and abrasions around the wrists and ankles, just as if he'd been tied up at some time."

My unease *must* have been obvious as he paused for effect, "The most unusual feature is that he was shot at close range, twice!" He paused, "And the bullets were from different firearms." He looked mildly at me and Bill.

I couldn't contain myself, "How horrible! It almost sounds like a gang killing, the Mafia or something out of the Kray's story." Bill was still being inscrutable as the sergeant looked sadly at me, "It does, sir. It does. I suppose this sort of thing's not in your experience, is it sir?"

Bill spoke very forcibly, "It most certainly is not, sergeant, I must admit I'm a little puzzled that you thought we might have some information on this terrible occurrence. We operate a perfectly normal," I nearly choked at the word 'normal', "legitimate business. We do not knowingly deal with any undesirable characters and would refuse to do so if we knew that there was anything not quite right." He finished up on such a note of righteous indignation that I was tempted to applaud.

The sergeant, shook his head sadly, "These are funny days, sir. You never really know." His voice tailed away. There was a pause.

He seemed to realise that nothing was going to come out of it, "Well, I'm sure that you want to get back to your, er, research, so I won't take up any more time. Thank you for your cooperation. I'll report back to the Inspector." He rose, shook hands and left. He must have felt the clamminess of mine and noted it. I went to wash as if I could erase some taint. As I came back, Bill had finished resetting the locks, "An astute man, our sergeant. He was watching you like a hawk."

I was weak, I felt drained, "I know, and I must have convinced him that I'm the biggest liar in the country."

Bill laughed, "He was so busy watching you that I was able to watch him. I'm sure he knew he'd get nothing out of us, but he simply came to tell us something and to see our reactions. I wonder why he did that?"

"Bill, I sincerely wish I knew, all this talk of spies has me ...;" He looked at me, I stopped in mid sentence, his eyes widened as I went on slowly, "I *knew* something niggled as you threw in that red herring of the Japanese. You remember the pot shot at Chasewater? It was two young Japanese who burst in and frightened the sniper away. It struck me as a bit odd at the time. I wonder if it wasn't just a coincidence." It was Bill's turn to look worried. Clearly he was thinking along the same lines as I was. Feeling very vulnerable I shivered. The office had become an icy place of uncertainty; we locked up and went our separate ways.

At home I cooked myself a huge paella, using all sorts of sea food, crab, scampi, even some cockles, and settled down with a bottle of Mosel white. I finished at leisure and collapsed into my sofa with the soothing tones of Chopin's Étude in G.

What with the meal, the wine and the wearying day, I felt myself drifting to sleep. I wondered if I would ever hear from Liza; her talk of finishing her jobs sounded like the end of her assignment and the likelihood of moving on. Retiring in a maudlin mood, I lay in the double bed thinking of the softness I'd felt as Liza had snuggled into my back that night. It seemed so long ago, almost another existence, as if I'd been reborn. It brought back the memory of the sexual awakening as Annie draped herself on to me another night. It was all gone now. I lay just thinking, down in spirit, finally weeping for the lost things of life and the unknown future lying in wait for me. Alone and deserted, I was a young boy rejected by his mother again. Life seemed to stretch empty and bleak for ever.

Chapter 41 Detonation.

It was still dark as I struggled to life. The cottage was silent. I glanced at the clock, which showed 05.15. I was sure something had awakened me. Inclined to put it down to the seafood, I tried to sleep, but there was a doubt that wouldn't be stilled. Groping for my dressing gown I groused and stumbled to the kitchen for a coffee. Managing to do it without disaster I sat sipping as an idea surfaced. It was the thought of the answerphone. Was that what had woken me? I carried the mug to the lounge. Sure enough the light was flashing, there was one message. I pressed the PLAY and waited. It was a surprise to hear Liza's voice; even through the machine there was a sombre tone, "Hello Bert, I shouldn't be doing this. I shouldn't worry you. You do worry, I know. The trouble is that I'm afraid. It's not being afraid of hurt or even death, it's the thought that I'll fail. I said I'd two jobs to do. One's cleared up. I've no regrets, I did what I had to and there's peace at last. My parents wouldn't approve of my methods, but I'm sure they can rest in peace now the betrayal's been ended. I can also be sure there'll be no more in the future; that alone gives me some pleasure. I've worked so long on this project; there have been so many obstacles and so much scepticism. But finally I stand at the point of truth. Tomorrow I put the final test into operation." There was a catch and a gulp, "By six I'll either be proved right, or well, it won't matter. I wish you could have been with me at the test, it would have meant so much, so much. But it's not possible for so many reasons. If all goes well I'll see you in three days at Chandler's at eight for a champagne celebration. If it fails... Please go there yourself and drink to my memory. Then forget me, I love you Bert." The message ended, the silence weighed on me stiflingly.

Stupefied, I was suddenly aware of the coffee burning my fingers as the mug tilted, unheeded. Cursing I went to the kitchen and ran cold water over my fingers. My tall clock showed nearly 5.30 am. The message rang in my ears, "By six I'll either be proved right, or ..." Throwing the towel on the kitchen worktop, where it slid unheeded to the floor, I ran up the stairs, ripped off the dressing gown and threw on slacks, sweater and moccasins. Still dragging on my sweater I raced down the stairs to the garage and into the Rover.

I howled down the lane, ignoring the thuds and bangs from the rough track. The grey sky was lightening as I squealed through the crossroads of Whittington. Thankfully there was no-one about that Sunday morning, so I was parking the car in Lichfield at 5.58. My breath rasping, I raced across the car park, regretting my general unfitness, but it was far too late to worry now.

There was a glimpsed movement as the service door opened at the Cathedral, a dark robed figure slipped in. I remembered the Dean and his early prayers.

In the far corner of the hotel car park was the BT temporary hut. There were lights within and there was a muted throb from the generator.

I stood still.

Now that the moment of decision had arrived, I hesitated. At the back of my mind was the ever present fear of rejection, if I went barging in would I be welcome or not; was there not an element of secrecy that demanded no interruptions?

The clock started to chime six; it started me on a dash across the open space, but I was halted by the ensuing events. The lights in the hut dimmed and the generator took on a deeper, throaty sound, it seemed to be struggling and slowed a half tone. A clutch of heavy cables ran from the hut to the trench and then to the Cathedral; I stopped in an awe struck, frozen stance as one of them started to glow a dull red. The generator was now struggling as if it was climbing a steep hill.

It was pure animal instinct that made me throw myself to the ground as the lights in the hut dimmed even further.

I can still see the scene as the events ran in slow motion. In reality it took a fraction of a second, but it was drawn out and imprinted on my mind for ever.

There was almost simultaneously, a clap of sound as if it was the end of the world, a flash of the most intense brilliance from the main spire of the Cathedral, that swelled until it touched the two smaller ones and flashed straight across the horizon, a blue-white streak of energy unleashed in a thunderbolt such as nature never produced. But what filled me with utter terror of the power and ferocity released was the heat, the compression wave, the ear-shattering sound and the earth-shaking explosion from the opposite end of the car park. I felt as if I was being squeezed flat by the force and yet at the same time having the breath sucked out of me. I don't know how long I lay there, but it could only have been seconds. It felt as if it was the end of my world.

Raising my head, ears still ringing from the blast I looked in horror at the hut, or at least where the hut had been. There was little to see, but a smoking platform, split as if struck by a giant axe, surrounded by debris, still fluttering or crashing to the ground. I was also conscious of other sounds, bells ringing, water spouting and crashes as of falling walls. Horrified, I stared at the new, unfinished Conference Centre. It was a wreck. The roof had lifted and twisted, fountains of water spouted from ruptured pipes, flames were starting to flicker from the inside of the heaps of unidentifiable rubble.

Staggering to my feet I tried to run to the hut, but my legs were rubbery, my left leg, in particular was hurting. I looked with shocked disinterest as at someone else's leg to see a gash and blood. I struggled on, but then stopped. It was totally useless. If Liza had been there, she was gone, there was nothing left. And then I saw a movement and heard a cry as of a wounded animal; I struggled across to the figure, hoping and praying.

I neared it and stopped nauseated by the shapeless horror of a burned body, that still bore the remnants of a white coat. In among the debris, looking up at me in agony was the burned face of the man who had been with Liza in the hut. I turned away and was sick. I flopped on the ground and must have passed out.

Then I vaguely remembered lights in my eyes. I was passing along an echoing corridor, there were voices, activity and finally came blissful sleep.

* * *

It was the clatter of metal wheels that woke me. Disorientated, for a second I panicked, but then the memories flooded back. And with the memories the pain. My left leg was hurting; I reached under the bedding to scratch it, but met the resistance of a bandage. The terrible events of the night came back as a physical rawness, that made my skin ultra-sensitive. The memory of the burned figure moaning in the wreckage of the hut scorched my battered brain and made me shudder.

Slowly, steadily, achingly with increasing awareness my surroundings took shape. I was in a private ward, the door closed, the bustle and movement of the outer ward muted and distant. Lost and slightly nauseous, I felt for my watch, but it wasn't there. Sunlight filtered through the heavily curtained windows. Hunger added to my discomfort. The door opened and a slim nurse entered, her face registered satisfaction as she saw I was awake, "Feeling better now, are we?"

I grunted, "I don't know about you, but I'm feeling battered."

She laughed, "Well, you're obviously on the mend. Feel like some lunch?"

"Lunch? What happened to breakfast?"

She was sombre, "You were sedated for your own good. You were thrashing about and calling; Lena or something."

Glancing at her watch, she brightened, "It's now midday and we're so glad to see that there's nothing serious. I'd suggest something simple, like soup and roll for now until the anaesthetic wears off. OK?"

Resignedly I nodded, but spoke before she could leave, "Was there anyone else found at ... at the scene? A man or ... a woman?"

Solemnly she nodded, "There was someone, an older man than you, but he's seriously ill, you won't be able to speak to him for some time. But that's all, no-one else."

I sat up, it hurt, "Are you sure? There was no-one else under the debris?" She turned a concerned face to me, "The place was blown to smithereens, there was nowhere for anyone or anything to be hidden. You can be sure of that. There was no-one else there at all," her face softened, "Your friend Lena must have left earlier, lucky for her."

I didn't think I could sink any lower. This was the end. I was still sobbing when lunch was brought. It was taken away and I was given a pill that brought blessed oblivion.

Chapter 42 Picking up the pieces.

It was dark and quiet when I emerged from the drugged sleep. The nurse watching me came and felt my pulse, "That's much better. Now don't try to sit up yet. Would you like something light for supper? Supper? Where had the day gone? Hunger and the drugs had made me nauseous again; I needed some carbohydrate to ease the bodily pain. The mental pain was a totally different matter. Struggling up I wheezed, "Could I have chips or potatoes and something? Chicken, ham, anything?"

Her relaxed expression said it all. She helped me to sit up properly, it wasn't quite agony this time, "I'll find something. I'm so glad you're feeling better."

What she could not see was the utter, inner deadness that lay leaden in my heart. I had to eat to live, but was there any point in life now? She was efficient and practical, no doubt she thought a good night's sleep and food was all that was needed. For my part I could see no future at all. My tears had dried, but my grief was just beginning.

But she could not see this; to her I was on the mend. She swept out with a crackle of stiff apron before I could speak again. As she clicked along the corridor, I heard her say, "In there, but don't stay long, he's tired."

Expecting to see Bill I looked, but was startled to see the bulky figure of Al Clinton squeeze in.

He grinned at my surprise, "How's the casualty, walking?"

I recovered enough to speak normally, "Not tried it yet, I've only just woken up." A smile started but died instantly, like everything else, it hurt, "At least all the bits are there, nothing's fallen off."

He laughed, a deep, solid sound of pleasure, "Gee! That's what I like about you Brits, tough as nails under all that effete."

I winced at the word, 'Brits', "I'm English, not a Brit," I retorted shortly.

He really did laugh at that. He then sat down, the humour vanished, "I've come to say Goodbye, old buddy. Tomorrow I'm off back across the pond. Must get back to the plant and see what they've been up to while I've been over here."

For some reason I felt as if I was losing a friend. In a way he was. He was responsible for my meeting Liza.

Sincerely I said, "Sorry to hear that, but I suppose we can't stand still, there are things to do."

My voice trailed away as I recalled Liza's words - *two jobs to finish* - it now seemed so final.

He sensed my introspection, he probably also knew why, so it was no surprise as he went on, "She was a great gal. I admired her a lot; she had guts and knew what she had to do." He sounded sad, "It was a shame she didn't live to pick up the pieces she expected to."

I did not quite know what to say to that, so I stayed silent.

He looked at me steadily, "She had this great thing for you and her," I was taken aback at this, "she was looking forward to having swept aside all the hurdles and finding the peace she'd been denied by Stefan. I believe she told you that he came back as George the late and unlamented?"

I simply nodded; I was too choked up to speak.

"There'll be a lot of people sleeping easier in their beds now that he's no longer about to work his particular brand of treachery. There were many people who had cause to see him removed from the scene."

"Like Annie?" He just sat, sad eyed, so I went on, "*was* she FBI?"

"I guess I don't need to answer that one. She had the strongest reason, but she also made the mistake of underestimating him. Liza didn't"

I stared, "You mean?"

He was all at once stony faced, "She wasn't the only one by far, you don't ask too deeply into that."

I suddenly remembered the *two bullets*, from different guns found in George's head. I looked at Al and it came into my mind what he'd said when we first met; he described himself as a rodent eliminator or some such words. He had also said he was a chemical manufacturer. Mistakenly I'd assumed it was one of his products; perhaps it wasn't so. I looked at this big, powerful man and wondered just what he was capable of. It seemed wise to take his advice and not probe too deeply.

He fished a card from his pocket, "Like I said before, if you're ever tempted to visit the States, do look me up, I'll help in any way I can." He shrugged, "I think it's the least I can do."

He stood, blocking out the light, "Well, I guess I'll just get along, I've some packing and settling up to do tomorrow." He started to turn to go, but stopped and looked back at me, "By the way, I never did thank you for the help in tracing the forebears. I'm still not sure, but I *think* I've found a link to Roger de Clinton. Sure hope I have. He was quite a guy, a real trouble shooter. Like me in some ways."

He held out a big hand, "So long. Our paths may cross again sometime."

He swept out leaving me with the maelstrom of thoughts and unanswered questions. I was not sure I wanted to really know the answers to some of them or if I would believe them if I did.

Shortly afterwards I was still mulling over the mess when Bill came in with Sheila, clutching a bunch of flowers and a bag of grapes. They were both clearly delighted to see me sitting up. Sheila gave me a hug; like everything else at that time, it hurt.

She said she was sorry, as a Sister, she should have known better: I reassured her that it was only my feeling sorry for myself. Sheila was blooming, she had a subtle something that made her seem, well, sort of very feminine and alive.

I wasn't kept in suspense as Bill beamed, "You can congratulate us, Bert. Sheila's expecting our first." Sheila flushed with a freshness to her cheeks; she really did look good.

I congratulated them sincerely, but inwardly I was cold. Would I ever have the opportunity?

Bill was looking at me with a mixed expression; he knew what I was thinking and was sorry for me.

It was at that moment that I began to live again. How could I spoil their life and the new life in Sheila with my own misery? They had it all, I had nothing. But was that any reason to cling on to the pain, making others miserable too? There are tragic people like that, there have been classic stories of deserted women who refuse to let go, men who harbour grudges all their lives. I did not want my life to be another Great Expectations or Moby Dick with me at its centre, killing others' happiness.

Sheila's glowing face brought my own loss to its right proportion. Liza was gone. My own distress was personal, a ghost to be faced in the dreams of the nights of loneliness that stretched away endlessly. I had to tread that path alone and let them go to their fulfilled existence together. My mind was made up, Liza was mine, if all I had was dreams, I would not destroy theirs. Bill had Sheila to care for, not me. I knew from the wrinkles on his brow that he was concerned. It would be so easy to be a tragic figure like another Miss Havisham or Captain Ahab.

But that would have been selfish.

I took away Bill's look as I asked, "I suppose you'll want that rise you're always pestering for now that there's all that expense?"

He was flustered, confused even, "No I wasn't."

He didn't know what to do with this sudden change, it disturbed and unsettled him. Silencing his discomfort I interrupted him, "And another thing, it's high time we took on another pair of hands. This has made me think how vulnerable we are with just the two of us. We've been lucky up to now, but if either one of us was killed or seriously handicapped, the firm would be in trouble."

Bill turned to Sheila, "I think it's affected his brain, you'd better call the doc. He sounds to me as if he's rambling." All three of us laughed. In my case it was forced.

"I'm coming to my senses, Bill. I've been too self-centred for too long. You can start a trawl for some up and coming youngster to join us and soon."

There was a thumping of crutches in the corridor and Teddy Wilson hobbled in, "I hear you've been in the wars, dear boy. Thought I'd call to see what you've been up to. I managed to escape when Sister's back was turned."

Bill stood to offer his chair, but Teddy waved him back, "Easier to stand right now. Having a family gathering? Thought I heard merriment as I came."

Bill smiled, "He's off his rocker. It must have affected what little brain he had, he's talking of giving me a rise, him the original Scrooge, *and* taking on a new employee to ease the crushing load on yours truly. He'll be normal soon and it will all disappear."

"Not a bit of it," I said, "It's simply an insurance and good business."

Teddy was pensive, "Do you really want someone? To help that is."

Beginning to enjoy being the tycoon I said confidently, "I certainly do."

"What age and experience?"

Bill leaped in, "Young, blond, good looking and cheap!" he gasped as Sheila nudged him.

I spoke firmly, detecting a reason behind Teddy's question, "Someone young, before they get all the bad habits from big business, big ideas from unions and before their creativity is stifled. Most of all he must fit into the team. If he doesn't, then out he goes. The pay will be negotiated, but, contrary to my *new partner's* comments, it will be interesting."

Teddy grinned, "Well said. Now it just so happens."

He was interrupted by the combined groans of disbelief from Bill and me.

He continued, "There's a new graduate in the Computer Faculty that I and the head of department have been watching with interest. I think McCall might just fit the bill. Interested?"

Breathless with the speed of events and the late hour, I suddenly felt tired and drained. Sheila recognised the signs and brought the visit to an end. As they were trooping out, my supper arrived. It awoke my hunger as I smelt the aroma of Chicken Supreme. Bill looked longingly, but was ushered out by an impatient Sheila. Teddy was roundly scolded by the Sister and sent packing as fast as his crutches allowed.

I began to nod before finishing the very good meal. Dozing and thinking, I had the feeling that life had changed irrevocably. When the small remains of my meal were taken away by an approving nurse I drifted into a deep sleep.

Chapter 43 New Blood.

The next morning the specialist hustled and pummelled me, and announced that I could go home that very morning. I wasn't anxious to be thrown out, but I didn't feel bad at all; even my gashed leg was only sore. So it was that I drove myself home very sedately and soberly, thinking of the events that had lead up to this time. As much as the past I thought of the future, a future that now seemed to be empty and soulless. The period pre-Liza and pre-Annie had seemed to be complete, satisfying and fulfilling: now life was hollow and pointless. For yet another time in my existence, I found myself let down by women. The trouble was that I was in a severe state of self-pity, bordering on depression. It was no good telling myself that neither of them would have made my life complete, I wasn't even a convincing liar to myself.

As I drove slowly over the bumpy track to my cottage, my remote sensing system registered an unexpected visitor, so I stopped before the cottage came into view. There was a dark grey Ford Cougar parked in the drive. I looked through my binoculars and recognised the military set to a head that could only be Colonel Heward. Carefully and painfully retracing my steps, I started the Rover and drove to the door as if I hadn't seen him. Greeting him with more than my normal warmth I invited him in to the lounge, settled him into a chair and made us both a coffee; for once he was on edge and declined the Earl Grey. He came straight to the point, but I was disturbed to see a grey pallor to his face that spoke of some deep-seated disease.

"I have been recalled to see you on a delicate matter, following the unfortunate demise of our agent Miss Vancyk; I have taken the liberty of calling on you at home as there is the need for the utmost secrecy and understanding."

He levelled his eyes, now more than ever like steel spikes and continued in his precise manner,

"I will be honest in saying that we have never been close, but I have always had the highest regard for your work and loyalty. It is for that reason that I persuaded their Lordships that you warranted a full explanation."

This was very disturbing, it was clear to me that there was an explosive situation developing. I'd always tried to keep out of the field work that I designed my wares for, it now seemed that it was about to swallow me whether I wanted it or not.

"Mr Fradley, I am about to request you to sign an oath of secrecy beyond the Official Secrets Act. This document is at the behest of the board, but in my view is completely unnecessary ..."

It was a sort of back-handed compliment I thought, that is until he went on, "... it is intended to safeguard the service from any attempt by you to profit from what I am about to say. It is unnecessary, because if there is the merest hint of your allowing a single word to leak out, you will be eliminated without warning."

The impact of those words hit me solidly as he paused, "Do you understand this?"

Aghast and furious I stared in disbelief, "Then, for God's sake, why tell me?"

"Because," there was censure in his hard eyes, "you have been unduly close to Miss Vancyk and you might have found out or have stumbled on the true nature of the project. Partly I am telling this for your own good and partly because I respect your integrity. I know that if this is made official, you will not fail." *Thanks for the compliment,* I thought.

He continued before I had chance to retort, "Miss Vancyk had filled in the usual Dependent's Allotment form. As she had no dependents and no other relatives close to her, she made you out as her sole beneficiary; she has left you the entire estate, both real and movable. It is my duty to present to you the documents relating to her effects and property."

My head began to spin as he continued, "I have drawn up a list of the known assets, without taking an inventory of the flat in Sussex Square. I consider that to be private and should be left to you to settle as you see fit." He pushed across the table a pitifully small document, showing the earthly worth and achievements of Liza. He also placed on the dining table a document headed TOP SECRET and written in the most bureaucratic jargon, I didn't hesitate, but signed it without reading it fully. If the Colonel was correct, then I would be watched and listened to night and day. Although up to then, I couldn't see for the life of me, not altogether the most comforting of expressions, why it was necessary. He handed over a bulky A 4 envelope containing various cards, keys and financial statements. I dropped them on the table unopened. He then looked me in the eye again, and for some reason, I shivered.

His voice was cold and quiet, but it shook me to the core, "Miss Vancyk was engaged on the most sensitive and potentially most powerful weapon that we have ever been offered. You were the constructor of part of it, the transmitter that was placed on the main steeple on the Cathedral." He paused as he drew a deep breath, "She had made the discovery of the potential as a result of her friendship with Professor Wilson's investigations into the Ley Lines. Most people considered he was crazy, so we let that belief continue unchecked." Pausing for breath he looked me straight in the eye. His inner strength hit me. The word, 'fanatical' came to mind.

Breathing easier, he continued in that scalpel-like voice, "Miss Vancyk, however, saw that there was the potential to use the natural carrier wave, of extremely long

271

oscillation, to transport solid matter instantaneously, or at least at the speed of light, from one place to the other. It was the unsuccessful attempt to transport herself last Sunday that caused the disaster that ensued."

He paused to blow his nose with a spotless handkerchief as the meaning began to filter into my brain.

Liza had been trying to send *herself* by radio to somewhere else.

I almost began to laugh thinking about Star Trek, *Beam me up, Scotty!*

But it was no laughing matter, it was an utter failure and the cause of the death of the one love I'd ever had, and would probably never have again. I couldn't believe my ears. Such science fiction belonged to the realms of escapism and fantasy. I must have stared open-mouthed, for the Colonel spoke with an almost human timbre, "The board were sceptical, if not derisive about the whole concept, but she wore them down enough to be given a minute budget to test her theory."

He grimaced, "Even the necessity of using Lichfield Cathedral, with its position on the most powerful of the lines and the almost unbelievable feature of the three steeples forming the required tripole aerial arrangement, was the result of immense and secret negotiations, that would have defeated me." The admiration was genuine I was sure.

Heward confirmed it, "Can you imagine the power of being able to send and retrieve not only agents, but ordinance?" Unable to take it in, I flopped into the settee as he outlined the potential, "Imagine being able to send nuclear weapons instantly and, with no danger to our own personnel, anywhere in the world. The weakest link in the nuclear deterrent is the delivery. Bombers can be shot down, missiles intercepted. This would have been unstoppable, a truly irresistible threat." There was genuine regret in his voice, "But it was not to be."

He stood, "I really am most sorry to have lost her. She is irreplaceable and will be missed in The Firm. I can only offer my condolences and say that I feel a personal loss."

I can't recall what I said then, I just wanted to be alone, I *had* to be alone to take it all in. Sitting in the deepening, unlit twilight, I was totally overwhelmed.

It hasn't happened often, but I sat and wept. The immensity of my loss was only just beginning to become clear.

Chapter 44 A New Beginning.

The following morning I went through the envelope containing the keys and cards. There was a very upsetting moment when I found the keys to the Porsche; I didn't think I could ever bring myself to either drive it or sell it. There was very little cash in the accounts as shown by the statements and there was an unusual swipe card that seemed to have no identification mark. There was a small bunch of keys, with a label, 'Flat in Sussex Square, Ditton'. Looking at the pathetic pile of remains, I made a sudden decision. I rang Bill and said I was taking the day off. He didn't seem to be surprised, but said he would like me to be there the following day as Alex McCall was calling then with an endorsement from Teddy Wilson and a request to make up our minds swiftly. Alex had been offered a very tempting position with Microsoft, who were pressing for an early answer.

I promised to be there.

Throwing the envelope into the Rover I set out for the hurly-burly of London traffic. It took me over two hours to find the Square and another half to find somewhere to park, Thames Ditton was crowded. I was bitterly regretting my snap decision by then, but I'd arrived so I might as well go ahead.

The flat was up a wide staircase, the door seemed at first glance to be ordinary enough, but I was unable to find any of the keys that fitted. It was then that I noticed in the ornate moulding round the frame, what seemed to be a badly fitting piece high on the left. I took out the swipe card and slid it in the crack; there was a click and I could push the door open. It was very ponderous, the reason was clear as I entered; it was over fifty millimetres thick and had a dull grey edge like a safe door. The heavy door shut slowly behind me, where it stopped with a solid thud.

The feeling that I was intruding was very strong, it was like violating some holy place, I stood and looked trying to imagine Liza and failed. Some faint perfume reached me; I saw the neatness and nearly walked out. Pulling myself together with an effort I wandered round the three rooms.

The living room was fitted with Hi-Fi, TV, DVD and a PC: there was little in the way of decoration, but it was all in understated elegance.

It was in complete contrast to my very well-used and lived-in cottage. The kitchen was clinical, the bedroom was in a soothing lilac, with concealed lighting, the soft furnishings were muted and calming.

I could imagine Liza spending most of her time there. Back in the living room I was drawn to the PC. Out of curiosity I switched it on and called up the e-mail. The screen said, ACCESS DENIED. I thought, *'what did I expect?'*

Wondering if there was a clue in the personal effects, I looked through twice but all I found was a card with 'A Fradley IV.' I shrugged, might as well try it.

To my amazement it worked.

I trawled through the usual rubbish and was about to bin the lot, when there was a cryptic note, that I assumed was something from HG, it read

"B 1 6 10 50 5: 999 . M" The sender's and the server's locations were not given. I tried the usual tricks, but all I got was ACCESS DENIED. The only other fact I could obtain was the date and time of receipt, it was 11.30 pm two days after the explosion. I noted the facts and sat staring at the message. Who was M? Was 999 some form of emergency signal? Was B 16 an American bomber? By now I was tired and confused, still with the feeling that I was impinging on her privacy, so I printed the e-mail, shut down the PC, pulled the door closed behind me and fought my way back to the sanity of Lichfield.

The following morning I went to the office in the manner of Shakespeare's schoolboy, 'like snail, unwillingly'. Passing the Oxfam shop I saw my tweed still hanging forlornly on the rack. On an impulse I went in and bought it for £1; I think they were relieved to be rid of it.

At the office I was met by Bill, who was rather nervous. It seemed that Alex Mc Call's imminent arrival was unnerving him. As it was the first time he'd interviewed a potential employee, it was understandable; it was so many years since I'd interviewed him that I was almost as keyed up as well. I showed Bill my copy of the cryptic message, his opinion was that it was certainly a code, it reminded him of the messages when Liza cancelled the 'buyers visit', but he wasn't in the mood for games just then.

The door bell rang and we both jumped a foot, anyone would have thought it was us that were after the job, not the other way around.

We looked at the monitor, stared and looked at each other. Was this Alex Mc Call? It suddenly struck us that Alex was not exclusively a male name. There was no doubt about the sex of the caller, her long blond hair was plaited in a swinging, heavy braid, she wore a print, cotton dress, carried a straw bag and was very pretty. I looked at Bill, "I thought you were joking when you said 'young, blond and good looking'!" He had gone red-faced, "How the blazes am I to interview that?"

I smirked, "As junior partner, you'd better get used to it, or you'll be done under the Sex Discrimination Act." For an eternal split second I nearly broke down. I remembered Liza with her hair in a pony tail standing there. It took all my willpower to keep control.

This was going to be hard to try to keep my grief hidden. It was touch and go whether or not I cancelled the whole thing right there. But there was Bill to consider too as I'd pledged to myself in the hospital.

He groaned, "Sheila'll never believe me."

I pressed the button to admit her, "You'll have to start thinking quickly; I think I'll go for a stroll while you do." His horror-struck face made me burst out laughing, "Only joking, Bill, only joking."

The girl swished in. Her dress was long. It swung demurely and attractively as she entered. She looked inquiringly at Bill. "Mr Fradley?" He indicated me. She appeared a bit disappointed, but she held out a slim arm; she wore no jewellery.

I took the proffered hand, her grip was firm, warm and confident, "Professor Wilson asked me to give you this." She rummaged in the straw bag and gave me a small envelope.

I indicated our visitor's chair; she gracefully subsided into it.

Facing her I thought of Liza sitting there and wondered how long my resolve could last. Everything was in hiatus waiting for me.

Having to say something I tried banality as the surest and safest line to take, "Would you like tea or coffee? I can't recommend Bill's coffee, but you're welcome to try it."

She laughed easily, I could see that she could quite quickly grow on you, "I would prefer weak tea if you have any."

Inwardly groaning I asked, "Earl Grey any good?"

Her eyes widened, "Lovely!"

Bill was already half way to the kitchenette, his relief giving his feet wings.

I read the note, 'This is to introduce Alexandra Mc Call. I have no reservations in saying that she has been one of the most outstanding pupils I have ever had. She has a mind that is uncluttered and clear as well as being a very shrewd analyst of any situation. Teddy.'

As if reading my mind, she grinned, "I gather Teddy played one of his jokes on you - you weren't expecting a girl, were you?"

From my expression it must have been obvious that she was right, but I was saved as Bill arrived with the coffee and tea in double quick time.

I blinked, where had he got the tea pot and china cups?

We drank our brew and chatted about her life at the Poly, she'd been assiduous, had a first class honours in Electronics, her social life was uncomplicated, she had two close girl friends and a feeling for one of the fringe of boys in her year. But she was mostly involved with a Stafford church that was supporting a clinic for the blind in India. She was very enthusiastic about it. Much more so than about the boy friend. While she'd been drinking and chatting, she'd been looking round without being intrusive.

I asked, "Did Teddy Wilson give you any idea what we do here?"

She said a little guardedly, "Nothing definite, but he hinted that you were in some microprocessor research." She hesitated, seemed to make up her mind, "It was his watch that intrigued me. He couldn't resist telling me of his adventures. By the way he's now able to walk using one stick and getting better every day."

That was good news to me. "What do you think of our office?"

She flushed very slightly.

"I saw you looking. Only natural, there's no offence taken. What do you think?"

She drew a deep breath, "Well, it's not Microsoft for sure. But it looks as if people work here." She brightened, "It's tidier than the lab at the Poly!"

Bill laughed at this: I let my face soften; the tidiness of Liza's flat surfaced in my mind. I couldn't laugh too much yet. The ice was broken; I was beginning to like this breath of fresh air. I started to think we needed her more than we thought as I spoke, "For a start I must explain that we are engaged in very sensitive work, so first off there isn't a lot I can tell you at this stage, but tell me what you think of this."

I gave her the little grey bug, now rescued from the Oxfam shop that had started these events.

"What do you make of that?"

She was at first somewhat taken aback, but peered closely at it, "Is this what you do?"

I looked at Bill as I shook my head, "No. It was stuck on my jacket by someone I haven't identified. Just tell me, what it is and what it's for."

She looked very closely, "Well. Without being too sure, I'd need some equipment to be certain, but it looks like something out of James Bond. It's carefully made and so small it could easily be overlooked. I suppose the material attached to it is from your jacket?"

I nodded, she went on, "There's so much miniaturisation these days. I can only assume it's either a tracing or audio device." She peered even closer, "I think you've opened it and you know what it is." There was a closeness in her face as she asked carefully, "Are you a spy or agent or something?"

Bill was trying hard to hide his amusement as I shook my head, "I am something, but I'm definitely not a spy. Now. What would you do with it?"

There was a hesitation, "I would satisfy my curiosity and try to disassemble it. It's very high-tec, so it would be difficult and need the right tools, but I'd certainly have a go."

Taking it from her I sat down, "If you wanted to design your own, how would you go about it?"

She was looking somewhat uneasy, but replied clearly and decisively. In so many ways she achingly reminded me of Liza, she knew what she was doing. If we employed her it would be hard. The thought came unbidden that perhaps this could cauterise the wounds, make me sane once more.

She continued a bit uncertainly, clearly thinking as she spoke, "I'd write a program for the mainframe, specify just what I wanted it to do and design the circuit. Then I'd draw the chips I needed, download them to a laser cutter and cook them into a solid state unit that couldn't be disassembled without destroying the entire device. The finish would depend on the use."

She stood, "This is going too far, I wasn't aware I was being recruited into M I 5, I think I'd better go."

One of the features of being the Managing Director of a small firm, whether you see it as an advantage or disadvantage depends on your outlook, is the need to make swift decisions on less than the full facts. I'd often done this in the past using little more than a gut feeling. I had this gut feeling now! I liked the girl, her ability and freshness of approach. Instinctively I trusted her integrity. The feeling that we needed her was strong and there would be only one chance.

I stood to face her. She was pretty, even in the solemn mood she was experiencing then, "Please sit down and listen, Miss Mc Call, I want to explain things before you make a decision." She sat warily.

"I've been a little unfair to you, in not giving you warning of our work. The trouble is, that as the work is so sensitive and unknown to most people, I wanted to test your outlook and trustworthiness above other considerations. It's obvious to you that we are in the business of clandestine surveillance; we have been for years. If I do say so, we are very good at it. The trouble, as you know, is that there's so much available in the microprocessor field that it's hard to keep ahead of the opposition."

I paused and looked at her, "Our work is almost exclusively for the Government, but we are merely the technicians. From the very short time we have spoken, I feel that you're exactly the person we need to breathe new life into our designs. I am my own boss, Bill is my best friend and I've decided to make him a partner for all the years we've been together." Bill shuffled somewhat at this.

Looking at them one at a time, I continued seriously, "This is a small team and must stay that way. If you feel that you can work with us, you would bring new ideas and techniques, but you would have to work as a team member. It goes without saying that absolute secrecy about our projects is essential. Finally, we cannot offer you the prestige of Microsoft, nor the expense account, but you would be an equal member of the team and you won't starve. If you want time to think, I'll give you as long as you need."

She blinked, "I'm not sure what to say. I'm a bit bewildered."

For two minutes she was silent, two of the longest minutes I've ever waited.

I was about to stand to let her leave, when she smiled and stood.

She held out her slim arm and her hand with the delicate fingers, "I think it will be fun. To tell the truth, I was tempted by the big time, but if I was simply a tiny chip in a huge mainframe, insignificant and barely noticed, I'd be stifled. There's more to life than designing games for bored children and spreadsheets for lazy executives. If the offer's for a job, I accept it."

It was with relief that I shook her hand, "I'll draw up the contract tomorrow, you can come next Monday to be shown the ropes."

There was an atmosphere of celebration, which led me to pull out my copy of the e-mail from Liza's mailbox. "Tell me what you make of this. Bill thinks it might be a message."

She glanced at it, "It's some sort of transliteration code, it is simple really, it is: - 'To A F from L V ... er, im Oh! I'm .... dot 1,000 ... er Oh! of course, I'm OK!'"

I stood as if turned to stone, speaking in a hushed whisper, "Are you sure?"

It was her turn to look uneasy, "I *think* so, it's so simple, but I suppose there could be a code within a code. But the first layer is straightforward, B = 2 = To; 1 = A, 6 = F, 10 = X = ex = from, 50 = L, 5 = V. 999 = 1,000 - 1 = 1M = I'm and so on. Does it mean anything?"

Bill and I exchanged glances. I spoke carefully, "It might, but I can't gain access to the sender or server to verify. Thanks for the translation."

She hesitated for a moment, "I could try to locate them if you have the modem connected somewhere."

I dared hardly breathe, "It isn't here, but I can connect to it."

She put down her straw bag, "Should we give it a go?"

I indicated the computer, she sat at the keyboard and her fingers flew over the keys. I gave her Liza's site, she rattled away and the screen came up ACCESS DENIED. She rattled away again and again it came up ACCESS DENIED. She frowned and typed rapidly once more. Still the screen read ACCESS DENIED.

This time she pressed two keys together and the screen showed a very slow scroll in reverse. As it did so, a blurred and indistinct image slowly crawled up the shifting scan. I stared, fascinated, but I felt my blood turn to ice in my veins as I recognised it. NASA! Alex looked at me with a querying frown, "Is that what you wanted?"

I swallowed and managed to croak, "Yes."

Bill stepped in again and took Alex gently to the door, "You've been most helpful. I look forward to working with you next Monday. You don't mind it I don't see you down the stairs? Nice to have met you."

She left with a puzzled expression on her face.

He came to me, "Now what was all that about, you look as if you've seen a ghost."

I sat, shaken, white faced, "I think I just have. That e-mail was sent from NASA two days *after* Liza disappeared, it was on her own PC, where I would find it. And," I paused unsure whether or not I was making sense, "if you extend the Ley Line from Lichfield to infinity, it passes through Florida."

Bill gaped, his mind racing.

I jumped up, to pace up and down, "Can't you see Bill? She's alive, I know she is."

His face registered shock, disbelief and amazement, "I said it reminded me of the message cancelling the visit." He stopped confused, "But you saw the explosion yourself. It can't be. You're not serious about NASA?"

I turned to him, I must have seemed demented, he stepped back at my tortured voice, "I can't believe she's just gone! She's out there somewhere, I feel it here," and I touched my head, "I know what I saw, at least what there was to be seen."

I whirled on Bill, perfectly clear in mind as to what I had to do, "I *have* to go. I've got to find her, wherever she is, however long it takes. The business is yours, you've put enough in it to earn it, I'll be off tomorrow."

Nothing Bill said had any effect at that moment, but later I regained some of my sense. My grief had miraculously erupted into an irrational hope, lifted me from the deepest depths to the vision of heaven. It was ridiculous, but it didn't matter.

In my heart I knew that Liza was alive, that she was calling me, needed me.

Nothing else in this world mattered.

And this time I won't let anything take her away.

REPORT ENDS.

SAVED TO SECURE ARCHIVE CATEGORY 1AA (ENCRYPTED) A F IV

DOCUMENT ENDS

EPILOGUE.

Wearily I closed and saved the file. It had all seemed complete and simple then. Was the present set-up worth it all? As I warmed again to the memory of those still hypnotic eyes, those creamy, high-boned cheeks, V asleep upstairs, I was sure it was. With a grunt I stretched as the sun began to edge over the orchard; time to wake V and live again. As I turned to shut down the computer, another file name made me hesitate.
'The Zeus Club.'

I had been painfully aware that the frequency of pin point missile strikes on terrorist leaders was increasing. Al had lied to me then and still was. Could I, should I leak the contents?

Now that was something that I felt V should definitely not see. But that was for another day. The present was a lively four year old, a part of me and Liza. He was also our future. I prayed that it was going to be better than my past had been.